THE LOOK OF LOVE

Her back was to the window, but he could see the fine shape of her figure and the line of her shoulders. The amused tilt of her head and the sparkle in her eyes were quite perfectly reflected in the looking glass on the counter by her elbow. She had just removed the ridiculously wide-brimmed hat she had been wearing and set it on the counter. Even as he watched, she turned to her companion with another small ripple of laughter, offering him a view of her lovely profile.

Archer jostled his friend Holly trying to get a better look. *Oh, yes, she was a goddess!*

"Oh, by heaven, if you have any intelligence yourself you will move on now that we've seen who it is," Holly said. "I recognize her. You are quite right—she does have a charming laugh. . . . But she is the last lady in London you should want to get involved with."

The Rake's Mistake

Gail Eastwood

A SIGNET BOOK

SIGNET
Published by New American Library, a division of
Penguin Putnam Inc., 375 Hudson Street,
New York, New York 10014, U.S.A.
Penguin Books Ltd, 80 Strand,
London WC2R 0RL, England
Penguin Books Australia Ltd, Ringwood,
Victoria, Australia
Penguin Books Canada Ltd, 10 Alcorn Avenue,
Toronto, Ontario, Canada M4V 3B2
Penguin Books (N.Z.) Ltd, 182–190 Wairau Road,
Auckland 10, New Zealand

Penguin Books Ltd, Registered Offices:
Harmondsworth, Middlesex, England

Published by Signet, an imprint of New American Library,
a division of Penguin Putnam Inc.

First Printing, November 2002
10 9 8 7 6 5 4 3 2 1

Copyright © Gail Eastwood Stokes, 2002
All rights reserved

 REGISTERED TRADEMARK—MARCA REGISTRADA

Printed in the United States of America

In memory of my dad, Albert M. Eastwood, who taught me to sail but never got to see this story finished, and for you, my friends and fans, who kept asking, "When is the next one?" and waited patiently, never doubting. Thank you for your faith in me—it really helped.

Chapter One

The sound halted Archer Everett Drake, Lord Ramsdale, as suddenly as if a spell had washed over him and frozen him in his tracks.

In that moment, the clamor of the London street around him fell away unnoticed and even the startled exclamation of the companion beside him failed to penetrate his consciousness. All he heard was soft, musical laughter coming out of the open shop door to his left.

"I say, Drake, whatever is the matter?"

Sir Peter Hollyfield still addressed Archer as in their school days before Archer's father, the second Baron Ramsdale, succumbed to years of dissolute living and left his son to carry on the title. Clearly Holly had noticed nothing except Archer's abrupt stop.

Archer was slow to answer, still lost in his response to the laughter. Something had felt distinctly different in the instant he'd heard it, as if his heart had somehow lightened.

Just the moment before, he had been walking innocently enough along Bond Street, half listening while Holly recounted in overwhelming detail his latest exploits at the card tables in White's. Jostling eddies of slow-moving pedestrians crowded the pavements on this fine morning in late May. Beside them an erratic flow of carts and carriages rumbled and rattled past. The clop of hooves and jingle of harnesses formed a rhythmic counterpoint to the calls of street venders amidst the hum of human interaction, not to mention Holly's droning baritone. Yet the sound of feminine laughter had slipped through it all like the cling of a shop bell, straight to Archer's ears.

Could his brain be playing tricks on him? He had been back in England only nine days. As eager as he had been to return from the West Indies, he already missed much that he had left behind—island breezes, dark eyes, and a certain person's engaging laughter.

This laughter sounded confoundingly similar—warm, honest, and full of genuine amusement, not some missish *haut monde* titter artfully contrived. Husky and sensuous about the edges, it pulled at him like a siren's song.

"A moment, Holly."

Archer started for the shop door entirely oblivious to the fact that it was a milliner's shop filled with ladies of the *ton*. Only his friend's insistent tug on his elbow prevented him from actually stepping inside.

"Have you gone mad? Lambs face the wolf pack with more protection than you would have, stepping in there! What has possessed you?"

"Did you not hear it?"

"What?"

"That enticing laughter? I have never heard a more seductive sound. I must discover the delightful creature who uttered it." He made another move toward the door.

Holly had not released Archer's elbow. "Aiming to make a spectacle of yourself? By Jove, Drake, you must be mad. Mind you, I always suspected as much."

He grinned but tightened his grip on Archer's arm. "It's not a confectioner's shop, despite that eager look on your face. The sweets in there bite back, and are likely to slip the parson's noose on you faster than you can blink. I don't think you fathom just what a matrimonial prize you have become."

A physical struggle against Holly was pointless without a serious effort. Archer's imposing friend topped his own six feet of height by a hand's width and outweighed him by a stone or more, all of it muscle. Still, Archer resisted.

"I swear I have just been hit by Cupid's dart."

"What, again?" Holly rolled his eyes. "I swear he uses you for target practice whenever you set foot in Town."

He drew Archer back to the outside of the shop's bow

window. After looking furtively in both directions, he nodded toward the mullioned panes.

"I see no one who knows us coming along at the moment. Take a quick look if you must, although I don't see
how you will know which woman it is. You *are* daft, you
realize. You are just asking to set a fresh round of gossip
going. After the last time, wouldn't your mother love
that?"

After the last time Archer had caused gossip, his great-
uncle, the Marquess of Huntington, had shipped him off to
the family's estates in the Caribbean for a three-year exile.
His mother had given it her blessing.

"Devil take my mother and my sisters along with her."
Archer had missed his family but not their overbearing tendency to meddle in his life. Now that he was back, they
were starting on him again. "Let Old Nick take the gossips,
too, while he's at it, and give them all something better to
do! Then he'll be too busy to bother with you and me."

Dismissing them all with a disdainful shake of his head,
he turned to the store's multipaned window. The distorted
images of Bond Street and his own and Holly's fashionably
attired forms reflected in the wavy glass made it difficult to
see into the shadowed interior. He stepped closer and, cup-
ping his hands around his face, scanned the inside of the
shop, peering between a pink satin bonnet and a plumed
silver evening turban displayed on stands in the window.

"She must be near the entrance or I would not have
heard her laughter," he said. The sound had not been loud.

"It would serve you right if she's the one over there by
the display case looking at gloves," Holly said gruffly, peering in beside him. He wore his tall-crowned silk hat
straighter than Archer did his beaver, and the brim bumped
against the glass. "That's Lady Brumborough, and she not
only outweighs me by three or four stone, she's very
married."

"Takes it seriously, eh?"

"And sees to it that her husband does, as well."

"A tyrant? God save us!"

"Indeed." As Holly began to chuckle, Archer heard the
light laughter again. He jabbed his friend in the ribs to
silence him.

"There, waiting to make a purchase at the counter! The one wearing that dark blue spencer. She does not seem to find this hat business a serious undertaking, which only goes to prove she is as intelligent as she is beautiful."

Her back was to the window, but he could see the fine shape of her figure and the line of her shoulders. The amused tilt of her head and the sparkle in her eye were quite perfectly reflected in the looking glass on the counter by her elbow. She had just removed the ridiculously wide-brimmed hat she had been wearing and set it on the counter. Even as he watched, she turned to her companion with another small ripple of laughter, offering him a view of her lovely profile.

Archer jostled Holly trying to get a better look. *Oh, yes, she was a goddess!* Young enough, yet with no hint of the schoolroom about her—past twenty, he would say. Slim yet delightfully curved, with a slender, graceful neck. Her small head was crowned with glorious upswept dark chestnut hair revealed perfectly by her momentary state of bareheadedness. She seemed as full of vitality as the sun.

"Oh, by heaven, if you have any intelligence yourself you will move on now that we've seen who it is," Holly said. "I recognize her. You are quite right—she does have a charming laugh. She is altogether quite charming—too charming by half! And widowed, too. But she is also the last lady in London you should want to get involved with."

"Why is that?" Archer asked, resisting Holly's attempt to drag him away from the window.

"Because," his friend replied with a dramatic pause, "that is *Lady Wetherell*. She is infamous—and rumored to be quite the courtesan. Has a scandalous history. You won't find her received at any of the respectable tables in town."

That information only quickened Archer's pulse and piqued his curiosity. The lady in question was not only beautiful, but tastefully, even impeccably, attired—a perfect picture of respectability and style. Was it for show alone?

He continued to stare while he fired questions at Holly. "Rumored to be? Infamous? Is she a courtesan or isn't she? Who is her current protector?" Considering it, he could picture her with someone easily enough—those slender arms and graceful hands, the arch of her neck . . .

There did seem to be something inherently sexual about her, despite the modesty of her appearance.

"Hmm, I don't seem to be discouraging your interest."

"Answer!"

"All right, I will tell you all I know—if you'll come away from that window. Look, here come those bounders Bicton and Timmsbury. They'll see us in a moment. I can hear it already: 'Guess who we found in Bond Street with his nose plastered against a milliner's window.' And can't you picture the betting book at White's? You have barely arrived in Town and already the speculation over your behavior will become the subject of everyone's attention. I promised your great-uncle I would look out for you. You are supposed to walk the straight-and-narrow path!"

"What, are you my keeper? You are no shepherd—"

"And you are no lamb, that's certain. Come on, let us walk up toward Weston's."

It galled Archer to think his family trusted him so little. At twenty-six the heir presumptive to the Marquess of Huntington hardly needed a watchdog. While he would admit his past behavior had been less than exemplary at times, he thought it was no more so than that of many fellows who needed to sow some wild oats and had both the time and the funds to do so.

Well, not *much* more so. Surely a little scandal was to be expected in everyone's life!

He took one last look through the shop window, then yielded to Holly's insistent tug, but only because he did not wish to cause further friction between them.

"I'll come along, Holly, but we're only going to loiter across the street and pretend to peruse the snuffboxes in Crandall's," he said. "I want to steal another look at the lady when she comes out."

Inside the shop, Daphne D'Avernett Stanwell, Lady Wetherell, waited for the salesclerk's attention. She had not meant to laugh out loud, but her attempt to stifle her amusement had failed completely. She supposed it did not matter, as she was already condemned for her behavior no matter what she did. There was, she knew well, a certain freedom that came along with a reputation like hers.

"You are right, Mattie, that last one did look quite as though I'd put an inverted coal scuttle on my head! But this one would protect me and at least three other people from the sun, rather like wearing a roof." Another bubble of laughter escaped. "I shall go back to the very first one—the simple one with that lovely blue ribbon and the single plume dyed to match. *If* the girl intends to wait upon us, that is."

Daphne would not leave the shop without making her purchase. She was accustomed to the stares and whispered comments that followed her when she went out in public places. She had schooled herself to ignore the way such treatment made her feel. Surprised that the women still in the shop so late in the morning had not all walked out the moment she entered, she had barely resisted the temptation to chase them all out like a flock of foolish hens. Now that she had made her selection, she did not expect to wait long to pay for it. The shop girl would undoubtedly wish to be rid of her as quickly as possible. That could be accounted as an advantage, could it not? She was quite ready to leave, now.

Moments earlier she had placed the enormous gypsy hat on the wood-and-glass counter, and as she did, a movement in the looking glass by her elbow had caught her eye. Two men had been outside the shop window, peering in quite unashamedly—or rather, one had peered in while the other tugged at his arm. They were dressed like gentlemen, even if they did not behave as such. The first was attractively broad-shouldered and trim-waisted, tall and wearing a blue coat, while the other was even taller, built more like a sturdy peel tower attired in brown. She had been unable to see them well as their faces were in shadow, but even as she looked, they had quit and moved on.

That was just as well for them, she thought, for she'd had the uncomfortable sense they had been ogling her. She might have delivered a few choice words to them when she stepped outside, and wouldn't the gossips have loved that? *Men!* Too often they behaved worse than the women.

She took her old bonnet from her maid and stuck it back on her own head rather ferociously. Could she not simply enjoy an outing and the plain pleasure of buying herself a new hat? That springtime ritual, learned at her mother's side, was Daphne's tribute to her mother's memory and always sent her back to her own work refreshed and inspired. An artist herself, Daphne appreciated creative talent when she found it in the work of others.

Besides, the shop itself was a visual feast of color and texture that never failed to delight her. The shelves and counters overflowed with plain and colored straws, silks, ribbons, feathers, flowers, finished and unfinished hats and bonnets in a multitude of styles, as well as a variety of elegant accessories. The faint scent of the straw resurrected memories of her childhood years on a country estate, before her life had turned upside down. Surely she had as much right to be here as anyone else.

Happily, none of the other women in the shop had made comments or had even acknowledged her presence. She hoped they would continue to keep their claws sheathed until she could finish making her purchase and leave.

The young milliner's assistant came over. Daphne quickly indicated the hat she had decided upon, paid for it, and arranged to have the package delivered to her home in Chelsea. As she made her way to the door, ladies drew away, gathering their skirts as if they feared contamination by a touch from hers. Lady Brumborough leaned toward the woman beside her and whispered very audibly, "I can't imagine what need *she* has for a new hat! Didn't think women of her sort actually got out and about in the daylight very much."

Stung, Daphne stopped for a fraction of a second. Such meanness was not worthy of any response, and she hated to show any sign that it bothered her. It was nothing new. Yet she could feel the color rising into her cheeks with her anger. Her husband's consequence had protected her from such behavior for a welcome interval while he was alive.

She knew better than to slap Lady Brumborough in public, much as she would have liked to. What a shame that she could not defend her honor by challenging the woman to a duel! The fantasy of skewering her on the end of a blade held great appeal. Daphne knew she should settle for sending a scathing look in the woman's direction and walking out with her head high, but she simply could not. That insistent troublemaker inside her would not let it be. She turned and advanced toward the offending woman.

"Why, my dear Lady B," she said, affecting a presumptuously intimate tone. "As usual, your concern is so kind! But as you would know, of course, we all must do our part to keep the good milliners like Madame Michaud in business, mustn't we—even at the cost of some beauty sleep?"

The shock of being addressed in such an outrageously familiar manner and being included by intimation in a common sisterly circle with someone like Lady Wetherell looked as though it might make Lady Brumborough faint. Her color had drained quite satisfyingly, and Daphne imagined there would be a nice little stir of gossip speculating about just how well the two women knew each other after all. She smiled and sailed out the door with her chin up. A bad reputation did have its uses.

Outside the shop, she squared her shoulders and looked up at the sky, determined to sweep the incident out of her mind along with so many others like it. The bright cloudiness of the day gave everything a silver light, beautiful in its own way. It made her fingers itch for a paintbrush. She thought of how surprised the biddies in the shop would be if they had any idea just how much she actually treasured the daylight, and why! As she and her maid started up the street toward their waiting carriage, Daphne managed a smile at the irony. The day was coming, she was determined, when those same women would rue their hasty judgments and see her in a whole new light.

Chapter Two

Dodging between a draper's cart and an elegant green curricle drawn by prancing matched chestnuts, Archer and Holly had crossed Bond Street and taken up a position in front of Crandall's window across the street from the milliner's shop. Turning to check his view of the doorway where Lady Wetherell would come out, Archer discovered with a stab of dismay that crossing the street had not saved him and his friend from encountering Mr. Bicton and Lord Timmsbury. Those two young men had ducked through the traffic to cross the street as well and proceeded to greet him and Holly with an enthusiasm that Archer thought was far from warranted.

Perhaps Holly knew these fellows better than he did. His own acquaintance with them was slight, hardly enough to merit the trouble of crossing the street to pursue a conversation. They wanted something, if he did not miss his guess. He had become quite adept at reading people during his time in the islands.

He tried to hide his annoyance and pretend he had nothing better to do, all the while keeping an eye out for Lady Wetherell. He hoped she would not leave the shop before he could rid himself of his unwelcome company.

In the meantime, he would have to wait to hear what Holly could tell him about the lady. He scarcely attended the conversation, replying mindlessly to the usual courtesies while trying to keep the milliner's shop door in sight over

Mr. Bicton's well-padded left shoulder. Every time the fellow shifted his position, Archer shifted his as well.

"Are we dancing, Lord Ramsdale?" Mr. Bicton finally inquired.

"What? No. Walking. Er, waiting. Actually, Sir Peter was considering going into Crandall's. Needs a new snuffbox." Archer hoped Holly would catch his hint. He pulled out his pocket watch and looked at it pointedly. "Afraid we haven't much time. Appointments, you know."

"Oh, well then, wouldn't want to detain you," Lord Timmsbury murmured. As lean as Mr. Bicton was plump, he reminded Archer of a fox cub, inquisitive but at the same time crafty. "It's just that I hear you're building a new boat to enter in the Duke's Cup in July. Heard she's to be something a bit out of the ordinary."

Ah, Archer thought, *so that's his game.* No doubt Timmsbury was planning to wager on the pleasure-boat race and was fishing for information that would give him an edge.

"Picked up a few ideas about sailing yachts, did you, during your time in the islands?" he prompted when Archer did not respond. "Not going to build some knife-nosed capsizing crate like your late friend Haverthorpe, are you?"

Archer stiffened, and the back of his neck prickled. In an instant he had stepped around Mr. Bicton and stood nose to nose with Lord Timmsbury.

"That remark, sir, was uncommonly ill-judged," he snarled, fists clenched at his sides. He and Richard Haverthorpe had sailed together often and shared an interest in improving the performance of sailing craft. After Archer had gone to the West Indies, Haverthorpe had drowned in the lower Thames while trying to prove the benefits of a boat with a radically unconventional design.

"Haverthorpe was a rare fellow of vision and conviction, besides being a friend," he continued, controlling the urge to plant his knuckles in Timmsbury's overly inquisitive face. "A *close* friend. But perhaps I did not hear you correctly."

Holly inserted his considerable bulk between the two men. "I'm certain that is the case," he said pointedly, staring at Timmsbury as he eased Archer back a few steps. "Lord Timmsbury would never be so idiotic as to insult a friend of yours and incur your wrath, Drake, unless he had a death wish, of course."

Timmsbury paled, and that was enough to help Archer regain control of his emotions. Truly, he knew better than to cause a scene in the middle of Bond Street.

"Who'd you say was building the new boat for you, eh?" Mr. Bicton put in helpfully.

"I didn't say," Archer replied with ice in his tone, but then a new idea occurred to him. Desperate to get rid of the two men, he drew Bicton closer and lowered his voice.

"Wouldn't want to risk word getting around to the competition, don't you know? Can't say what, but she does have a few innovations in her design. It remains to be seen, of course, how well those will work sailing here in the Thames. You understand why I can't divulge the details."

He hoped that crumb of confirmation would be sufficient to satisfy the men. Common courtesy demanded that they let the subject drop, not that Timmsbury had shown courtesy in his remarks. Winning the race was desperately important to Archer, but it was equally important that no one should know that. He raised an eyebrow at Holly, hoping he would jump back into the conversation and help him out.

"I say," Holly responded dutifully, "do you know, I believe I saw Sir Ellison Tolley down by Sam's Bookshop and Library when we came by there. I hear he's planning to enter for the Cup with a new boat, also."

Brilliant, thought Archer. Bicton's and Timmsbury's faces lit up at the prospect of gleaning information from another race participant. The two men bid him and Holly a hasty adieu and went off to hunt down a new quarry.

"What a plumper!" Archer said to Holly as soon as the others were out of earshot. He was grinning now.

"I know—the things I do for my friends! Did the trick, did it not? They had us trapped here, and I was afraid you would pop Timmsbury's cork. And just in time—look, here comes the lady."

They watched as Lady Wetherell came out of the milliner's shop with her maid in tow and started up the street. A passing dray loaded with crates blocked the men's view for a moment, and then they could see the women getting into their waiting carriage, a stylish maroon vis-à-vis with yellow wheels.

"Utterly magnificent," Archer rhapsodized.

"I'm not so certain about the wheel color."

Archer punched Holly on the arm, even though he knew the teasing was intentional. "Dunderhead! The lady! Did you see how she sailed out of that shop with her head held high? It was as if she were quite above everything."

He truly did not think he had ever seen a more beautiful woman. The charm was more than her physical appearance—she seemed to radiate a spirited liveliness that drew him. He wondered how Holly could be immune to it.

"Hmmph. Those who are beneath everything have to put on airs, I suppose," Holly muttered. "Beauty cannot make up for a lack of character, you know."

"Perhaps I define character differently than you, my friend. Come now, you promised to tell me all about her."

Once Lady Wetherell's carriage passed them and continued down Bond Street, Archer and Holly started up in the other direction, toward the mews where they had left Archer's own carriage. Dodging fellow pedestrians and keeping an eye on the uneven pavements kept them occupied as they talked, although most people made way for them, an advantage of walking with Holly.

"You said she was a widow. How long?"

Holly sighed. "Oh, probably a full year and more, now."

Past the mourning period. "Hm, that's good."

"I doubt the late Lord Wetherell sees it that way."

Archer smiled. "If he sees anything." He imagined that anyone married to such a beautiful woman would be grieved indeed to leave her behind. "Poor fellow. What can the lady possibly have done to make her so reviled?"

"Seems to have an unerring instinct and appetite for scandal. There's quite a list of her supposed lovers, for instance."

"London is full of merry widows free to love whomever they please. That should not put her beyond the pale."

"It is hardly discreet if one's liaisons are public knowledge, and I assure you, the list connected to her is recited over cards in all the clubs. It is very long. Then, of course, rumor has it that her amorous career began even before she was married."

"Is that the worst of it? For a woman that beautiful, I'd need more than the paltry threat of hearing my name on that list to discourage my interest. Why, half the names might be there only for bragging."

"I needn't remind you that discretion and propriety are still the rule in our circles. Certainly she did not even see fit to wait until her mourning period was over to begin entertaining again after old Wetherell died."

Archer supposed he must not look dissuaded, for Holly hardly paused for breath. "Her marriage to the viscount was itself a scandal, I gather. You and I were still at Cambridge then. They say he was a besotted old fool in his sixties. She was a penniless chit of eighteen, orphaned, and only seven years older than his son! But one need only look at her to understand how easily she could have brought the old man around. Wetherell no doubt figured he was old enough to damn society and do as he pleased."

Holly stepped around the cart of an old woman selling apples and Archer dodged behind him. "If she'd been an heiress and he a pockets-to-let duke, no one would have been even slightly shocked," he argued. He did not add that he thought damning society and doing as one pleased should not be dependent upon age.

"Well, that's not the worst." Holly moved ahead with dogged persistence. "Before her marriage she worked as an artist's model."

Archer's reply died in his throat. Models were no better than—and often were—common prostitutes. The idea just did not fit with his impression of the lady.

His mouth must have been agape, for Holly said, "Shocking, eh? I thought you would find it so. There is a family history of scandal there. As I understand it, her father caused several, too. I don't know the details, but they say he was a gentleman artist who ran through his wife's money and then gave up his status to enter into trade, founding an art academy."

He stopped walking and faced Archer. "They say he had the talent to be accepted into the Royal Academy but lacked the required moral character. Is it any wonder that his daughter should have the same failing, given the example he set for her?"

Archer felt the muscles in his jaw tighten. That was the same flawed reasoning that led everyone to believe he would end up an irresponsible wastrel like his own father. "You cannot hold the daughter to blame for the sins of her father. Look at my own father. Not exactly a shining example of moral rectitude."

"Ah, but at least your father sank gracefully into debt without resorting to trade. And, by Jove, he never put any member of your family to *work!*" Holly's face reflected a thorough distaste for the very idea, bred into him through countless generations of aristocratic ancestors. "And such work! Can you imagine a man who would so use his own daughter?"

"Given the number of streetwalkers in London, there must be many."

"But not *gentlemen,*" Holly protested, the note of horror still in his voice. "He had to know putting his daughter to such a use would ruin her."

Archer simply could not accept the story. "Can you verify any of this?"

"Well, I've not bedded her myself, if that's what you want to know. But where there's smoke there's usually fire," Holly replied darkly.

"I never knew you were such a gossip, Holly. Worse than a woman!" Archer tried to put a teasing tone into his words, but underneath he was feeling unaccountably testy. He didn't know why this matter of Lady Wetherell had instantly become such an obsession.

"What? What? Swords or pistols?" Holly pretended to take offense. "Watch your words, friend. I would not take that comment from anyone but you."

"Because you know I can beat you at either of those."

"So I should choose cards, or fisticuffs?"

Archer laughed. "God forbid you should beat me at cards any more than you already do." But he was not to be distracted. "You said there is a stepson?"

They had reached the entrance to the stable mews and turned into the shadowed archway.

"Yes, from the viscount's first marriage." Holly's words echoed hollowly, as did the two friends' footsteps. "The lad is just old enough to be getting into all sorts of wrong company and trouble. Has an affinity for the gaming tables, I've heard, although I haven't yet played against him."

Emerging into the paved courtyard, Archer signaled to

the stabler to fetch his carriage as he absorbed this information. "That is too perfect, old man. Sounds as though the lad could use a steadying influence. Perhaps I can rescue him."

"You would stoop to such an old ploy—using the son to get to the woman?" Holly gave Archer a disapproving frown. "Can you not see why an involvement with her is out of the question?"

Archer tried to look brightly angelic. "Can you not believe I might simply have the lad's welfare in mind? Or do you assume the lady wouldn't welcome my interest? Now I should be insulted! You will admit I have some talent with females."

"You can't afford to get burned by scandal this time around."

"What scandal? I do not plan to marry her. And she is not married herself. Do you doubt I can be discreet?"

"It isn't *your* discretion that worries me. Somehow, word of her affairs always seems to get about."

Deaf to his friend's concern, Archer added, "I suppose the plan does depend. How do she and the stepson rub along together?"

Holly answered with obvious reluctance. "Apparently well enough. Old Wetherell named her the boy's guardian. The lad has not yet reached his majority."

Eyebrows raised, Archer gazed at his friend. "A woman guardian? That is unusual enough, but one with such a reputation? Unimaginable! I wonder what he was thinking. If there are other relatives, they must have been positively apoplectic. This whole thing intrigues me more and more." He turned to watch his horses being led out of the stable block.

"What makes you think you'll have time for a dalliance?" Holly asked a little desperately. "Won't you need to use your time sailing the river?"

"Perhaps she likes to sail."

"You are *not* thinking. Suppose she is the leader in the lad's dance toward ruin? Listen to me, Drake. Did you love the West Indies so much that you wish to be exiled there again? Any involvement with Lady Wetherell would be disastrous for you—the last thing you need!"

"She sounds like the perfect mistress to me." Archer

grinned, but Holly positioned himself directly in front of him and began to poke him with a finger for emphasis.

"Lord Huntington will have my hide to decorate his study wall, I say. If you care nothing for his opinion and power, what about his purse strings? He could cut you off in a trice. Need I remind you that the reason you're here in London is to find a bride?"

"That is my family's thinking, not mine. I have my own priorities, and the parson's trap is not among them—not yet."

"By Jove, I smell rebellion. I thought a dash of cool English air would make you sensible after all that hellish tropical heat. If you are so randy, let me find you a lovely opera dancer—no one would so much as bat an eyelash over a liaison like that. I don't relish being caught in the middle of this."

"If you would not make rash promises to my relations, you wouldn't *be* caught in the middle, my friend."

Archer's glossy new town coach stood ready to receive him. He and Holly would part here as Archer was headed for his family's residence in Fitzwarren Place and his friend had business elsewhere.

"You keep telling me Lady Wetherell is the last woman in London I should get involved with," Archer said as he mounted the steps of the carriage. "If you will sleep easier, I'll promise she will be just that. The *last* woman I get involved with before I submit to the leg shackles for life." *A last stab at independence.*

Holly groaned and shook his head. "I should know by now that there's no dissuading you from a course once you are set on it." He started to walk away, but at the last moment he turned his head and looked Archer straight in the eye.

"I am thoroughly serious, Drake. You'll regret it if this idea hasn't left you when you wake up tomorrow. Pursuing this could be the biggest mistake you ever make."

Archer cocked an eyebrow and answered with an irreverent grin. At this moment, the idea of courting Lady Wetherell—disaster or not—filled him with the same excitement as the prospect of a good sailing race, and he loved to race more than anything. *Challenge made life worth living.*

"A mistake, Holly?" he replied. "When did you think I have ever made any of those?"

Chapter Three

Minutes later Archer's carriage halted on the flags of a small courtyard in front of his family's large stone town house. He gave a nod of acknowledgment to the footman who let down the carriage steps for him and gave another to the one who opened the highly polished front door as he climbed the steps of the imposing residence.

Definitely, he needed to get his own Town rooms—especially if he was going to carry on a dalliance. Coming here made him feel as though he were eight years old again. A man needed privacy as well as control over his own comings and goings. Thank God for Westwater, his uncle's retreat on the bank of the Thames in Fulham, a few miles west of London. Without that sanctuary, he would be residing here under his mother's control and supervision just as if he really were that small boy again.

His mother, he reflected, had not yet had time to realize that his three years in the Caribbean had changed him. He had arrived there an unwelcome interloper whose stay was known to be temporary, yet he had wanted to be useful and make a contribution. He had exercised patience, never one of his strongest qualities, studying the people around him, the situation, and the operations of his great-uncle's plantations.

Amazingly, he had begun to see how he might offer suggestions and exercise some authority without appearing to be a threat to those who were established there long before he came and who would remain there after he left. He saw how arrogant it would be for him to come in and make sweeping changes. The situation had required delicate handling, and he knew he had done well. But did his family know?

There were far-ranging tensions and issues that put the scent of upheaval in the Caribbean air, and he looked forward to sitting down with his great-uncle to talk about these things, man-to-man. That was about the only aspect of seeing the old man he did look forward to with pleasure. For the most part he was relieved that the marquess was not yet in London.

"Good day, my lord. The ladies have been awaiting your arrival. They are in the blue salon."

He handed off his walking stick, hat, and gloves to a third waiting footman and headed straight for the stairs, unmindful of the elegance of his surroundings. The inlaid floor of black and white marble squares gleamed in the soft light filtering down from the skylight above the stair hall. The stairs themselves rose from the ground floor in twin arcs of graceful steps with ornate wrought-iron railings and met at a landing before ascending further. Archer started up the right-hand stairway, taking the shallow steps two at a time quite easily with his long legs.

He did not, however, fling wide the double doors of the blue salon in a dramatic gesture of arrival when he reached them. He opened one door quietly and slipped into the room.

His mother stood silhouetted at a tall window, slim and erect with her back to him. His sister Winifred, all blond curls and flounced white muslin, was arrayed on the pale blue–striped satin sofa prattling on about something with chorused support from their youngest sister, Caroline. Caro, with her dark hair, looked far more like a sister to him and behaved more like him, too, he thought, as she surveyed the tea tray in front of her, seeking a choice morsel. How they ever noticed the click of the door when he closed it behind him he could not guess, but silence fell instantly. His mother turned.

"Here you are at last, Archer. We have been waiting for you this hour."

He went to her and kissed her cheek, noting not for the first time the fine lines and betraying strands of gray hair that had encroached upon her in his absence. His mother was a handsome dark-haired beauty still, but time was her enemy.

"My apologies for keeping you waiting. I have been out and about with Hollyfield; among other things, I checked on the status of my new boat. I thought it would please you that I am making my presence in Town visible, at least."

He would not claim to have been attending to matters of importance—his mother would see right through such a fib, and his failings would only be compounded. Besides, he was well past the age of bending the truth to appease her. Or at least he thought he should be. She probably knew perfectly well that he had been dreading and postponing this session anyway. He tried to dampen his buoyant good spirits. *No sense arousing anyone's curiosity.*

Lady Ramsdale moved to a chair and with an autocratic wave of her hand indicated that he might as well be seated also. As he passed his sisters, he tossed a small packet to each of them and smiled at their gleeful cries. He had not forgotten to do their errands—embroidery thread for Winnie and sweets for Caro.

"Your sisters and I have been sifting through all the invitations that have been flooding in since the papers announced your arrival home," his mother said. "We have drawn up a list of the engagements we think would be the most suitable for you to attend. Although I cannot say that we are quite in agreement over all of them," she added, slanting a look at the young women.

He chuckled. "Most suitable—yes, of course. And have you left me any time to pursue plans of my own, such as sailing or spending time at my club?" He did not mention a different sort of pursuit that was fresh on his mind, of a certain beautiful courtesan whose laughter had enchanted him.

"I tried to tell them—" Caroline began.

"Well, what is really more important—?" Winnie said at the same time.

"Hush, girls. Ahem. We have only included on the list the engagements we thought you would find most enjoyable, Archer—ones with the brightest and loveliest young ladies likely to attend, for instance—"

"That have been approved or perhaps even hand picked by his lordship?"

His mother ignored him. "Or ones with a high chance of good quality music, for another instance."

"Or good food," Archer said. "Let us not forget the importance of a good meal to a man."

He tried to keep his tone light, but a certain edge had crept into his words. Their list would include balls, dinners, musicales, routs, evenings of theater, and endless dozens of other entertainments and soirees. These would present an endless parade of dangerous young women with marriage on their minds. The prospect was daunting.

"And I suppose that the social advantage to Winnie and Caroline has not been a factor at all in these choices? Or any thought of keeping me occupied and out of trouble?"

Of course, it was already too late for that. He smiled as his mother was forced to abandon her too-bright cheeriness.

"Well, naturally considering Winnie and Caroline is necessary, my dear. Winnie has waited all this time to make her come-out, and Caroline will be old enough to make hers next year. Having you home now only increases their consequence. Can you blame us if we wish to show you off? We have missed you terribly."

He could accept that as closer to the truth. His mother meant well, and he believed she loved him. His three-year exile to the islands had probably been hard on her—perhaps harder than it had been on him. While, God knew, he had missed his family, he had not found his time there insufferable, especially with amusing company to distract him. A mistress here in London would surely ease his discontent. For a moment, the sound of Lady Wetherell's husky laughter and a vision of her marching from the hat shop filled his mind, triggering a familiar longing.

"We will wait until Lord Huntington is come to Town before we hold Winnie's come-out ball, of course," his mother continued, jerking his attention back with a snap. She was too wise to make any mention of specific matrimonial prospects. She probably thought he would bolt if she pursued that subject, and she was quite likely right.

"When is he coming?"

"He has not said exactly."

"Mother, you know I intend to try for the Duke's Cup in July and to prepare with practice before that. I must have time to relearn the river and get a feel for the new boat once it is ready. I do not promise to attend all of these functions you have so carefully selected."

"There might be a few occasions that could be missed," she said, sounding almost conciliatory.

"Oh, but not the Todmartins' ball!" Winnie's desperation was unmistakable.

He could not resist the temptation to tease her. He had been surprised at how much he had missed his pesky sisters. They had grown into young ladies while he was gone. "What is so special about that particular ball, if I may ask? I might not be at all inclined to attend that one."

That set off a round of explanations about who would be there and who would not, and why it mattered and to whom, and he simply could not keep his attention on it. A vision of Lady Wetherell's upswept chestnut hair danced into his mind. Dark, glossy, and undoubtably soft hair. He longed to touch it.

The first thing I should do is discover which gaming haunts her young charge frequents. If I can put him into my debt, it might be reason enough to call on her about it. The thought crossed his mind that he might himself incur some debts following this course, although his skill at the tables was passable. Was the lad into deep play?

Archer ticked off in his mind the list of his recent expenditures—new wardrobe, new carriage, new draperies for his mother's dining room, not to mention the sleek new sailing cutter he had just made a payment on that morning, ordered before he had left the islands. It was nearly finished. He supposed he had been a trifle extravagant since arriving, hadn't he? Then with this round of socializing in the wind, there had already been bills for new gowns for his mother and sisters plus a hundred other feminine necessities, which he would never dream of denying them even if he might grumble.

Add to the list the usual expenses of wooing a new lady and it amounted to quite a sum, but he could cover it. He was *not* like his spendthrift father. Spending blunt you had was quite different from spending blunt you did not have. The monthly income his great-uncle was providing amounted to a princely fortune.

It was a bribe, of course, to ensure Archer's good behavior. But Archer had banked much of it, and even invested some. He did not have extravagant tastes or needs, for the most part. If the money stopped, he could still manage for some time on what he had put by. And there was the Duke's Cup, offering the largest money prize for a regatta anywhere in England. If he could win that, his path to independence was assured. In that sense, he saw his new boat as an investment, not a luxury. Not to mention that he had a point to prove—and a friend to vindicate.

Dismissing his momentary concern, he began to picture a leisurely cruise down the Thames with Lady Wetherell aboard that new boat. If he could judge by his own painful experience, half of the gossip told about her was likely not even true. Finding out which half could be very pleasurable, he was certain.

"Archer. Archer Everett Drake, you have not been attending a single word we've said."

"Uh, about the Finchleys' ball? When did you say it would be held?"

Caroline snorted in a very unladylike fashion. "We left that and are talking about vouchers for Almack's now, silly goose."

Despite a certain note of sympathy underneath her words, Archer felt he could not allow such irreverence. Reluctantly, he gave up a vision of a very relaxed Lady Wetherell trailing her delicate white hand in the water over the side rail of his new cutter and focused instead upon his youngest sister. He had yet to establish his authority in his new role with the family. "I'll thank you not to address the future Marquess of Huntington and head of this family as a silly goose, young lady."

He could see Caroline was not impressed with his sternness.

"Archer, please. We are only trying to help you," his mother said. "Could you not give us your attention for just these few minutes? It is necessary to make some decisions, for we must send replies to all these notes and cards. There are the requisite visits to be made and certain other social conventions that must be followed. I know it all seems trivial to you, but I assure you it is not."

At the pleading note in his mother's voice, Archer capitulated. He seemed to be doing a great deal of that since his arrival. In the islands, no one had told him what to do. He had been in charge. That, at least, had been refreshing.

He realized, however, that young Lord Wetherell could be expected to attend at least some of the events on his mother's list. The lad had a title and, apparently, some funds. He would not be entirely ostracized by the members of the *haut ton* just because he had a scandalous, beautiful, unacceptable stepmother.

"Let me see this list," he said imperiously, holding out his hand.

Someone was also waiting for Daphne when she returned from her shopping expedition. It had taken her rather longer to reach her destination, as she and her stepson shared a villa on the banks of the River Thames in Chelsea.

"Lord Thornhurst is in the library, madam, waiting to see you," her butler informed her. An elderly fellow with a face like a ferret, he was stooped and wizened yet sharp and alert. "I do apologize. He insisted upon waiting, even when I told him I'd no idea how long you would be gone."

She finished untying the strings to her old bonnet and handed it to him before she answered. Lord, give her patience! She had an idea why Lord Thornhurst had come, and also why he chose not to try again at some other time. In that case he might have to explain to his wife. She sighed.

"It is all right, Carmichael. I will see him."

"Also, this came for you." The butler looked even more apologetic, as if he felt responsible for what came in the mail.

She took the letter he held out to her, knowing the ordinary mail would be on a tray in her sitting room. A glance told her it was from Lord Pasmore, her stepson's uncle. No doubt another missive complaining about something she had or hadn't done. He was always threatening to drag her before the Chancery Court for her failure to be a fit guardian for his nephew.

"Thank you, Carmichael." She would not shock the old man by ripping up the letter unread right in front of him. Lord Pasmore's threats were not worth two pins. But before she headed for the library she had to know, "Is my step—ah, Lord Wetherell—at home?"

The man shook his head with a hint of sympathy on his face.

She attempted an unconcerned smile, as if she could actually hide her feelings. "No, I thought as much. I do not know why I even asked."

Robbie was so seldom at home anymore. His uncle's threats might not worry her, but Robbie did.

For the moment, however, she had to deal with her visitor. Clutching the unopened letter in one hand, she brushed back a stray wisp of dark chestnut hair from her temple and smoothed her skirt with the other, gathering her thoughts to focus upon Lord Thornhurst.

The earl was tall enough to lean one elbow upon the library's mantelshelf and was casually examining the Sevres figurines displayed there when she opened the door. At the sound of her entrance he hastily replaced the figurine from his hand and straightened up like a young lad caught pinching scones in the kitchen. Except that Lord Thornhurst was all of seventy years old, a gray-haired comrade of her late husband.

"Lord Thornhurst," she said with a sincere attempt to sound courteous.

He ambled over to her, moving awkwardly because he suffered from gout. "I thought I would drop by to see how you are faring, my dear. I am concerned for you, you know."

The letter crinkled as she tightened her grip on it. She was quite certain she knew where this conversation was headed. If she had a half crown for every time she'd heard a man make this speech since her husband's death, she'd be a very rich woman by now.

"It is very kind of you." *Or it would be if your motives were clear of any self-interest.*

He seized her free hand and kissed it, holding it a little too long. "I—um—you're looking well."

"I feel well, thank you." *Or I did until now.* She extracted her hand quickly and suggested he sit down.

"You haven't been entertaining of late," he noted, lowering himself into the nearest leather-upholstered chair. "Rather, I mean—that is to say—I noticed there haven't been any invitations for your lovely dinners here at Grove House in recent weeks."

She chose a chair placed directly opposite to his and did not answer. The comment wouldn't have pricked at all if he had not taken such care to reword it.

"I miss the engaging, intelligent company, the stimulating conversation, the food, and I miss you, my dear."

There could be a grain of truth in there somewhere. She bit back a laugh, reminding herself that he meant well, in his own twisted way. "I am flattered to think you miss my humble gatherings, Lord Thornhurst, and I am sorry, too. At first I thought it would be a fitting tribute to my husband's memory to start holding the salon again. He always did enjoy good food and a good discussion, particularly if it concerned the arts."

She had also naively believed that as a widow she might have been granted the freedom to resume her role of hosting them without censure. "However," she continued, "the dinners seemed to be causing gossip. Or to be frank, perhaps I should simply say they fueled new gossip."

Gossip alone would not have stopped her. However, the sheer number of her husband's male friends whose interest had proved to be something other than the arts, plus the jealous wives, formerly friendly, who suddenly no longer trusted her around those same husbands, had finally exhausted her patience. But she would not say that. "Life is difficult enough for poor Robbie, saddled with me for a stepmother. I felt I must stop."

"It is a shame. You are a supreme hostess—just one of your admirable talents, may I say? Yet if you cease to socialize altogether, you will be very lonely."

Ah, he was warming to it now. She doubted she could put him off his course, but she had to try. "It is not so bad. I am content."

She missed the companionship of her husband, but her life was relatively peaceful, which she was wise enough to value. Above all, she had privacy, which she prized after being put on display for so long, first by her father and then by her husband.

"You are in a vulnerable position now that you are no longer in mourning. Our new Lord Wetherell is still too young to serve as your protector, and you have no one else."

"I don't believe I need a protector, Lord Thornhurst,

although I do appreciate your concern." She was trying
hard to remain polite. She really ought to throw the fellow
out on his ear, but what a stir that might cause!

"Less honorable men than myself are very likely to seek
to take advantage of you."

As if he were not? But there was nothing new in that.
"Lord Wetherell had confidence in my ability to take care
of myself, sir. Clearly he would not have named me as
Robbie's guardian if he had not deemed me capable."

"Admirable in sentiment, but not at all practical. I told
him so myself. How is a woman to exercise any authority
over a young man? He should be in a university. Fortunately, he has the solicitors to handle his funds, and from
what I am hearing, 'tis a very good thing. What do you
know of his recent conduct, I might ask?"

He touched now on the very thing that worried her, but
she refused to show any vulnerability to this man. Problems
with Robbie were none of his concern. Fortunately, she
was spared the necessity of replying when he went right on.

"But watching over the young cub is not to my point.
Who will watch over you? You are still young—and so
beautiful, my dear. Not to mention I fear your reputation
makes you far more vulnerable than, well, that is to
say . . ."

She supposed she should admire his frankness in ad-
dressing that problem, even if he lacked the backbone to
finish his sentence. Perhaps she might have admired it, if
she did not think that somewhere in the depths (or shal-
lows) of his mind, he actually believed there must be some
validity in that reputation. And here was a man who had
known her throughout all five years of her marriage! If he
had such ideas, certainly it was no wonder that people who
did not know her thought what they did. A little knot of
anger began to tighten in her stomach.

"If I were not married, you must know I would be quick
to follow Lord Wetherell's example to provide for you. It
is the least a friend can do." He sighed deeply. "As it is,
my wife . . ."

Daphne knew very well. She knew the old fellow had no
idea he was insulting her or that he was as transparent as
glass. She knew the next thing he was going to say was
something she did not want to hear, yet the fastest way to

be rid of him would be to hear him out, thank him for his supposed good intentions, and then send him off before she said or did something she would later regret. That was among her greatest failings. She closed her fist around the letter in her hand, crushing it.

"While I cannot offer you my name, I could still offer you my protection, Lady Wetherell. I enjoy many of the same interests as your late husband, and truly, I am not so old as you may suppose. We have known each other these several years and rub along well enough. . . ."

She couldn't stand it. She held up her other hand to stop him before he could say any more. She held no illusions about her status in society. Only a fool in her position would hope to be married again, but demmed if she would become nothing more than some man's convenience!

"Please, Lord Thornhurst. I tell you, I lack for nothing. My husband left me very well situated, in every way he possibly could. I thank you for your *kindness,* but I do not need or want a protector.

"I would give the same answer to anyone, despite what the gossips say," she added, trying to soften the rejection. He really did mean well, in his own way.

"You mustn't think for a moment that I believe what they say!" he protested. "It is exactly to protect you from such things that I make my offer."

His hypocrisy was ludicrous; Daphne could not restrain herself. At least she managed not to laugh. "I fail to see how becoming anyone's mistress would *protect* my reputation," she said dryly. "No, Lord Thornhurst, it will not serve. And I think I must declare our visit at an end. There is nothing more to be said."

She rose, forcing him to relinquish his seat as well.

"I am sorry, Lady Wetherell. If you should change your mind at any time, please do consider the offer as standing open. . . ." The words were courteous, but the look in his eye suggested that she might be the one who would be sorry.

She ushered him toward the door with a sense of urgency, hoping he would say nothing more. She did not need any more enemies, but her tolerance for being insulted had limits.

When she heard him taking his leave in the front entry

hall, she smoothed out the crumpled letter from Robbie's uncle and ripped it into tiny pieces. She cast them into the library fireplace and watched them glow and catch fire on the hot coals. *Men!* The last thing she wanted or needed in her life right now was a man. *No, not even the last thing.*

Chapter Four

Shifting the reins of his curricle into one hand for a moment, Archer checked the scrap of paper on which he had written the directions to Lord Wetherell's home. He knew he had better tame his feelings before he arrived there. An elated grin was hardly the appropriate expression for a man calling to settle his previous night's gambling debt.

Archer's plan to woo Lady Wetherell was progressing at last. In the two weeks since he had first seen her, he had eluded the schemes of several matchmaking mamas and endured dinner parties, concerts, theater nights, and several balls in the company of his mother and Winnie. He had run across Lord Wetherell at some of these events and in between them had frequented the places where the lad gambled. Not only had he managed to make the young viscount's acquaintance but he had even become something of a friend and adviser to him.

Guidance was something Lady Wetherell's stepson desperately needed. The eighteen-year-old viscount showed a marked inability to judge his companions or even choose suitable persons with whom to engage in a hand of cards. The boy had gambled away a great deal of money and seemed bent on throwing more money after it.

In the same fortnight, Archer had neither won nor lost any great amounts of the ready at the gaming tables. Comforting as that might be, it had done little to advance his own scheme. However, last night he had finally been blessed with the perfect luck to lose a hundred pounds to the young lord. This turn of events had thrilled them both, albeit for quite different reasons. Archer had been forced to give the boy vowels, and honor demanded that he make an appearance at the lad's home today to pay up. Nothing could have suited him better.

Grove House was located in western Chelsea, on the bank of the Thames a short distance beyond the Battersea Bridge. When he'd received the directions, Archer had been delighted to find that he and Lady Wetherell shared access to the river. *No need for Town rooms.* Should his plans succeed, in future he could come and go with both ease and total discretion simply by sailing down from his residence at Fulham.

He hoped the lady liked to sail. Holly had been right that Archer needed to spend as much time as possible practicing his skills, learning his new boat, and refreshing his knowledge of the river. He smiled, thinking there were certain parallels with the process of winning a mistress.

He had visited his bank in the city this morning and now was headed west along the King's Road in Chelsea. He passed the road to Battersea Bridge and several more lanes that led to the Thames. At the far end of one he could make out the sun-silvered flash of the water and the red tip of a sail on a river barge. It was a glorious day to be out on the river, a day that truly felt and smelled like early June and the coming summer.

He experienced a quick stab of jealousy for the bargemen and thought, not for the first time, that the pleasures of their work must surely outweigh the dangers and hard labor. At least they had the freedom to choose it. He wanted only to exercise his own freedom while he still could.

Following the directions, he passed a new terrace of houses built across from open fields. At this end of Chelsea, farm fields still outnumbered houses, although the growth of London was slowly creeping out even this far. In the nearly two years since Napoleon had been shipped off to St. Helena, a depressed economy had slowed the growth but not halted it entirely.

Of course, Archer thought wryly, the Prince Regent preferred impressive projects like the new Vauxhall Bridge to homes for the city's overflowing populace. Under construction when Archer left for the islands, the bridge had opened last year. This year the Waterloo Bridge would be opened on the battle's anniversary in midmonth. Soon hundreds of London homes would be destroyed to make way for construction of Prinny's grand Regent Street. Perhaps the poor souls to be displaced would come out here to live in Chelsea.

Recognizing the direction of his thoughts, he grimaced. He was beginning to sound like a reformer Whig. He had better not share these views when he finally sat down with his great-uncle or the man might keel over from shock. At the end of the terrace Archer turned his matched pair of blacks into yet another lane that led to the river.

Lord Wetherell's villa was situated at the end of the lane on land running down to the water with open fields beyond. Archer noted that the old-fashioned grounds appeared in perfect order as he entered through the open gates and drove up the gravel carriageway. Meticulously tended garden beds and neatly clipped shrubbery ornamented smooth green lawns. A fringe of additional shrubbery and large trees stood between the gardens and the river, but the water could be seen glinting through the foliage. The house was a neat brick structure with large chimneys, built in the style of the last century. The windows and white trim gleamed in the sunlight, supporting the image of prosperity and order.

Archer had learned through discreet inquiries that the modest estate did not lack for funds—at least, not yet. If the young Lord Wetherell kept up his present ways for long, that could change. But for now, if Lady Wetherell was taking lovers, she did so purely for the pleasure of it, not for profit or from need. *Not truly a courtesan, despite rumors*. That idea pleased him. He could not recall a time when a woman had so totally ensnared his interest. Especially when he had yet to meet her! He shook his head, trying to quell his eagerness and summon a sober expression.

For a moment after he halted his horses, nothing happened. No one emerged from the residence; no groom appeared to take charge of his carriage. He was beginning to wonder if he should revise his opinion of the well-tended place when a young boy came flying around the corner of the house, still shrugging one arm into the emerald green velvet coat of his livery. With a look of apology, the lad skidded to a stop in front of Archer, bowed, and then approached the horses with appropriate decorum. At that point, the front door opened and a similarly clad footman drawn up as stiffly as the human form allowed acknowledged Archer's arrival.

Bemused, Archer left his cattle and equipage in the hands of the lad and ascended the steps to the entrance. He gave a surreptitious tug to the bottom edge of his buff-colored waistcoat and shook down his shirt cuffs, making certain their ruffled edges showed just the proper amount beneath the sleeves of his coat. He had dressed with great care this morning, trying the patience of his valet as he rejected the first several of the fellow's attempts to tie his cravat. His coat, of blue superfine and made by Weston, fit his frame to the fraction of an inch. Holly would have approved, especially given his frequent lamentation over Archer's usual carelessness about his clothes.

Unlike his oversized friend, Archer could normally afford to be less than fastidious. His untamable brown hair seemed to attract ladies' fingers the way his changeable gray eyes attracted their admiration. They praised his patrician nose, or his strong, square jaw, or his fine, broad shoulders, regardless of how he was dressed. Confident now as he stepped up to the door of Grove House, he handed the bewigged footman his card and inquired after Lord Wetherell.

"His lordship is not receiving visitors at this hour," the servant informed him frostily.

He smiled. He had expected as much. Counted on it, in fact. Lord Wetherell had consumed far too much claret last night to be up and about yet today. His head would give him great regrets when or if he finally did stir.

"I don't mind waiting," Archer said pleasantly. "We have some business to conclude, but there is no reason to drag the poor fellow from his bed. I can well imagine he will not be feeling quite himself today." As if he had only just thought of it he added, "Perhaps I might have a word with Lady Wetherell?"

The footman looked dubious at best, so Archer added, "There is a matter concerning her stepson. She does not

know me, but perhaps if you would mention I am an acquaintance of the young lord. . . ."

He did not need to press his case further. At the far
end of the entry passageway the lady in question appeared,
carrying her gloves and a basket full of late-blooming
quince branches. As she approached, Archer thought she
belonged in a painting representing the freshness of spring.
The color in the flowers echoed the pink in her cheeks and
the wide straw hat she wore gave her the look of a charming shepherdess. She wore a blue-gray pelisse that was open
down the front, showing a blush pink muslin dress beneath.

"I heard, Wilson. I will receive him," she said. As Archer
stepped inside, she untied the ribbons of her hat and removed it.

Seeing her now in close quarters only confirmed Archer's
first impression of her great beauty. Her features were
finely sculptured—her cheekbones high, her nose straight
and narrow, her mouth full and sensuously curved. Her
skin was like flawless ivory. Lively, intelligent eyes surveyed
him questioningly from under dark, slashing eyebrows that
dramatically accented her face. Thank God there was no
way for her to know his heartbeat had just tripled its speed.

She set the basket on a table in the passage. Touching
the blossoms almost regretfully, she said, "Have Ellen take
these to the kitchen and put them in water, please, Wilson.
I will tend to them in few minutes." Her voice had the
same enchanting huskiness as her laughter and made Archer think of sweet dark honey.

She handed her hat to the footman and exchanged it for
Archer's card. Curiosity and wariness played across her
face as she inspected it.

"Lord Ramsdale?"

Archer bowed politely.

"This way, if you please."

She led him into an anteroom off the passageway. It was
a modest but tastefully appointed chamber with paneling
painted a soft shade of gray. Morning sun poured in
through the single window. As he followed her into the
room he caught a whiff of her scent—an exotic suggestion
of jasmine and roses, but so subtle as to be from the soap
she used.

She gestured for him to take a seat, pointing toward one of the gilded French armchairs that matched the settee facing them. She seated herself across from him.

"I don't believe we have met, sir." It was a flat, brisk statement. Questions were in her eyes, not her voice. Those eyes were a luminous brown—the deep, translucent color of a quiet woodland pool.

"You are right, madam, although I must say I am delighted to have the opportunity."

She was clearly taking his measure, studying him, and to judge by her silence and the look in her eyes, was not instantly inclined to like or trust him.

"Your stepson speaks very highly of you," he added quickly, knowing she must be wondering why he had come.

The eyebrows went up and the scrutiny ceased. "I am surprised that he would mention me at all, quite frankly," she said, looking at him directly. "I cannot say that I have ever heard him speak of you, sir. You say it is concerning him that you wished a word with me?" At this moment the woodland pool looked very cold indeed.

Obviously, flattery was the wrong path to choose. Here was a woman who wasted no time on small talk or false pleasantries, but went directly to the point. She made no attempt to put her visitor at ease. She was clearly not at ease herself, sitting primly on the edge of her chair with her spine as straight as a mizzenmast.

Well, what had he expected? That as soon as she laid eyes upon him she would welcome him into her arms? He was not so foolish, but he supposed he had expected someone a bit flirtatious, a little interested—or at least a little warm! Warning bells sounded in his head; he thought he should proceed with caution.

"In all honesty, I must admit my friendship with your stepson is a relatively new one. I have only recently arrived in London after three years in the West Indies. Lord Wetherell seemed in need of a friend and our paths kept crossing. I enjoy his company. He is a good lad."

He paused to see how she would receive this and thought her rigid shoulders and wary expression softened a little. Encouraged, he added the good news, "He won a sum from me at the tables last night, and I have come to make good on my vowels."

She looked stunned. "He won?"

"Yes. Apparently that is unusual."

"You've come to pay *him*?"

The mixed astonishment and relief on her face hit him suddenly with the realization of his own stupidity. *By God, she had thought he was a creditor.* No wonder his reception was chilly! And he had lent credence to that by calling so early, like a common tradesman. Perhaps she'd even thought him a moneylender. But he saw the relief in her face quickly replaced by doubt.

"Dash it, I really do owe you an apology!" he said. "Coming by so early. I have forgotten I am not in the islands. You must have thought the worst! Can you forgive me?"

No lady of his acquaintance had ever resisted such a plea from him, especially when accompanied by his most charming smile, but he was not certain that forgiveness would be forthcoming this time. He plunged ahead.

"The truth is, as Lord Wetherell is still indisposed, I thought I might take this opportunity to express some concerns to you, in confidence. How much do you know of his friends and activities?"

The tiny crease that appeared between her brows told him volumes even before she replied. She looked more uncomfortable than ever, as if her seat were full of pins.

"I suppose I imagine more than I actually know, like many a mother." She did not look at him now, but stared down at the hands clasped in her lap. "He is seldom at home of late, and I admit that I have been concerned. I have heard a few—uh—reports."

He would wager she was more than concerned, if she had actually believed creditors might be coming to call at the house.

"You are wise to be concerned. He is moving in a rather fast circle that includes Lord Lyndham, Lord Bayhurst, and Sir Simon Fotheroy. They are a rowdy bunch with deep pockets and little sense. I've learned that under their influence he has come to owe some sizable sums to certain members of the *ton* who are not known for their patience."

"Oh dear. That is just the sort of thing I feared." She jumped up, as if the seat had become unbearable, and began to pace. When she noticed he had properly risen

from his own seat, she waved at him to sit again. "I'm
sorry. I cannot think well when I am still."

He was glad for that as he watched her move to the
fireplace and back to the sofa, admiring the way her muslin
gown and thin pelisse skimmed over her curves. She moved
with grace and smooth fluid motions, although her fisted
hands betrayed her agitation.

"I shall have to speak to him about this," she said with
obvious reluctance, more to herself than to him. "Whether
that shall have any effect remains to be seen."

He supposed her authority might not have been put to
any test in the time since her husband had died. He felt
true sympathy for her situation. "I have been thinking it
might help if, with your permission, I introduced him to
some different people—tried to steer him in some other
directions."

It was gratifying indeed to see how quickly her dejected
expression gave way to hope. "Could you do that? Would
you? You are kind to concern yourself at all."

"I would be happy to be of service." *And happy to include her in some of the invitations.* "However, I do think
it best if he does not know we had this conversation. Only
my deep concern overcame my reluctance to carry tales
to you."

*Well, it was the truth—his concern for the boy, plus his
concern to make her acquaintance.* "I could not help thinking how much I would want to know if it were my own son
getting into trouble."

"Yes, of course."

She paused by a painting of a ship cresting through waves
that hung on the wall behind her. "I do feel as if he were
my own son," she said softly, staring at the painting.

Her perusal of the painting brought it to his attention
and, despite the attraction of watching her, he was intrigued
momentarily by the picture. He rose from his chair again,
intending to inspect it himself.

As if his movement roused her, she turned back to him.
"How old is yours?"

"My—?" Archer was caught off balance.

"Your son," she said, regarding him curiously.

"Oh." Archer chuckled. "Purely hypothetical." He advanced a few steps toward the painting. It had to be a sign that she was thawing toward him if she was asking a personal question. "I have yet to tie the parson's knot. I meant that if I had a son, I would want to know."

It was true, he realized, although he had said the words with little thought. The very idea of fatherhood seemed less alarming to him, somehow, in this setting, or perhaps it was the effect of her company. For a fleeting second, he thought he'd actually felt a kind of deep yearning tugging at him, clamoring for his attention, but it passed quickly if it had been there at all. Well, at least now the lady would know he was unattached.

She moved a foot or two back from the painting, preserving the distance between them. "Your instincts are sound, then."

I've always thought so, Archer agreed to himself. His instincts were screaming that he and she were meant to be together, despite how she might act.

"Tell me about this painting," he said, partly to stop her from retreating. "It looks vaguely Dutch School, but I don't recognize the artist. That surprises me, as I collect marine art and fancy myself something of a connoisseur."

For a fleeting second, she smiled.

It was the first time she'd done so since he'd arrived, and it was hardly long enough. Archer wanted to see her do it again, to test if the room had really brightened.

"No Dutch master painted it," she said. "My father did."

"Your father? I am astonished." *So, at least one part of the story is true.* He stepped closer to the painting, examining it with heightened interest. That brought him closer to her and seemed to raise the temperature in the room.

"If you look closely, you can see the color is not right for the Dutch School," she added. "My father liked to experiment with pigments."

Archer did his best to stay focused, studying the brushwork and the colors. "It is extremely well done—the handling of the light, the translucence of the water, the sense of motion in the waves and sails. And there does not appear to be a line of rigging out of place." He was close enough now to catch her scent again.

She stayed, absorbed in the painting. "Yes. My father

was a genius. My late husband appreciated that better than most people. He studied under my father, but they were also friends. This picture was a gift."

She reached up to touch the painting with something that seemed very like affection. As her fingers traced the painted swells, he noticed a smudge of green staining her nails. In the next instant, unthinking, he caught her hand in his.

"Paint?"

He felt the shock go through her body, and saw it in her eyes, alight now with—was it alarm, or merely surprise? Then, unbelievably, she blushed. It was hardly the reaction of a practiced seductress.

"Y-yes. I . . . can't always get the color out."

He didn't know whether to drop her hand as if it were on fire and apologize for his forwardness, or keep hold of it as if touching her was the most natural thing in the world. He did not want her to think the paint repelled him. Her hand felt deliciously small and delicate in his, radiating an astonishing heat. A fierce surge of desire washed through him in response. He fought down the urge to pull her into his arms. How much more that would have shocked her!

For a long moment neither of them moved, each frozen for a different reason. He was both fascinated and thoroughly shaken, trapped now in a limbo from which he could neither advance nor retreat. What to do? He returned his gaze to her fingers, to give her a chance to compose herself.

An eon passed before she broke the spell, summoning a wry chuckle from some unexpected depth. "The green is especially charming, do you not agree? Gives me the look of growing fungus—like aged cheese left too long."

He couldn't stop his own chuckle. Who could possibly have expected her to say such a thing?

Seizing the advantage, she stepped back, twisting her hand and taking the decision from him. He released her at once but hastened to take up the conversation.

"So you are a painter as well!" It made sense that an artist's daughter might also be an artist. The possibility and his discovery of it pleased him.

"It is nothing. I dabble."

"Somehow I doubt that. That looks to me like the hand of a serious artist. I'd like very much to see your work.

Perhaps one day you'll permit me? In the meantime, I apologize if I shocked you—I did not mean to."

He did not expect an invitation now. She had just begun to warm to him a little and he had bungled that badly. He gave her a way back to neutral ground. "Your father was very talented."

"He was never given the credit he deserved." She said it in an odd tone of voice and turned back to her chair. "You said you are a collector?"

It was his cue to return to his own seat and allow the change of subject. "I have been since I was your stepson's age. It is one of my weaknesses."

Now there was an opening! A coquette might have seized that opportunity to explore what other weaknesses he might have, but Lady Wetherell did not. The guardedness had reappeared in her face, although it warred with an enthusiasm she apparently could not restrain. She seemed genuinely—and only—interested in his paintings. "How large is your collection? Which artists have you?"

Her questions gave him a perfect opening to advance his own cause. "I have been fortunate to acquire some great masters, I am proud to say, including Monamy, Cuyp, de Vlieger and even van de Velde. I would be honored and delighted to show them to you sometime." *Perhaps his goal might not turn out to be so difficult after all*! "I also have—"

He was interrupted by the arrival of Lord Wetherell. Despite the obvious efforts of the young man's valet, the immaculately turned-out viscount looked every bit as miserable as Archer had expected. No perfectly tied cravat could make up for the dark circles under his eyes or the slump of his shoulders.

"Morning, Daphne, Ramsdale." The words were not slurred but the lad winced as he spoke them, indicating the state of his head.

Daphne—her name was Daphne.

"Oh, dear. Robbie, do sit down."

Archer felt a pang of guilt as he looked at the suffering lad. If he had insisted last night, he might have stopped the boy from overindulging, or he might have convinced him to head home a little earlier. *But then I wouldn't have lost that last hand of cards or had this chance to meet the lovely Daphne.* He might have waited many weeks indeed for an invitation from the lad or some other legitimate excuse to call.

"Perhaps you might order coffee, Lady Wetherell," he suggested helpfully. "I don't believe tea will be sufficient to put the lad to rights this morning."

"Yes, you are right, of course." She rose quickly and went to the bellpull that hung by the doorway.

He watched her, trying to decide if her name fit her.

She hesitated for a moment, then asked, "Will you have some also, Lord Ramsdale? Or tea?"

It was not exactly an invitation. Her tone told Archer that despite having found a common interest, or perhaps because of his rash behavior, she was still uncomfortable in his presence.

The young viscount roused himself at that. "We'll go into the library. We've some business. Send coffee *and* tea."

"You needn't move on my account," she said quickly. "Indeed, Robbie, you look as though you might do better to stay still. I'll have the tea and coffee sent in to you here, and will leave you two to your discussions."

She looked as though she'd prefer not to, Archer thought, noting the way she lingered by the door. Studying her face, he did not flatter himself to imagine it was on his account, or rather, *favorably* on his account. That little crease in her forehead had returned and in it he read a mother's uncertainty.

He rose and took a step toward her. *Trust me,* he wanted to say. But instead he could only say courteously, "It has been an honor and a pleasure to meet you, Lady Wetherell," offering her a well-practiced bow. Perhaps it was just as well she gave him no opportunity to kiss her hand, given what had happened between them earlier.

She nodded curtly. No friendly or coquettish smile, no veiled encouragement. "Lord Ramsdale. I must get back to the poor quince branches I sent to the kitchen, before Cook decides to stew them or some such."

With that, she fled. There was no other word to describe her exit.

Chapter Five

Daphne leaned against the doorframe in the passage for a moment after closing the anteroom door behind her, trying to marshal her chaotic feelings.

"My lady, is anything amiss?"

Ever-vigilant Wilson was on duty, of course, hovering nearby in case anything was needed. "Nothing amiss, Wilson, thank you," she replied. *At least, nothing that you can remedy.* "But the gentlemen need tea and coffee, and some breakfast for Lord Wetherell, please."

Nodding, the footman headed off toward the kitchen, and Daphne followed slowly.

What was wrong with her? She had been inconceivably rude to Lord Ramsdale. Granted he had called at an unseemly hour, but he had come with good intentions, to pay his debt and to offer his help. She had been horrible to him, even after he had disabused her of her initial mistaken notions.

She hated to admit to herself what she had thought. Upon his arrival she had sent her young assistant, the groom Jamie, flying off to perform his duties while she gathered up her basket and branches and headed for the house filled with equal measures of dread and determination. She had charged into the house ready to do battle with a creditor who hadn't the courtesy to send a note. The only reason she could imagine for a personal visit was that the fellow hoped to extract payment from her in a nonmonetary form. He would learn how wrong that was!

Filled with such thoughts, she had been completely un-
prepared when she met Lord Ramsdale in the entryway.
The waves in his dark hair and the fringe that fell over his
forehead when he bowed had instantly charmed her. When
he straightened, his striking features had finished the job.
Thick, dark eyebrows hovered over deep-set gray eyes. A
strong, square jaw and straight, aristocratic nose balanced
them. It was a manly face, lit by a boyish smile that she
imagined melted many hearts. Most women probably found
the combination irresistible.

Confound the man! Why did he have to be so attractive?
Why could she not have gathered her wits once she learned
his true purpose, at least enough to thank him? Why could
she not have taken the time to make herself presentable
instead of rushing in from the garden? Never had she been
so flustered simply by meeting a man.

She glanced down at her skirt, realizing she had never
so much as checked to see if she had twigs and leaves
clinging to it. She should have made him wait while she
excused herself. How long did it take to don a lace cap?

Of course, she had compounded those errors when he
touched her. At the moment his hand had seized hers, molten fire had poured through her veins, triggering a kind of
intense yearning unlike anything she had ever felt. She had
been so stunned she had stood there like a dolt instead of
snatching away her hand, and only seconds later had she
felt alarm that he would make such a bold move.

Now as she hurried down the stairs toward the kitchen,
she rubbed her fingers against the folds of her skirt. She
could still feel a residual tingling from their contact. What
must he have thought? Had he recognized her physical response? If he had not already heard the rumors people
spread about her, this encounter would doubtless make him
a believer once he did.

The question was, could she—should she—believe he
wanted only to help Robbie? She must not assume that
every man she met wanted to take advantage of her. Yet
she had not failed to notice the way his gaze had followed
her during their interview. She had seen that kind of hungry
look too often not to recognize it. She could not shake her
suspicion that Lord Ramsdale was not being completely
honest.

Four faces turned expectantly to her as she entered the kitchen, and she attempted to paste on a smile to cover her inner turmoil.

"I'll just reclaim those branches and get them out of your way," she said to Cook, eager to retreat to the quiet sanctuary of her studio. "Thank you for seeing to them."

Cook nodded. "I'm making his lordship a bit of toast. Thought it might be best to go easy on his poor stomach this morning."

"Yes, I quite agree."

Wordlessly, Cook and Ellen, the maid-of-all-work, began to prepare a tray under the watchful eye of Carmichael. The elderly butler would serve the gentlemen himself.

Daphne turned toward the quince branches, now resting in a heavy bucket of water. Carmichael signaled to the footman with only an inclination of his head, quite as if she had spoken her intention out loud.

"Are these to go up to the studio, your ladyship?" Wilson inquired.

She had to permit the footman to carry it for her. While she did not desire company just then, his presence did allow her to ask to be informed the very moment Lord Ramsdale left the house.

She would do well to stay far away from the handsome baron. She did not quite trust him—or perhaps she did not trust herself. Regardless, as she followed Wilson up the servant's stairs she could not help hoping the lord would still honor his offer to help Robbie despite her foolish behavior. Weaning Robbie away from a bad set of friends was something she truly did not know how to do herself.

Once Wilson left her, Daphne set to work shifting the quince branches into a tall blue pottery vase. Her studio was a large square room on the northeast corner of the house with a huge north-facing Palladian window her husband had ordered installed just for her. In a patch of late-morning sun that still slanted through the windows on the east wall, a long-haired, mostly white cat with gray markings lounged on a painted canvas floorcloth.

"I must confess I am a little rattled, Roquefort," Daphne confided to the cat. She hunted among the shelves filled with collected treasures, selecting several other items to form a still-life composition. "I have been blinded by the vision of a very handsome gentleman—other than you, I mean—and what's more, when he leaves I have to have a very serious talk with Master Robert."

The cat stretched and shifted his position, apparently unconcerned that he might have a rival for his mistress's admiration. He was one of the very few things Daphne had been able to bring with her from her old life.

She glanced at a large canvas standing on an easel in the corner of the room. A marine painting similar to the one downstairs in the anteroom was taking shape there, as yet unfinished. "I wonder if that last layer of glazing has had enough time to dry. I mustn't rush it. But I shouldn't try to work on my masterpiece until I can focus my concentration, anyway, eh, old fellow?"

The painting was intended to showcase the best of her talent. It was to be the key that would open the doors to the prestigious Royal Academy, the picture that would qualify her to study there. It was a crucial step on her future path. But for now she chuckled and reached down to scratch behind the cat's ears. "I hope none of your cat hairs are stuck to it! I really shouldn't allow you to come in here, but I know it is your favorite room."

With a sigh she removed a pewter tankard she had tried in her arrangement and put it back next to a small box that had been her mother's on the shelf above her worktable. "That's not the shape. It wants something round."

Unfortunately, the pewter color reminded her of Lord Ramsdale, whose eyes were nearly the same shade as the tankard. *Oh, dear.* Could she not get the man out of her mind? That he shared her interest in art was downright dangerous. She had caught herself fantasizing about having him as her own friend, not just an acquaintance of Robbie's.

That temptation was simply too cruel. If she was not careful, she might start dreaming of love and marriage and children and all sorts of things she could not and would not ever have. Why torture herself? Achieving social acceptability through her artwork might be an impossible enough goal by itself.

She settled for a squat silver teapot with a nicely rounded shape and after making a few more adjustments for the light, got out pencils and paper to begin her sketch. But the only image she could visualize on the blank paper was Lord Ramsdale again. Drat the man!

Not long after, Wilson reappeared to inform her that the baron had taken his leave and was no doubt stirring up dust in the drive at that very moment. Daphne set aside her materials and hurried down to intercept her stepson before he could disappear somewhere.

She found him still slumped over in his chair in the anteroom with the food on the breakfast tray before him mostly untouched. He looked up at her with a most pathetic expression and only made half an attempt to stagger to his feet when she came into the room.

She sank quickly into the nearest seat to save him the effort.

"Hullo. I assume you have been up for hours?" he said, moving his head gingerly.

"As always."

"And at what time did my friend Lord Ramsdale arrive?"

"I was in the garden when he arrived, so I am not entirely certain, but I think it was about ten."

She paused, thinking of how to direct the conversation. She had promised she would not betray Lord Ramsdale's confidence. But perhaps talking about the baron would lead Robbie to share something about his other friends—and his troubles. She got up again and approached the tea tray hopefully.

"Is he always so inclined to flaunt convention?" she asked, lifting the teapot experimentally. A satisfying slosh told her there was still some left. "That was an unseemly hour to come calling, business or not."

The idea that Lord Ramsdale would not be ruled by rigid social codes appealed to the part of her that rebelled against them, too. But was such a man a wise companion for Robbie?

There were extra cups on the tea tray, probably in case one of the gentlemen had wished to sample both beverages. She selected one and poured herself some tea. "I cannot imagine a man quite so eager to discharge his debts." *Yet that, surely, could be counted a virtue.*

"How long have you known him? What do you know about him?" she asked, returning to her seat. She hoped she did not sound like an inquisitor.

Instead of bristling with annoyance, Robbie turned to her with a cautiously teasing smile. "Ah, did you find him interesting, then? I see that you were forced to play the hostess to him for some time before I managed to pry myself from my bed."

"That is not why—" she began to say, then flustered, cut herself off. She would have denied that she wanted to know more about Lord Ramsdale from her own interest. Yet what *would* she say? That she wanted to know only for Robbie's sake, because she did not trust his choice in friends? That she and the baron had hatched a plot to steer Robbie in better directions? Ridiculous as it was, perhaps she should allow Robbie to think she did have some interest in the man. It might make it easier for her to encourage their connection and also make certain it was in truth as desirable as it seemed.

She did not have to contrive the faint tinge of embarrassment coloring her cheeks. "Well, um, perhaps," she said, hastily amending her reply. She took a sip of tea.

Robbie was looking at her quite intently. "You did!" he crowed with an altogether uncalled-for note of triumph in his voice, then winced.

"Now Robbie, do not make a muchness out of nothing," she cautioned, unwilling to carry the ruse too far. "It seems he has an interest in art—marine art particularly. In fact, he claims to have a considerable collection, although that is not so unusual. But we found we shared an interest."

"That is famous! I knew I liked him."

"Well, I don't believe having a collection of marine art by itself qualifies someone for sainthood. I will admit that, despite his apparent inability to tell time, it is honorable that he appeared so promptly to pay his vowels."

"Ah, you needn't take that high tone. I can see very well that you liked him. It is written all over your face, whether you admit it or not. I shall invite him to dinner."

"You shall not!" *Oh, dear.* This conversation was not going the way she wished. She spoke more sharply than she intended. "I am still your guardian and I have some say in the matter. You are not thinking things through."

Robbie's expression of delight turned black in an instant. It had always amazed her how quickly his moods could change. Daphne tried to gentle her tone.

"While I am pleased to see that you have at least one friend you feel is presentable enough to bring home with you, you simply *must* stop to consider the circumstances and consequences of these matters. If we were to invite him, you know the Vicious Biddies would start up the gossip immediately. His name would be linked up with mine. The fact that there's nothing to it would never stop them. They always seem to know who comes and goes here, and they always cast it in the worst possible light."

"We should simply damn all the gossips and do as we wish!" Robbie said, scowling down at the floor, his black look unabated.

"It seems to me we do that frequently," she replied gently. "However, not when someone else will be dragged through the mud with us. We have to recognize how what we do affects other people."

He glanced up at her, defiant. "I see it, you know, when you lose patience with toeing the line. Don't you think I lose patience, too?" He was actually upset enough to lurch unsteadily out of his chair. "And I don't appreciate your casting aspersions on my other friends."

"It is hard on you to be saddled with me for a stepmother," Daphne said with gentle sympathy. "I am sorry for it. But this is not about us or what we wish to do."

Robbie was immediately contrite. He approached and took her hand. "I did not mean what I said as a complaint. I would not trade you for any other stepmother in the world."

She squeezed his fingers in reassurance. "And I would not wish for any other stepson." Affection and sympathy filled her heart as she watched him return to his chair and ease himself down into it with great care. This was not the best time to try to have this discussion with him.

"I only said what I did about your other friends because I know nothing at all about them. Really, Robbie, it seems to me if they were as upright and respectable as Lord Ramsdale appears to be, then at the very least you would mention them occasionally in conversation. You are always off with them. Who are they? What happens if they lead you into trouble? Would you come to me? I worry. But I worry because I care."

"I know."

She fiddled with her teacup. "You know that your uncle keeps threatening to challenge my guardianship in Chancery Court. Empty threats, those are—he cannot prove any of the charges he would like to lay against me, since all of them are untrue. But do you understand how much it would help if your own behavior were more circumspect? You are never at home, Robbie. I never know what you are about, or with whom. There are so many ways a young man can fall into trouble!

"I hope Lord Ramsdale is indeed a good friend, for he no doubt has the benefit of experience. I am sorry you cannot invite him to come for dinner, but it would be exceedingly unwise."

Robbie frowned, his mulish expression showing clearly that he was unconvinced. "By your reasoning, then, you will always live in isolation, can never have any friends, and will never be able to socialize ever again. By that, don't you realize, the Vicious Biddies win? You shouldn't give in. It gives the appearance that they are right.

"What's more," he added determinedly, "you should permit other people to make their own decisions if they choose to associate with you, despite whatever consequences might come of it. I think you push away people who might be willing to tolerate the gossip."

It was a long speech for someone who definitely looked a bit green about the gills. Somehow, Robbie had twisted the conversation around to be about her, and now he was finished. If Daphne had hoped for more about either Lord Ramsdale or any of Robbie's other friends, she realized now she would not get it. She had squandered her opportunity by saying too much, turning her casual inquiry into a lecture, and had received something of a lecture herself in return.

"I still feel dashed miserable," Robbie said. "I think for now my only activity will be to retire again and nurse my head. So you needn't worry over what I'm about."

Daphne watched him rise from his chair and shuffle slowly to the door, shoulders slumped.

"I think I have learned not to drink so much claret all in one evening. And as you are insistent, I shan't invite Lord Ramsdale to dinner." He slanted a quick look at her. "But I am glad you liked him."

Chapter Six

Archer had hatched a plot with Lord Wetherell. He waited several days before putting it into motion, but that was as long as he could force himself to wait. On a breezy June morning with pale sunshine that lit the sails on the Thames and silvered the surface of the water, he eased downriver in his great-uncle's little sloop *Ariadne*. A southwesterly wind and an outgoing tide carried him along effortlessly.

He could relax and enjoy the exhilaration of running before the wind, as this part of the river had a good deal less traffic than any part below the Battersea Bridge. The old wooden bridge with its low, narrow openings barred all but the smallest vessels from the upper river. "Shooting" the fast currents under the bridge with the attendant risk of capsize or collision was a noted danger of navigating the Thames for any boats that could pass through—one Archer would have to practice before the upcoming races. But not today. Today he was only going as far as the landing at the foot of Lady Wetherell's garden.

With both wind and current sweeping him along, coming in there would require some attention. As he sailed closer he noted the landmarks—the farms, marshes, and country manors that still graced this section of the river. Soon the chimneys and roof of Grove House appeared above the leafy tops of a clump of poplars, and he saw the masonry pier that marked the landing.

He trimmed his sail to slow his speed. Just as he came opposite the stairs and pier, he pushed the rudder hard over to turn the *Ariadne*. As the current carried the boat, he made a second turn and completed his final approach upwind with just enough headway to gently kiss the pier.

Ha. Driving a carriage was no challenge at all compared to the precise demands of sailing. He smiled with satisfaction, justifiably proud of the skills he'd acquired through long years of practice. If only he could be sure his plans for Lady Wetherell would work as neatly. He could not remember a time when he had so completely failed to elicit some interest from a female who interested him. Was the one woman he wanted in London the one woman who was immune to his charms?

Well, he would not be discouraged by the chilly reception he'd received. Challenge made every prize more worthwhile. Once he had secured *Ariadne*, taken in her sail, and put out the canvas fenders to protect her from scraping the pier, he jumped from her deck to the stairs and headed up the path toward Grove House.

Daphne was in her studio attempting to work on her so-called Royal Academy painting. With a frown of concentration she slid a tiny bead of gray paint along the edge of a dark green wave with the tip of her brush, adding a highlight to the stormy sea on her canvas.

For a painting that was so important to her plans, it definitely lacked something. If only she could determine what! Only the best artists were accepted to study at the Royal Academy. Of those, only those deemed good enough to be allowed to exhibit there were considered worthy of further recognition. Among that group, only a select few were granted actual membership in the Academy with the accompanying prestige, acclaim, and success. Only two women had ever been admitted as R.A. members, and they had both been founders.

Well, what good were goals if one did not aim high? Daphne sighed. Coming from where she stood socially, she would need such lofty achievement to overcome her past.

Wilson knocked at the open door. "Excuse me, my lady. Lord Ramsdale is arrived, asking for his lordship. Unfortunately, Lord Wetherell stepped out, and asked me to refer Lord Ramsdale to you if he came by."

"Did he, indeed?" That was odd. What could have called Robbie out so early in the day, especially if he knew Lord Ramsdale might call? For that matter, why would Lord Ramsdale again be calling so unfashionably early? Daphne thought she smelled a rat. *Not very subtle, Robbie.*

Unwilling to be manipulated, her first impulse was to simply send the baron on his way without seeing him. But then she thought two could play at this game. It did seem unfair to be discourteous to the man yet again.

"If he does not mind waiting, Wilson, make him comfortable in the front drawing room, and I will be with him shortly." She would make no mistake this time, but would change out of her painting smock, wash, and make herself totally proper and presentable. He could always choose not to wait.

As she wrapped her brush in a soaked cloth to keep it moist, she wondered why he had come to the house again. Surely he could not already owe Robbie another debt?

"Can he be so bad at playing cards?" she asked Roquefort, her ever-present companion in the studio. "It is highly suspicious. But if Robbie were in some new trouble, he would send a note, and I doubt he'd be calling on Robbie instead of me. Perhaps it is nothing."

She carefully put away her paints, then hurried to her room, reaching back to untie the fastenings of her smock as she went. She splashed her face and washed her hands with tepid water from her washstand, taking care to scrub her nails. Stripping off the old muslin she had been wearing, she pulled a pale green day dress with long sleeves and a modest bib front from her wardrobe and slipped into it, fumbling with the front closings in her haste. Then she twisted her dark chestnut hair into a coil and pinned it up with a handful of pins—not the neat job Mattie, her abigail, would have done, but she did not want to take the time to wait. A lace cap trimmed with green ribbon finished the transformation. "There. Perfectly respectable," she told her mirror.

When she entered the front drawing room Lord Ramsdale was standing with his hands clasped behind his back, studying the artwork hung on the far wall. Four Dutch marine paintings from her husband's collection were displayed there in heavy gilt frames above the wainscoting.

She paused for a moment before greeting him, taking in the way his stance emphasized the breadth of his shoulders and the pure masculinity that emanated from him. Today he was clad in a brown kerseymere coat and tan inexpressibles that appeared to fit his form so snugly she wondered that he could move. He turned to her with a smile when she spoke to him.

I was wrong, she admitted to herself begrudgingly. *Handsome is hardly an adequate description of him. With that smile he is, well—bedazzling.*

Before she could gather her wits again, he had crossed to her and bowed over her hand in reply to her greeting. It was perfectly proper. He did not hold her hand any longer than he should. Was she a tiny bit disappointed?

Aghast at the very possibility, she summoned a polite smile and quickly offered him the nearest chair so that he would have to sit. She took the one that faced it a good five feet away.

"I am surprised that we should have the honor of another call from you so soon, Lord Ramsdale," she said, keeping her expression as bland as possible. "I hope and pray it is not an indication of your luck at the tables?"

He laughed. Not a perfunctory laugh, either, but a lovely, deep baritone laugh that showed he apparently was delighted by her small jest. She felt the reverberations all the way down to her toes.

"Not at all, madam, I assure you. I came to take Lord Wetherell out for a sail, which is the reason why I have come, once again, at such an early hour. I find I must apologize to you again, and for the same failing as the first time. It is very humiliating," he added, looking very like a rogue and not humiliated at all.

Dear God, how was anyone supposed to resist this fellow? She tried to be stiff and formal. "Very well, you are forgiven, especially since you apologize so artfully." Now where had those last words come from? "As Wilson has informed you, my stepson is not here."

"Yes. I am surprised. I thought we had an understanding that if the weather was fine we would go out this morning. I cannot imagine a finer day for sailing than this. The breeze is fresh, and the sun is warm. The tide is perfect, and the river is looking its best."

"It is a shame," she agreed. He made it sound very appealing. "It is not like Robbie—Lord Wetherell—to be undependable when he has an engagement." *Unless he has some reason.* "Perhaps he mistook the day?"

Lord Ramsdale shook his head. His dark hair curled around his ears in a very attractive way. "I thought our plans were quite clear, but apparently not."

He paused, then looked at her with an unmistakably speculative gleam in his eye. "I came down from Fulham in my great-uncle's little sloop. She is tied at your landing at this moment, just waiting for a passenger. Could I interest you in a sail? It is a shame to waste the opportunity."

He had sailed in those perfectly fitted pantaloons? She bit her tongue before the thought could slip out. She would love to see what it was like to sail on the river. But was this exactly what Robbie had hoped for? Something was definitely afoot.

The real question was whether or not Lord Ramsdale was party to the plan. Had he really come for Robbie, or could he and Robbie have conspired together? Did she trust him? It all came back to that unanswered question.

"Thank you, but I think not," she answered, aware that she might just be unwilling to trust anyone.

"Oh, come," he said, flashing that persuasive smile. "If the proprieties concern you, let me assure you it is no different than going for a carriage drive in the park. The river is a perfectly public place. Although," he added in a softer voice, "at the same time it is unlikely we would even be seen by any high sticklers of society."

Did he know of her trouble with the gossipmongers? Had he truly found an outing that might be proof against them? Her resolve to resist temptation weakened.

She realized that going with him would offer an excellent chance to learn more about him. It could also be a chance to discover if he was truly honest in his interest in helping Robbie, or if he expected something from her in return. If she conducted herself with perfect decorum and he made so much as a single wrong move, she would know her distrust might be justified.

You would be alone with him, cautioned her inner voice. *You won't be able to walk away from him out on the water if he misbehaves.*

No more than I could in a moving carriage, she answered back. *At least I would know.* She could take care of herself. And as he had just said, the river was a public place.

"Have you ever sailed on the river for the pure pleasure of it?" he asked.

She shook her head. "I've been ferried by watermen, of course, going to Vauxhall with my husband. I've never sailed."

"In that case, I positively insist that you come. You can have no idea of what you have been missing." The eagerness in his face at that moment made him look very boyish indeed. "It can be utterly peaceful, or quite exhilarating—sometimes both at once. Not to mention it is the only way to really see and appreciate the beauty of the river. As an artist, I know you would appreciate that."

He raised his eyebrows as she still hesitated. "It is perfectly safe, I assure you. I have been sailing since my childhood and am as skilled a captain as you may find. No harm will come to you."

"All right, for a short time. Just allow me fetch my bonnet."

He looked extremely pleased when she rejoined him minutes later, wearing a dark green corduroy spencer over her gown and a small chip bonnet securely tied under her chin. She was just pulling on a pair of thin kid gloves.

"I thought a shawl might get in the way with the wind and all the ropes," she said, "and I thought a hat or large bonnet might prove to be quite a hazard to navigation."

"A very intelligent observation, Lady Wetherell. You have the makings of a fine sailor." He chuckled. The warm look of approval in his eyes was disconcerting.

She avoided looking at him again until they had made their way from the house down to the landing. There she stopped, realizing that although the boat was securely tied to the pier, clambering on board would require some assistance. *His* assistance.

"It is a shame there's no such thing as sail boys who will hold one's boat while you pay calls or run errands, like the lads who hold one's carriage horses for a penny," he was saying, apparently unaware of—or unconcerned by—her dilemma. "The small inconvenience of having to take down the sail and put it back up is nothing compared to the vast pleasure and other advantages offered by a good sail, however."

His pantaloons must have been made from knitted stockinette. She watched him leap effortlessly across a three-foot gap between the stairs and the boat deck, a feat she had no hope of copying with her long skirts and shorter legs. The boat dipped and rocked under his weight, but he steadied himself with a casual hand on the forestays and seemed perfectly accustomed to the motion.

Unfortunately for her, the closest stairs were several feet lower than the level of the boat's deck and covered by water, while the pier itself was several feet above the boat thanks to the outgoing tide.

"You must allow me to help you," he said, turning back to her. "You could jump from there and trust me to pull you aboard, or let me lift you up from the lower stairs, but it might be easiest if you go up above on the pier. If you are not worried about soiling your dress, sit down and let your legs hang over the edge, then you can just drop down and let me ease your landing onto the deck."

He made it sound so straightforward, but the very idea of any such contact between them sent a ripple of heat through her and made her feel as though her insides were twisting in knots. "Perhaps this is not such a good idea . . . ," she began.

"Never tell me you are afraid to sail! I would not believe it," he said, his gaze sharpening with challenge.

"Of course not." She was not one of those backward ninnyhammers who still thought sailing for pleasure risked life and limb for nothing. Did he deliberately misunderstand her hesitation? What she feared was something quite other than sailing, but she certainly couldn't tell him.

She marched out to the end of the pier and sat down after brushing a clean spot on the stone, letting her legs hang as he had instructed. "Now just slip off," he said. "I'll guide you. You'll not end up in the water, I promise."

She aimed for a spot on the deck just in front of him. He braced himself and with ready arms caught her around the hips as she came down, letting her ease down the rest of the way against his body until she gained her footing. The boat dipped under their weight and she clung to him as he lifted her down into the sloop's cockpit. It was outrageous, but was it deliberate? She struggled for breath, nearly paralyzed with shock.

"Steady?"

She couldn't form words to answer, so she simply nodded. Could he be so unaffected? The sensations she'd just felt were shocking but delicious. She was quite certain she had felt every inch of his hard male body, and still felt as though rockets were shooting off in her brain and every other part of her own body. Maybe he was so used to being with women he truly thought nothing of having her in his arms.

He took her by the hand, guiding her to a seat. She was already so giddy that the warmth from his hand only added a few more ripples of sensation. She struggled to regain her composure.

"It will be a bit tricky setting off with wind and tide against us," he said with a note of apology in his voice, quite as if nothing extraordinary had happened. "I'll have to put you to work—will you mind?"

"And here I thought you wanted a passenger, when it was crew you needed all along. A shabby business, sir!" she exclaimed in mock protest, determined to pretend that nothing had happened.

He gave a quick shout of delighted laughter. "Shabby, me beauty? Shabby? Indeed, I am an infamous rogue pirate and I've hoodwinked ye to work on t' high seas at me side. But 'tis a life of adventure, I'll warrant ye, and there could be treasure in it." He raised one eyebrow ridiculously high and stroked an invisible beard. She could not help laughing at his foolishness.

He set about preparing the sail and instructed her how to take in the fenders when he gave her the command. "This is called the tiller," he added, showing her the long polished wooden handle sticking out from the back of the cockpit. "This is what steers the boat. When I go forward to cast off—uh, that is, to untie us from the pier—I want you to hold this in exactly this position. Can you do that?"

She nodded.

"It may try to pull away from you. Be firm and determined."

"I am quite proficient at that," she declared.

*   *   *

She was. As Archer loosened the ropes and shoved against the masonry to push the nose of the boat out into the current, he saw her suddenly clutch at the tiller with both hands as it tried to move. For a moment the little boat moved sideways with the current, but then the wind filled the sail and they swooped out toward the center of the river on a starboard tack. He studied her expressive face, chuckling when he saw her react with surprised excitement to the sudden power that struck the boat. He settled himself on the upwind side and took the tiller from her.

As the angle of the boat to the water steadied, her excitement faltered visibly, alarm creeping into her brown eyes.

"Is it—is it supposed to *tilt* like this?" she asked, her knuckles white as she gripped the coaming, the wooden edge that rimmed the cockpit.

"Yes. It gives us better speed, which we need going upriver against the forces of nature. Fear not—I can adjust it simply by changing our angle to the wind." He moved the tiller, and moments later the boat headed up enough to lose some speed and level out a bit, but he quickly set it back as it had been so the force of the current could not overwhelm them.

"I can also adjust it by changing the angle of the sail." Here he let out the sail a little, with the same result. "You must relax. Trust me. Close your eyes and listen to the sound of the water and feel the wind on your face. You will get used to the sensations and your unease will dissipate."

She looked as if she did not believe him, but she did as he bade her. Watching her, he could almost see the moment when she finally did begin to relax. Her death grip on the coaming eased and her face softened. Her position became less rigid. Dear God, she was such a beautiful creature! It had taken every ounce of his willpower not to take advantage when he had held her in his arms.

He had wanted to hear her laugh again—had wanted that husky velvet warmth to touch him and seduce him the way it had that first day on Bond Street. He wanted to show her and share with her the rapture that he'd always found when he'd sailed with his island mistress in the azure waters of the West Indies. He and Janetta had shared a special bond of passion and affection that was more comfortable than love and left their hearts unscathed. It was something he hoped to find again.

And what about the beautiful Lady Wetherell? Had anyone ever claimed her heart? Had she loved her husband, a man so much older than she was? Or had she given her heart recklessly to someone else, and had it broken into pieces?

He studied her now, shamelessly drinking in the ivory smoothness of her skin, the sweep of her eyelashes, the fine arch of her dark eyebrows. Her mouth looked soft and full of passion, made for kisses. She was vibrant, alive, enticing. He wanted her, but she possessed a reserve that he instinctively knew he must heed. It was too soon to expect the easy camaraderie and laughter he had enjoyed with Janetta. This was only their second meeting. He would need to be patient.

She was smiling by the time she opened her eyes again. "You were right," she said, sounding perfectly surprised. "It is quite unlike anything I have ever experienced. How did you describe it? Both peaceful and exhilarating."

Gratified, he smiled back. "You can trust me. I know what I am doing."

She lifted an eyebrow but made no comment. Instead she looked around. "Goodness! We are already almost to the other side of the river. I had no idea."

"The sail was one of mankind's better inventions," he said warmly, "rather like harnessing the horse to save walking. Rowing is such a slow and laborious business, compared to the efficiency of sailing. But now we must prepare to come about."

"Come about?" She looked alarmed again. "What is it? What must I do?"

"Why, nothing at all, dear lady. It only means we are about to turn and set our course toward the other bank, before we run aground in the mud! The sail will shift over to this side, and I will shift myself over to that one."

He suited action to word, pushing the tiller toward her and timing the other movements in a smooth coordinated process. The canvas sail flapped noisily until it filled again on the other side of the mast. Moments later, he was sitting beside her.

Mere inches separated them. How easy it would have

been to "accidentally" position himself so that they sat thigh-against-thigh! He could even have claimed it was necessary for the proper distribution of weight in the boat. Tucked into the corner of the cockpit, she had nowhere to go. He swallowed, fighting temptation.

"Goodness, we are going even faster now," she exclaimed. A beautiful flush of pink colored her cheeks, and a sparkle of excitement lit her brown eyes.

Was it only from the new speed on this tack, or had it anything to do with him? He would have given anything to know. *God, how much he wanted to kiss her.*

Daphne reveled in the sensations of the warm sun on her shoulders, the rhythm of the boat moving through the water, and the amazing sense of power in harnessing the wind. The faster the boat went, the faster her heart beat, and right now it was positively racing. She refused to believe it had anything to do with how close Lord Ramsdale was sitting to her just now. She felt as though they were flying, and she wanted nothing so much as to cast off her bonnet and let the wind flow through her hair.

Of course, that was just the sort of behavior that would send a wrong message to Lord Ramsdale. She had to admit that except for the one moment boarding the boat—doubtless quite unavoidable—he had acted the perfect gentleman. But who could blame him for anything he might do if she revealed herself to be an improper woman full of sensual desires? *She might just as well kiss him.*

Surprised and dismayed that such a thought would even cross her mind, Daphne tried to inch a little farther away from him, but of course there was nowhere to go. She was already pressed as far against the corner of the cockpit as possible.

"Would you like to take a turn at the tiller?"

He was looking at her intently, and she prayed that nothing of her thoughts could be read on her face.

"Oh, yes!" she said, grateful for the diversion.

He proceeded to show her. "The first thing is to position your hands correctly. I think you'll want to use two hands, at least until you grow accustomed to the helm. Try it with one hand here, and the other—like this."

He placed her hands on the wooden shaft, her left near

the end of the tiller where his had been and her other closer in. His hands covered hers, but only for a matter of seconds. The warmth she felt through her thin gloves could as easily have been from the sun-warmed wood as from him.

However, she had to lean forward to reach the tiller, and her left arm now stretched right across his flat abdomen. He did not look as though he minded one bit.

"Um. That is a bit awkward for you, is it not?" he said with a grin. "We'll have to shift forward. You won't have the proper leverage sitting back in the corner like that."

He hitched up along the shelflike seat toward the midsection of the boat. She followed, but misjudged how slight a distance he was going and suddenly found herself firmly hip to hip against him.

"Oh! I beg your pardon." She hastily moved back several inches. "There. Is this all right?"

She saw a flash of amusement cross his face and could tell by his expression that he bit back the first reply that came to him. "Yes, that should do," he replied, his voice deep and determinedly serious. "Are you quite comfortable? That is important. You look very elegant in the seat of control."

She felt neither elegant nor at all in control—not of herself, at least. However, he patiently explained the principles involved in steering the boat—how the rudder worked, how to keep sight of a chosen landfall to maintain course, how to compensate for changes in the wind and current. Gradually she forgot her awkwardness and began to concentrate fully on her task. His enthusiasm was infectious.

He stretched out his long legs and leaned back against the coaming, putting his hands behind his head. "You have a natural talent for this."

She couldn't help smiling. Taking the tiller was like taking the reins of a spirited horse. Through the warm wood in her hands she could feel the force of the water pushing against the rudder, challenging her mastery over it. She felt deliciously one with the boat and the river. As she looked ahead to mark her heading, the wind tickled the curls around her face.

"What a shame that Robbie had to miss this." She sighed, for the moment feeling utterly content.

Chapter Seven

"We will need to come about very shortly," came Lord Ramsdale's voice. With a start, Daphne realized they were yet again getting quite close to the mudflats that stretched out toward them from the opposite riverbank.

Instantly, uncertainty bordering on panic replaced her lovely contentment. "Oh, heavens. What do I do now?"

"Remain calm," he said with an impudent smile, "and above all, do not let go of the tiller. Now, push the tiller—slowly—away from you. I will take care of the rest."

She did as he instructed, then admired his agility as he easily reset the sail, adjusted the lines, and moved back to the other side of the cockpit. Could she ever learn to move about a boat with such grace? The breeze had freshened, increasing the tilt of the boat rather alarmingly. The water seemed only inches away. He advised her to move to the upwind side next to him, a feat that she accomplished bravely if rather unsteadily.

Now he was the one sitting back in the corner, and she sat beside and just forward of him, guiding the boat on the next leg of its zigzag course up the river. She was careful to preserve the invisible barrier of space between them, despite how much more relaxed she had begun to feel.

A barge approached them, heading downriver, and Lord Ramsdale took charge for a few moments until it had safely crossed in front of them. The rough-looking crewmen all waved and called out their admiration for the trim little craft and its female passenger. The baron waved back.

"You don't even know them," she said, astonished and blushing.

"You mustn't mind. On the water, everyone waves," he said simply, his boyish smile lighting up his eyes. They looked more silver now than pewter-colored. "And even the Prince Regent himself is not immune from comments. It is as if all the pretenses of society are stripped away here, and we all become merely humans. Very democratic, the river is."

"It sounds as if only Whigs and commoners venture out on it, then," she said, laughing.

He laughed, too, and she felt positively lighthearted. How could such a simple thing as a sail on the river affect her so profoundly?

They sailed on, and she was so taken with the sailing itself and with seeing the river as she had never seen it, she entirely forgot her mission to learn what she could about Lord Ramsdale. With each tack that took them farther upriver, she discovered more to know about the vagaries of tides and the river currents and about handling the boat, until finally they were within sight of the old wooden bridge at Putney.

"Are you hungry?" he asked her. "I must admit that I am famished. Something about fresh air and being on the water always seems to create a huge appetite."

She looked about dubiously, wishing he looked less as if he would like to devour her just then. "Did you bring a picnic?"

"I wish I had, for that would be a delightful solution," he admitted. "I shall the next time, I promise. But Westwater, my great-uncle's house at Fulham, is just up ahead on the right. We could stop in there and beg something from the kitchen."

She realized she had lost all track of time. "How long have we been sailing? What time has it gotten to be?" In truth, she had become so relaxed she was quite drowsy. The sun had climbed high in sky.

"It is noon," he told her, consulting his pocket watch. "Did you have afternoon engagements?"

"No. I just—well, I—no, not exactly." She had planned to paint. "I just did not think it would be proper to go off sailing with you for very long."

"Oh, there is that worry about propriety again," he said

with his annoyingly roguish chuckle. "Who even knows that we are out here? What are rules but something we follow to please other people? Out here, of all places, we are free to do as we please."

Up ahead she could make out the house he had indicated, a Palladian stone mansion on a rise above the river with green lawns running down almost to the bank. An octagonal summerhouse on a stone terrace perched by the water's edge, close by a dock and the pilings of an unoccupied boat slip. It looked very inviting, yet she wondered how many people would learn she had been sailing with Lord Ramsdale if they stopped in there. Would it be a mistake? He did not seem to think so.

"I'm afraid it will take us at least as long again to make the run back down the river," he said. "If I am not mistaken, the tide is turning. I have been so charmed by your company, I lost track of the time myself. Will you forgive me?"

"That is the second time today that you have asked me that." Her stomach rumbled. "I will forgive you if you can truly procure us something to eat. I discover that I am hungry, after all."

Now that her mind was not on sailing, she realized she had done little to accomplish her purposes in coming. Paying a call at his great-uncle's house ought to offer an excellent opportunity to make some discoveries, if she dared.

"The house is beautiful," she said wistfully. "The proportions are so classic! And it is situated so perfectly—there must be a lovely view of the river from all of the rooms on this side."

He took the tiller from her as she continued to gaze at the shore ahead. "The view of it from here is flawlessly composed. Has it ever been painted?" she asked.

"Not this view, no." He motioned to her to change her seat, as they were coming about again. "There is a view of the house from the north painted by Francesco Zuccarelli. I'll show it to you, if you like."

He headed the boat toward a point downwind of the dock. "Perhaps I should commission you to paint this view. It could be a gift for my great-uncle."

"You haven't even seen my work. How do you know I could paint a landscape of any merit?"

"I know you are an artist, and I've seen how you've been studying the shore while we've been sailing. I am not mistaken, am I? Would you think about it?"

"I will consider the possibility." The lovely scene attracted her, but the sketches and preliminary work she would have to do before creating such a painting would require more boating on the river, very likely with Lord Ramsdale. Was it really the painting he wanted? She was a fool for raising the topic. Yet the view begged to be painted.

They made their final approach and for the next few minutes were busy making the landing and securing the boat. Daphne felt like a seasoned sailor now and with the baron's assistance jumped lightly from the deck to the dock, which floated on a level with the boat. Lord Ramsdale only held her hand to guide her, quite as if he were assisting her from a carriage. *Nothing exceptional in that.* Fortunately, he was strong and steady, for the float swayed as she landed on it and she clutched at his arm to keep her balance. He had behaved in every way like a gentleman. Why was it so hard to trust him? Had the past made her so jaded?

The baron offered her his arm, and they began to walk up the grassy slope toward the house. Having her hand tucked into the crook of his elbow and held securely against his side gave her an odd feeling of warmth and protection. She liked it entirely too well.

"Robbie told me that your great-uncle is the Marquess of Huntington. I don't believe I've ever met him," she said, hoping to divert her thoughts. "Is he active in society?"

"No. He seldom comes to London at all. He will only be coming up this year because the elder of my two sisters is being brought out this season."

Daphne thought it was lovely that Lord Ramsdale had sisters. Perhaps Robbie would be invited to the come-out ball. But then an alarm bell sounded in the back of her mind. "The marquess is not currently in residence?"

"No, indeed. Do I owe yet another apology? I did not mean to give that impression. I am the only family member using the house at present. My mother and sisters prefer the town house in Fitzwarren Place, as does my great-uncle. He says Westwater is too big and ramshackle for his taste, but I believe the truth is that he gets lonely."

"You do not?" The words slipped out before she could stop them. Definitely the wrong words.

"At times," he replied, giving her a look that was both hot and hungry.

She stopped. "I think I should wait at the boat." She removed her hand from the crook of his arm and added, "You could bring our picnic out. We could eat while we sail back to Grove House."

He turned to face her, his gray eyes searching hers. "Now why would you want to do that? Here is your perfect opportunity to see my collection of marine paintings, and I wanted to show you that one of the house, as well. My entire art collection hangs in the gallery here."

She did wish to see his paintings, and she still wanted to learn about him, about his life. But—propriety! Her innocence was her only defense against lies spread against her. "You said yourself, your mother and sisters are not in residence here, and neither is the marquess. It wouldn't be at all proper."

His face was hard to read. Once again she thought she saw impatience flit across it before he masked it with his casual air. "There you are again," he chided her gently, "worrying about the rules. You are a widowed lady—are you not free to do as you please? Who is here to judge you, in any case? The servants here are paid very well and their tact and discretion is expected at all times. You need not fear them."

"As it happens, I care what *you* think," she said, trying to gauge his expression. "I am afraid you may have some wrong ideas about me."

There. For better or worse she had opened the subject. Perhaps her own frankness would encourage him to be honest with her.

"What sort of ideas might those be?"

Drat the man! Could he truly not know what she meant, or did he get a perverse pleasure in making her lay it out for him? His polite mask betrayed nothing.

"Oh, for instance, that I am the sort of woman who would think nothing of going off alone with a man to his residence." She couldn't prevent an edge of irritation from creeping into her voice. "Have you—that is, you might

have heard some things said. . . . Other people might have
misled you about me."

Well, that certainly had sounded lame. Honestly, what
was wrong with her when she was around this man? She
cocked her head at an angle and glanced at him askance,
still trying to perceive what was going through his mind.

"So you are not a 'merry widow' kicking up your heels
now that your mourning period is over?"

"No, I am not. I have Robbie to consider."

"Ah, yes. Your guardianship."

She was genuinely surprised. "You know of that? I suppose Robbie must have told you."

"Come. Let us walk and talk at the same time." He
tucked her hand back into the crook of his arm and began
to stroll up toward the house once again. "I thought it
prudent to learn a little bit about you if I planned to take
your stepson under my wing."

Her dismay must have shown on her face for he smiled
and gave her hand a reassuring pat. "I have not changed
my mind about helping your young charge."

A surprisingly strong sense of relief flooded her, making
her wonder just when his help and his opinion had become
so important to her. "You do not believe, then, that I am
a scandalously immoral woman leading the boy to his
own ruin?"

"Are you?"

"No."

"Well, then, that is all right. I needn't fear that you'll
corrupt me if I bring you into my home."

The conceit was so silly and her relief was so great, she
had to laugh, and then they had arrived at the house and
were crossing the parterre that ran along the entire length
of it. To resist entering now would seem absurd. How did
he manage to win her over every time? Maybe that was
what made him dangerous.

The house inside was elegant, if old-fashioned. A thin,
dignified servant who looked like a schoolmaster dressed
in a severe black frock coat and snowy white cravat admitted them through a set of French doors that opened into a
splendid hall with floor and columns of colored marble.
Light reflected off the man's spectacles, shielding his expression, but nothing in his demeanor betrayed that he had

any opinion about an unaccompanied woman arriving with his master.

He was either perfectly trained or else quite accustomed to the occurrence. The latter idea did not make Daphne feel better at all. Bowing respectfully, the fellow showed them into a sitting room furnished with crimson velvet draperies and dark wainscoting to the ceiling.

Daphne quickly forgot her self-consciousness as she looked about her, however. "I see nothing 'ramshackle' about this at all," she exclaimed as she admired the fine old furniture in the room. Thick and heavily carved, she imagined it was centuries old—even older than the house itself, perhaps. The hand-polished finish glowed in sunlight that poured through the tall windows.

"Do you like it? Then you will enjoy the other rooms," Lord Ramsdale said. Genuine pleasure lit his face. "I will give you the tour."

He took her by the hand and it seemed like the most natural thing in the world—a casual gesture that nevertheless set her pulse racing. If she pulled away, it would only call attention to their contact and make things feel awkward, tense. How such moments came and went between them amazed her, for she had never before experienced such feelings.

He led her through a passage and into the main stairway hall, lit by an ornate skylight two stories above them. A huge, glass-fronted cabinet on the wide stair landing displayed family treasures, but he pointed to the floor beside it.

"That ancient boot was supposedly one of a pair that belonged to Sir Francis Drake himself," he said. "No one knows why we only have the one. Perhaps some other branch of the family has the mate to it. I rescued it from the front entry hall, where my great-uncle was using it to hold umbrellas."

They passed through an elegant salon furnished in gold brocade and a large formal dining room with a massive display of family silver and a long, polished table that could easily have sat twenty for dinner. She imagined these rooms saw little use, lovely as they were. *This house should be full of laughing, contented people,* she thought, but did not say so.

His pride in the place was obvious as he pointed out particular Drake family treasures and recounted entertaining stories. In the process of the tour, she learned his family's history.

"You must have spent a great deal of time in this house," she said, charmed to see this side of him. "You know it so well."

"Yes."

For a moment the joy left his face, and she thought his gray eyes suddenly looked bleak. *So, the handsome baron has his own hidden pain,* she thought.

"Was your time here unhappy? You seem to love this house."

He shook his head. "I was happy here, for the most part. My father was not the best role model and caused his share of grief."

How well she knew that pain. *Something else we have in common,* she could not help thinking, feeling another bond between them. But he did not elaborate. He opened another door and motioned her through, dismissing the memories with a shrug.

The library was cavernous, lined with shelves of books that rose to three-quarters of the height of the walls. Paintings of mythological subjects hung in heavy gilt frames above them. Small, ornately carved tables stood against the bookcases, bearing more stacks of books, while a grouping of chairs and sofas looked comfortable and inviting in the center of the room.

A huge, heavy table dominated the far end of the room. On it Daphne could not help noticing a large folio of what appeared to be ship plans left open beside a series of sketches and a small pile of volumes with names like *Navalis Architecturalis* and *Treatise on Shipbuilding* lettered on their spines. This sudden revelation of how the man beside her spent some of his private time felt like an intrusion, yet it was exactly what she wanted to learn. What interested him? What sort of man was he? What were his habits? She pictured him laboring over the drawings by lamplight at night, alone except for the servants in this large, silent house. Was the loneliness that picture conjured up only a reflection of her own?

"Someone appears to have been hard at work here," she

observed, slanting an inquiring look at him. She was being ridiculous—she knew nothing about this man. He might bring women or entire parties here every night that he wasn't socializing in Mayfair, or even on the nights when he was. How foolish to imagine loneliness might be another common bond they shared. "Are you a naval architect as well as a sailor?"

An enthused smile lit his face. "You give me too much credit. I do have an interest in ship design, however. I designed the sailing yacht I am having built in Southwark. I have been corresponding with my builder for several years about this project."

"Several years?" Daphne was impressed. Had he not told her he had been in the West Indies? He must have been planning this boat all the time he was away. "This project must be very dear to your heart, then."

"Indeed." He looked away from her, down at the drawings on the table, and ran a finger over one of the pages. "It is part of a dream of mine—perhaps only a foolish fantasy, but one I must see through to completion."

She was not certain he would confide the rest of it, yet she wanted very much to know. She had a feeling that in this moment, she was privileged to have a rare glimpse of the true man who was Lord Ramsdale. She craved that honesty. As she watched his fingers move slowly across the curving lines of a ship's hull on the paper, there was something so sensuous about the gesture that a tremor ran through her.

"Tell me," she said, appalled when the words came out as a whisper.

He looked at her, surprise in his pewter-gray eyes. She did not know if it was because of her interest, her tone, or the fact that she was there at all. Perhaps it was surprise that he had almost bared himself to her.

" 'Tis no earthshaking thing," he said as if a bit embarrassed. "I'd like to see this new boat of my devising prove a theory and whip the tar out of all the other Thames sailing yachts. Capturing a fine prize like the Duke's Cup is not a bad way to do it. I dream of small victories."

Once again, she had a strong sense that he had held something back, despite the smile he gave her now. "What is your theory?" she asked, hoping to draw out more.

"Oh, something too technical and boring to fill up your pretty head." The smile did not reach his eyes. He reached again for her hand. "I shall have to take you out in my new boat. But let us continue our tour."

It was foolish to feel disappointed. Why should she want him to confide in her? Was she not the very woman who had told herself neither to expect nor to seek out a friendship with this man? She wanted to feel nothing, knew it was safer to feel nothing, but despite years of need and effort, she had never quite learned how.

He led her through more of the house until at last he brought her to the gallery, stepping aside to usher her into the room. She caught her breath when she saw the display of paintings. The room was as long as two large drawing rooms set end-to-end, with north-facing windows along one side. The walls were paneled like those in most of the other rooms, but nestled within the framework provided by the panels hung paintings, one above another almost to the ceiling and covering every available space. The sheer number of paintings alone astonished her.

"Why, I feel as if I am at the Royal Academy," she exclaimed with a soft chuckle, although in truth the room triggered her memories of Summerwood. She had been very small when she had lived there and her memories were mostly vague, but the image of a room much like this one was vivid in her mind. She supposed most of those paintings had been sold along with the house when her father's impracticalities had forced them to leave.

She hardly knew where to begin looking. The pictures here appeared to be grouped by subject or type—sporting pictures, horses, pastoral landscapes, exotic foreign locales, mythological settings, historical and biblical scenes. Lord Ramsdale took her hand again and led her first to a group of portraits.

"Some of my redoubtable ancestors," he said, waving his other hand at the lot staring down at them. Walking along the section, he pointed to various candidates, naming several sea captains and admirals among them. "Here is my favorite, of course," he said, stopping. "Sir Francis Drake himself, with the Golden Hind behind him. You can see I come from a long line of sailors."

A moment later he stopped again. "Now this—this is my

great-uncle as a young man about my age. Handsome fellow then, was he not?" He quirked an amused eyebrow at her. "Now, some people hold that I resemble him somewhat."

"Fishing for compliments, sir? I reserve the right to withhold judgment," she said with a smile. But it was true; he did resemble the handsome dark-haired marquess.

"Now, come along down here. I promised to show you Zuccarelli's picture of Westwater. Here it is."

The picture hung above the carved rococo fireplace and mantel in an obvious place of honor. Slipping her hand out of his, she moved closer in order to inspect the work. Zuccarelli had been a founder of the Royal Academy during one of his visits to England. The treatment was highly romantic and exquisitely done.

"It is very lovely," she said. "Your family is justified to be proud of it. But the view from the river is even better. I am surprised he did not choose it."

"Perhaps he never saw it. Perhaps that view was meant to be painted by you."

Was it? Did she believe fate sometimes worked that way? Certainly the vision called to her.

"I would especially value it if it was done by you," he added quietly. "Your own interpretation, in your own style—uniquely yours, for me."

The soft words spoken in his deep voice sounded extremely intimate. Daphne felt the physical response to him trying to unfurl within her and fought against it. Her head knew that involvement with this man would mean disaster for her, even if her heart did not. Yet his words touched the edges of her passion for painting. Perhaps she could paint the scene from memory alone? She would view it again when they left.

"I will consider it," she said. "In the meantime, you promised to show me your collection of marines." Distraction was her best strategy just now. Looking along the gallery walls, she could see paintings of ships and seascapes farther down. She moved toward the end of the room before he could try to take her hand again. "Are those yours, or is your great-uncle also a collector?"

"Ah, I was saving the best for last." He followed her. "One day all of these pictures will be mine, so it seemed to make sense to hang mine here along with the rest. This house has the best gallery among all my great-uncle's properties."

There must have been at least thirty marines. The first one she came to was a dramatic storm scene by Jan Porcellis. She studied it closely, her excitement rising. This was painting as she knew it best, thanks to her father's own passion for it. She moved from one painting to the next, admiring and commenting.

"Look at this one by de Vlieger," she said, delighted by a tranquil scene of boats at anchor. "And you even have one by van de Cappelle." Caught up in examining the paintings, she paid little heed to where Lord Ramsdale was standing. When she came to the corner at the end of the wall and turned to the next painting, she bumped right into the baron standing there.

"Oh, I beg your pardon!" She stepped back hastily. What would he think if she kept running into him? First in the boat, now this. She felt a flush burning her face.

He chuckled, the deep sound affecting her like a physical touch. "No, I beg yours. I should have realized I would be in your path." He did not move, however, and she wondered if he meant for her to move around him. She made the mistake of looking up at him.

"I wish you could see how lovely you are," he continued. "Your face is so animated with enthusiasm, you positively glow."

"I glow?"

"Yes, quite. You did so when we were sailing, too, when you were excited and absorbed in your task."

She did not know what to say. They stared at each other for what felt like a full minute. He seemed very near. Had he moved closer? Heart pounding, she suddenly thought he might be going to kiss her. Before she could panic at the idiotic notion, however, he stepped back and motioned for her to proceed.

She slipped past him and inspected the next two paintings without really seeing them at all. By the time she came to the third one in the grouping, her equilibrium was returning and all she still lacked was concentration. Something about that third painting of a large pleasure yacht engaged in a rough sea quite suddenly gathered all her attention into focus, however. She peered at it intently, her pulse quickening.

"This is by Van de Velde, is it not?" she asked, trying not to sound as puzzled as she felt. "It is an original?"

"Yes, why?" He stepped closer.

"Oh, it's nothing. I just wondered if perhaps it might be a well-done copy."

"It had better not be a copy. I purchased it at auction from the Beaufort Galleries. I don't mind saying I paid handsomely for that painting, too. It is by the elder Van de Velde and supposedly dates from his first visit to England. If you look closely you can see the Dover cliffs on the horizon. It is among the rarest in my collection."

Such "ship portrait" paintings by the elder Van de Velde during his years in England were very rare indeed. Daphne knew of only one other, in her husband's study at Grove House. But she doubted that the elder Van de Velde's recognizable painting style and pallet differed greatly during his first sojourn in England from his better-known military pictures. The brushwork, mood, and subject were not what bothered her about the one before her now. What bothered her was the tone, and as she studied the colors that had been applied to the canvas before her, sweat began to moisten her palms.

"You do not affect to carry a quizzing glass, I suppose, my lord?"

"Is my lack of fashion so obvious?"

"Oh, dear, I did not mean—"

He chuckled. "Allow me to surprise you. My friend Hollyfield aspires to turn me into a fashionable fribble like himself someday. While I am not dandified enough to use it, I confess that I have one in my waistcoat pocket." He extracted the small magnifier and handed it to her.

Through the little lens, Daphne studied the pigments on the canvas in close detail. Mixed among the expected strokes of somber gray-green and yellow, she saw unexpected and almost unnoticeable flecks of brilliant blue—a most particular blue that was very familiar to her.

"What do you see?"

D'Avernett blue, she thought. *Father's blue. A color that definitely should not be there.* Aloud she said, "Something curious. Perhaps I am wrong. . . ."

Remain calm, she told herself, echoing Lord Ramsdale's instructions to her when they were bringing his boat about. *You will* not *tell this man your father's signature color appears in this painting.* She did not doubt her eye for color, but what she saw made no sense to her.

The next two pictures were by Van de Velde the Younger, more famous and more prolific than his father. He used a brighter palette and Daphne moved on to his pictures to examine the shades of blue in his work. She scarcely knew if she hoped to find the same blue there or not. Perhaps the color her father had invented was not as unique as they had thought. The alarmed racing of her heart seemed to have expanded to every part of her body.

"There is something—I can see it in your face," said Lord Ramsdale. "Tell me."

What she needed was to go home. There she could examine the elder Van de Velde painting in her husband's collection and compare it to what she had just seen.

What then? She truly did not know. She could tell no one of the connection to her father. But she had to say something to Lord Ramsdale.

"Your prized painting by Van de Velde the Elder appears to have some unusual tints in it, but perhaps it is only a trick of the light," she said guardedly. "It is certainly the work of a great master." What sort of master she could not say.

"Which is a polite way of saying you suspect my picture is a copy, after all," the baron said, moving very close to her. Before she knew what he was doing, he had slipped a finger under her chin and turned her face toward his. "Is that not so?"

She could not lie, staring into those silver-gray eyes. Her racing heart tripled its speed, if that were possible. The very air around them felt charged, as if they stood in the midst of a lightning storm.

"All right, yes, I think it might be," she whispered, wondering at the intensity in his eyes. Was he was angry or about to kiss her? She knew she should back away, but she seemed to be riveted in place.

For an endless moment they stood there; then once again he released her abruptly, as if he'd suddenly changed his mind. "If you know of any way we could be certain, let us discuss it over food. I am still famished and we have post-poned our picnic long enough."

With the moment broken, she worried about the consequences of her admission. How could she protect her father's reputation if the painting proved somehow connected to him? How could she explain her suspicions without dragging in his name and work?

She would pray all the way home that she was wrong.

Chapter Eight

Daphne and Lord Ramsdale discovered that the tide had indeed turned while they lingered at Westwater. Over hurried refreshments in the summerhouse, Daphne explained about her husband's Van de Velde painting and her idea to compare the two, then carefully steered the conversation to safer topics.

Now as they set off to sail back to Grove House, opposing forces of wind and current ruffled the surface of the Thames and rocked the *Ariadne*. The sun flirted with racing clouds, rendering the afternoon warm and cold by turns. Daphne shivered, buffeted by her own contrasting emotions.

Lord Ramsdale looked both so virile and at ease at the helm of the boat, his strong hand resting lightly on the tiller. Would that she could feel so relaxed! Instead she felt torn apart, wanting to get home as quickly as possible yet loath to end this rare idyl. She could not afford such a pleasure again. This man had the power to turn her entire world upside down. She had already known that pain twice in her life. She was not about to risk it again.

"You are so quiet," he said, easing the boat's course with a small adjustment of the tiller. "I hope you are not feeling unwell?"

"Unwell?"

"We are encountering a bit of chop. Some people find the motion can have, er, an unpleasant effect, especially if they have just eaten."

"Oh! Oh, I see. Heavens no, I am quite enjoying myself."

It was true, as long as she shut out everything from her heart and mind except the sailing. The rhythmic splash of the water curling at the sides of the hull and the bucking motion as the boat crested the small waves thrilled her now as much as the smoother sound and rhythm of their earlier voyage.

She attempted a smile, hoping to cover her inner turmoil. "Perhaps I should have been born a seaman instead of— of . . ."

"A woman so beautiful she takes my breath away? Now that, indeed, would have been a terrible waste." He was looking at her warmly again, his eyes like molten silver in the bright afternoon light.

If only he would not do that! He had been such a perfect gentleman all day, she had almost begun to trust him, except for the strangely charged moments like this one.

"Or an artist," he added, "with the talent to capture this river view of my home? That would have been a terrible loss as well. . . ."

Her head jerked up at the reminder. Lost in her other thoughts, she had almost forgotten to look at the view of Westwater again, to commit it to memory as indelibly as she could.

"You are kind, even if you do indulge in flattery." She studied the riverbank now, taking in the colors and light and shapes of the scene before her, trying to capture the picture in her brain even as the boat continued on and the angle of the view slipped away.

"You have decided to paint it, haven't you?" he asked gently.

"Yes. I cannot resist." Giving in to one impulse did not mean she would give in to any others, however.

"I will be happy to bring you out here at any time you wish to work on it."

"That should not be necessary, although I thank you. I believe I can do it with what I have stored in here." She tapped the side of her bonnet. *I will have to.* "However, I do want to thank you for convincing me to come sailing with you today. You were right—I did not know what I was missing! I cannot remember the last time I enjoyed something so much."

He raised a dark eyebrow, managing to look both roguish and extremely doubtful at the same time. "That is strong praise indeed. I can think of at least one greater pl—well, never mind. I am very glad to have helped you discover this. I must warn you that it is very addictive."

"Is it?"

"Next time you will be begging me to take you out."

"I never beg." Addictive it might be, but for her there could not be—must not be—another time.

He had been teasing, but now he sobered. "Will you truly not need to see the view of Westwater again?"

"I will remember it," she said firmly, wishing she believed it. "When the painting is finished I will send word to you."

"I see."

Did he? He said nothing more for several minutes, although she could feel his gaze upon her. She did not dare to look at him, lest her resolve weaken.

They sailed on in quiet punctuated by the slap of the water against the hull and the creak of the timbers overhead. When they were almost back to Grove House, she said, "There is one thing we still have not discussed, if I may presume to raise the subject."

"And what might that be?" he asked with what she now thought of as his indulgent smile. The sensuous curves of his mouth distracted her for a moment, sending a little curl of heat down through her body. Good heavens, had she already begun to recognize his different ways of smiling?

She pulled herself back to her question. "Do you have a specific plan for helping my stepson? If you do, might I be privy to what it is?"

She hoped she had not offended him with her reluctance to sail again. She only wanted to be certain he understood that helping Robbie was separate from socializing with her, for the good of all concerned.

"You are already privy to it, in a way," he said, his smile broadening. "I plan to make a sailor out of him. We Thames yachtsmen are made out to be eccentric but for the most part harmless. That is more than I can say for his current batch of companions."

Her surprise must have shown on her face, for he continued. "I cannot claim that we never wager, but you will find few habitual gamblers among us. The group includes some wealthy cits, even tradesmen, but also some who are conspicuously *haut ton*—Lord Ponsonby, for example, and Lord Grantham."

The sail began to flap noisily, and he paused to adjust it. "That's not to mention those who practice maneuvers in their bigger yachts in the Lower Thames when they are not sailing off the Isle of Wight. Uxbridge—that is, Lord Anglesey, now—has always been an avid yachtsman, and the loss of his leg at Waterloo has not dampened his enthusiasm a whit. Young Wetherell will find himself in some exalted, if eccentric, company indeed."

"Goodness. I had no idea! Although I must say you do not strike me as eccentric. Are you?"

He chuckled. "I do not think so, although some people might disagree. Shall I ask how I *do* strike you?"

Wary of where this question might lead, she shook her head, hoping he would not press her. She must not—*must not*—ask flirtatious questions. He was only too quick to follow up on the slightest encouragement!

"You do understand that my stepson has no sailing experience?" she asked, retreating to safer conversation.

"Yes. If you wonder that I am so willing to teach him, I confess that I am not entirely altruistic. I need a crewman. My new boat will take two hands to handle her in a race. A young, agile fellow like your stepson would be a great help to me."

His plan was admirable, introducing Robbie not only to new people but to an entirely new pursuit. She felt some of her doubts about the baron dissolve away, like the loosening of a too-tight corset. He must truly have been coming this morning to take Robbie sailing, after all. This whole day's outing must have been just what it seemed, a momentary impulse on his part. The sense of relief that filled her was surprising, for she hadn't realized how much of her trust she still held in reserve.

"It sounds splendid," she said. "I am also happy to learn there is some benefit to you in all this, in return for your kindness."

She did not add aloud, *It all makes more sense to me now, seeing another motive.* Instead she added, "Having had a taste of it now myself, I cannot imagine any other outcome but that Robbie will love it. I had better become accustomed to the idea that before long he will be wanting a boat of his own."

And that he will be out on the river doing what I should like to do myself.

Much to Daphne's dismay, the baron insisted on seeing her up to the house upon their return, even though it meant taking down the sail and securing the *Ariadne* to the Grove House pier. He wanted to see the Van de Velde painting in her husband's study for himself, he told her.

"However, I must not stay long," he added, to her relief. "As usual, my mother and sisters have filled my evening with engagements. I must still sail back to Westwater to make ready."

Daphne would have preferred to examine the painting alone, but she could not think of an adequate reason to insist upon it without arousing exactly the sort of suspicion she hoped to avoid. She tried to affect the lightest of attitudes, as if it all mattered very little to her.

As they entered the house Wilson greeted them, his well-practiced dignity for once tinged by something bordering reproach. "My lady, young Lord Wetherell was asking for you, and I could not tell him where you had gone or when you expected to return."

Daphne chuckled. "Turnabout is fair play, if you should ask me. It quite serves him right, and once you told him Lord Ramsdale had been here, I'm certain he figured it out for himself. However, you may tell him I have returned. He is welcome to join me and Lord Ramsdale in my husband's study."

She led the way to the small, tidy room her husband had used as his private sanctuary. She seldom came here except to go over household accounts or other business—after all this time it still smelled of her husband's pipe and was so full of his presence it gave her the eerie feeling he might walk in at any moment. In her loneliest hours she missed his company so much she ached, and being in this room always made the pain worse.

Just now, however, she strode in purposefully, intent on examining the much-prized painting that he kept on the wall beside his desk. She had not gone three steps into the room before she stopped cold, heart pumping. The Van de Velde was not there. There was simply an empty space on the papered wall where the picture normally hung—a perfect rectangle of colored Chinese landscape less faded than that surrounding it. What did it mean?

Remain calm, she told herself, words that seemed to have become the catchphrase of the day. Perhaps the servants had simply removed the picture for cleaning. Perhaps Robbie had decided to hang it elsewhere, although she was surprised he had not consulted her. Either of those instances was preferable to what she feared. She tried to slow her frantic heartbeat. She must ask, but do so calmly. She must not let on that her concern was anything beyond ordinary.

"What is it?" Lord Ramsdale asked from behind her, no doubt alarmed by her sudden halt.

"It's very odd," she said, choosing her words with care. "The painting is not in its usual place." She stepped aside and gestured toward the empty space on the wall.

"Perhaps it has only been taken down but not removed," he said reasonably, looking about. She checked behind the desk, and he peered behind a standing cabinet. However, even a more thorough examination quickly showed that the painting was not anywhere in the room.

"You must think we run a very disordered household. I assure you, that is not normally the case." Daphne tried to cover her alarm with a show of embarrassment. "Will you wait in the drawing room while I find out what has become of the picture? If I cannot locate it in a few minutes, perhaps we can postpone our viewing until another day."

The baron agreed and Daphne went off in search of the servants. Questioning them required every ounce of tact she could muster—it was a bad business to make servants feel they were being accused of anything. She trusted all of them, but could not hide her impatience when they knew nothing at all about the missing painting.

"Not that it was missing, or even *when* it went missing? How can it be that none of you know?" she exclaimed in frustration. "Does no one dust my husband's study, or clean the lamps or lay a fire in there? I'll grant you it does not see much use these days, but it is not altogether abandoned."

Ellen, the maid-of-all-work, raised a hand timidly. "My lady, it would be my job to dust and clean in there. But his lordship told me I needn't."

"When was this?"

The young woman looked distraught. "I—I'm not certain. Perhaps a week ago? Or two weeks?"

Ah, Robbie. Daphne had suspected—feared—that he was behind the trouble all along. It had been three weeks since she had last been in the room. Robbie must have counted on her avoidance to give him time to—what? Pawn and then reclaim the picture, so she would never find out? Well, now she had.

She found him in the morning room—he was stretched out on the elegant French chaise longue, sound asleep and snoring softly. No wonder he had not joined her and the baron in his father's study. He looked innocent and young, and the sight of him softened her anger and frustration for a moment, until she steeled herself again for her task. This was not a time to be gentle and understanding, she was certain. Robbie needed a firm hand if he had sunk into this much trouble.

She shook him awake, wondering what she should say to him. Would he tell her the truth, or try to lie? His deception hurt her more than the loss of the painting.

"Robbie, wake up. I must talk with you."

He rubbed his eyes, looking about in confusion. "Huh? Daphne? What is the matter?"

"There is something very wrong, Robbie, and I believe you can tell me about it. The Van de Velde painting is missing from your father's study. Will you tell me what has happened to it and why? I have reason to believe you know."

He sat up very straight, fully awakened. "The Van de Velde? Uh . . ."

She waited, watching his face as he tried to decide what to tell her. "Start at the beginning and tell me everything," she prompted. "Whatever the trouble is, I think we had better work together to solve it now, even at the cost of your pride." She bit back her disappointment in him, knowing that now was not the time to express it.

He groaned, then looked down at the flowered carpet

between his feet. "I wanted to spare you the worry. I was so certain I could solve it myself. It's just that, instead of improving, things keep getting worse. Each thing I do seems to cause more problems instead of solving any."

He rubbed his face with both hands, pushed back his wheat-colored hair, and then looked up at her with true anguish in his eyes. "I thought I could take care of it," he said again, as if the progress of events mystified him.

She pulled a lightweight armchair out of its position in the neat half circle of matching gilded furniture so she could sit close to him. "It is all about your gambling losses, if I don't miss my guess. Am I right, Robbie? They became too much to handle?"

He nodded, mute with misery.

"Did you borrow to cover them?"

Again he nodded. "I might have won it all back on the turn of a single card!"

"How bad is it? Did you have to borrow again to cover the amounts you originally borrowed? And then more?"

She spoke softly. She knew how the downward debt spiral worked and how deep it could get. She knew that the deeper the spiral got, the tighter it wound around the failing victim. She had seen her father fall into his and wallow in it for years, sometimes rising partway out, only to fall back in. He had never gone to debtor's prison, but the possibility of that had hovered over them like an ever-present shadow from the time she was old enough to see and understand such things—from the time they had had to leave Summerwood. Her life had altered forever in that single day.

"You could have asked for an advance on your quarterly allowance," she suggested, suspecting that she already knew the reason why he had not.

He shook his head and groaned again. "I owed too much," he whispered.

"You went to the moneylenders?"

"Yes. Then, to pay them, I made some private arrangements."

"Oh, dear."

Her father had had those kinds of friends, too—friends only too willing to help out, except later their idea of help-

ing changed, and their idea of repayment time changed,
and many of her father's most valuable assets had ended
up in the hands of such eager, grasping "friends."

She realized suddenly that she was whispering, too, bent
toward him like a coconspirator. She straightened up and
spoke in a normal voice. "Who wanted your father's Van
de Velde?"

With an awful twist to her stomach, she remembered the
look of passion on Lord Ramsdale's face when he had
showed her the one in his gallery—the counterfeit one. If
he knew, if he had wanted a genuine one . . . But then why
would he have been so eager to see a painting he already
knew was gone? To see if she knew what Robbie had
done? To see if they had sold *him* a copy?

"It—it wasn't Lord Ramsdale, was it?" She knew the
suspicion was absurd.

"No!"

The vehemence of Robbie's answer reassured her, and
she sank back in her chair in relief. Short-lived relief. The
idea of having sold anyone a mere copy brought with it an
entirely new worry.

What if her husband's Van de Velde painting was no
more genuine than the one hanging in the Westwater gallery? If Lord Ramsdale had innocently purchased a counterfeit painting at great expense, could not her husband
have been fooled the same way? She wished now with all
her heart that she had paid more attention to it, had examined it closely the way she had studied Lord Ramsdale's
painting. But there had been no reason!

"Botheration. Botheration." She shook her head. "What
do you know about your father's Van de Velde, Robbie?
Had it been in the family for a long time?" She held her
breath, hoping his answer would eliminate her biggest fear.

"He bought it while he was studying with your father.
There's probably a record of it in his papers somewhere."

That was precisely what she had not wanted to hear. A
family heirloom of long standing would have been unques-
tionably authentic.

Quite unconsciously, she got up and began to pace. What
if both paintings were counterfeit, and the new owner of
her husband's painting somehow discovered it was a forgery? Could Robbie prove to that new owner's satisfaction

that he had not known? What if the other person thought Robbie had purposely sold a counterfeit rather than part with the precious original? What if it turned out her father was indeed somehow connected to the paintings? Her head was beginning to pound harder than her heart.

"Robbie, we simply *must* get that painting back. There is more at stake than you know."

Her stepson looked positively disheartened. "I sold it to Lord Ainshaw," he admitted at last. "He would never sell it back to us. He wanted it more than anything else."

Absently Daphne rubbed a finger along the bridge of her nose, a habit when she was thinking hard. Having a chance to authenticate the painting was the only way to know how bad the trouble was.

"Very well. Somehow we must find a way to examine it. Do you know what Lord Ainshaw planned to do with it?"

"His art collection is famous. I am certain he planned to hang it in his private gallery."

"So all we need is to be invited to view his collection. That should be easy."

Robbie looked up at her sharply, and she realized her heavy sarcasm had shocked him. She sat back down in her chair, dejected. She had as much chance of being invited to see Lord Ainshaw's art collection as she had being invited to tea with the queen.

"Now I think it is *you* who is not telling something," Robbie said. "I was a fool to sell Father's prized painting, and I am truly sorry for deceiving you. That was worse than foolish; it was cowardly. But obviously it matters even more than I thought. Yet what could be changed simply by viewing it again?"

Daphne pulled herself together with an effort. "Let us take one problem at a time," she said. "Did Lord Ainshaw's purchase of the painting discharge your debt to him?"

"Yes—in a devil's bargain weighted all to his advantage."

"Oh, I've no doubt of that. Do you still owe anyone else?"

Robbie squirmed. "Well, uh, actually, yes. A few."

She sighed. "I do hope you've learned a lesson from all this. Make up a list with the names and the amounts you owe, please. We will give it to your father's solicitors and

let them take care of it, which would have been the right
solution from the start. You do understand that now? Perhaps your embarrassment over this will be sufficient to
keep you from ever getting into such a coil again. I hate
to say so, but you must learn to be less trusting, Robbie.
Many people take great pleasure in the misfortunes of others, and many of them are happy to lead you right into
those misfortunes. You may trust that I know!"

"Yes, all right. I will, I do, and I will try," Robbie replied, not too abashed to try to answer all of her speech at
once. "Now will you explain about the painting?"

How could Daphne explain without dragging her father's
name into the question? Robbie and anyone else would
want to know why she suspected Lord Ramsdale's picture
was a forgery. Could she, who valued honesty so much, tell
part of the truth and be convincing? Could she tell it
quickly? Lord Ramsdale was still waiting.

"Lord Ramsdale owns a painting by the elder Van de
Velde, also," she began carefully. "I saw it today. The trouble is, it did not look quite right to me. I think it is possible
someone swindled him. The only way to know is for me to
look closely at your father's painting and compare the
two."

"You mean you think Lord Ramsdale's is counterfeit?"
Robbie's voice rose a notch, reflecting both surprise and
excitement. At least he did not ask where she had seen it.

"It *may* be," she corrected, although in her heart she did
not think she was mistaken. Her eye had been trained in
color perception from a very early age.

"What frightens me more is the possibility that if Lord
Ramsdale's painting is a forgery, perhaps your father's
could be, also. And what if Lord Ainshaw should discover
that? Oh, Robbie, there is much potential here for disaster.
You could be accused, and find yourself in much deeper
trouble than you ever bargained for. As I am your guardian, we would be cast into the briars together. Even if we
were to solve that problem, I am convinced your uncle
would gleefully seize the opportunity to finally prove to the
Chancery Court that I am unfit. Given his influence, he
could probably muster enough outraged support to get his
case heard sooner rather than later, and I fear your own

preferences would be set aside since criminal fraud would be involved."

She did not add that her credentials as an artist and those of her father would no doubt make her doubly suspect, even without any direct link between the counterfeit and her father. Neither did she mention that a scandal of such dimension would undoubtedly close the doors of the R.A. to her forever, whether she was found guilty or not. She, who had so little respectability, could lose every tattered shred she had left and with it her dreams and the one thing that made her life worthwhile—Robbie himself. Would her one path to respectability become her road to ruin instead? If only she had never seen Lord Ramsdale's painting!

"We must determine if the paintings are authentic or not."

Robbie did not ask her what made her suspect a counter-feiter had been at work. She was at least relieved and even a little flattered to think he had that much faith in her knowledge. Lord Ramsdale, she was certain, would not hes-itate to ask, and she was quickly realizing that there would be no solution that did not involve the baron.

"We will need to speak with Lord Ramsdale," she said, more to herself than to Robbie.

"Must we?"

Robbie's squeak of protest caught at her heart. Revealing his folly to his new friend would probably hurt Robbie's pride most of all.

"I am sorry, Robbie, but yes. He is in a position to help us sort this out. He has the entrée to places I could never set foot in on my own—places like Lord Ainshaw's private gallery. And, as Lord Ramsdale is cooling his heels in our drawing room at this moment, there is no getting around it. He already knows our own Van de Velde is missing."

Chapter Nine

Archer had two fingers in his waistcoat pocket fishing for his watch at the moment Lady Wetherell returned to the drawing room with her stepson trailing along behind her.

The expression on her face did not bode well for the missing painting, and the hangdog look on the lad gave a clue that he had something to do with it all. Archer, rising from his chair, guessed the story in an instant.

"My stepson, it seems, has sold the Van de Velde," Lady Wetherell announced with admirable calm. Only her eyes betrayed her feelings. In their brown depths Archer thought he could perceive not only distress but also fear. Was there something more at stake here than he knew of?

"Let me guess," he said, taking pity on the boy. "Pawned it to cover your gaming losses?"

The young fellow shook his head. "Worse," he said with a voice that shook in his embarrassment and misery. "If I'd pawned it, I could at least redeem it. I sold it to Lord Ainshaw."

Archer whistled. "Who will add it to his already-extensive collection." Although he knew the boy was not his responsibility, Archer felt that somehow he should have or might have forestalled such a circumstance. He had not guessed the boy was in as deep as that.

"Do you know him?" Lady Wetherell asked. "Robbie seems certain that we cannot buy the painting back from him."

"The earl and I have been rivals bidding on pictures at

numerous auctions," Archer said, thinking of sizeable bids he had lost to the other man. He could not offer her much comfort. "Lord Ainshaw is very acquisitive. His determination seems matched by the depth of his pockets."

"Botheration!"

"Of course, I could try to negotiate with him, if you would like me to try," Archer added quickly. The more ways he could make himself useful to this pair, the better for all involved, as far as he could see. Lady Wetherell's immoderate language amused him—he did not think she was even aware of her exclamation. She appeared to be thinking hard, rubbing the bridge of her nose absently and beginning to pace back and forth on the pale rose-and-gold flowers of the Axminster carpet.

"No," she said at last, "although I do thank you for the offer." She seemed to have reached some firm conclusion. She stopped pacing and turned to him. "I have some thoughts on this, and there are some ways in which you might help. But I know you are pressed for time right now. Could you come by tomorrow so we could discuss it?"

A sense of elation overtook his disappointment at her refusal. She was actually *inviting* him to return. Surely this was progress!

"If the weather is not inclement tomorrow, I should take Lord Wetherell out for his first sail, since he missed his chance today. The sooner we begin his training, the better." Archer kept his gaze steady on Lady Wetherell lest she sense any conspiracy between her stepson and himself. "I could come early, if you wish, or stay afterward."

He fixed his most winning smile upon her, hoping she would choose the latter option. Staying afterward would give him a longer time with her, more private and possibly more rewarding.

"Come early," she replied promptly.

"It might be *quite* early," he emphasized, "given the necessity to consider tides and weather."

"You've already seen that I am an early riser," she answered, not the slightest bit put off. "Early-morning visits from you seem to be becoming a habit here, at any rate."

The following morning Daphne sat in dappled shade by her easel in the garden, trying unsuccessfully to concentrate on the images on her canvas and the colors on her brushes rather than any thoughts of what she was planning or how it might affect her. A breeze ruffled the green canopy of leaves above her head and set patches of sunlight dancing along her arms and across her work.

All her firm resolutions of the previous day were overthrown now by her need for Lord Ramsdale's help. *I can resist his charm,* she reasoned, dabbing pale yellow ochre onto a flower petal in her picture. The slow deliberateness of the motion was quite at odds with her state of mind. *I will only do what is necessary, and only be with him the smallest amount of time.* If only she could believe that he had no interest in her!

Unfortunately, she was also not comfortable with either the idea of using him or the effect her plan would undoubtedly have upon him. *I have been used by others for almost my entire life. Why should I hesitate to do the same to someone else now when I need to?*

For a moment she saw Lord Ramsdale's smiling gray eyes in the midst of her scene, instead of flowers. Handsome, kind Lord Ramsdale, so willing to help. He would not refuse her request, but he also would not recognize the damage his reputation and standing among the *beau monde* would suffer from his kindness.

As soon as they were seen together, there would be talk. To be charged with indiscretion and identified as someone's mistress was hardly a change for her, but he would be condemned for flaunting his ladybird in public and having the bad taste to get involved with the notorious Lady Wetherell. For him, the talk could be damaging indeed.

You have no choice, she told herself sternly. The potential scandal connected to the paintings would be far more disastrous than any harm to the baron's reputation. It was essential that she solve the questions about their authenticity, both for Robbie's sake and for her own. She could not bear the thought that her father, as brilliant and committed to his art as he had been, might in some way be involved. She only hoped she could investigate that possibility without revealing it to anyone.

Truly, the course she had decided upon was flawed and full of risks. She had not even considered how the baron might interpret her sudden desire to spend time with him after she had made her opposite intentions so clear yesterday. However, she could see no alternative. She and Robbie had spent their entire evening sifting through her husband's records to discover when and from whom he had purchased his Van de Velde painting. The information they had finally found did not eliminate her doubts.

There was one thing for which she was grateful, however—viewing Lord Ainshaw's collection could be done in private. She would not have to venture into a full-blown gathering of the *beau monde,* where she was not welcome and where there was always the risk of running into certain former students from her father's classes. Students like Morgan Laybrook, for one, who in the past had caused her so much trouble her father had dismissed him from the D'Avernett Academy. None had caused difficulties for her while her husband had been by her side, but now? It was true that she had no one to protect her now. One indiscreet run-in with Laybrook or one or two others whom she would never call gentlemen and she could disgrace herself again with an entirely new scandal.

Archer did not mind in the least being invited to return to Grove House earlier than he had planned. Surely it was a good sign that Lady Wetherell had asked him to come at all. The morning mist had already cleared away, and he was fortunate to have a second day that was perfect for fine sailing. As he guided the *Ariadne* to Chelsea with one hand on the tiller and the sun on his face, he thought again about the lady and their previous day's outing.

The woman surprised him. The vivacious, laughing beauty he had spied in the hat shop that first day had shown herself in moments while they sailed on the river, but there were walls around that lovely, lively sprite—walls built from experiences he could only guess at. Would he ever be able to earn her trust?

What he really wanted was to sweep her up into his arms and convince her by kisses that they were destined to be lovers. He had danced such a patient, careful dance yesterday! He could not count how many times he'd had to stay his hand before it brushed her shoulder or touched her hair. He had watched her and watched her, looking his fill, studying the way she moved her hands, the way her eyes lit up when something interested her, the inviting way her lips pursed when she was thinking.

Was he obsessed? He'd felt like such a schoolboy, uncertain of his words and actions. He had tried not to betray the depth of his passion for her, lest he frighten her. She still seemed wary of him, and although he did not understand the reason for it, he would continue to go slowly. He would need to know this young widow much better before he could hope to read all of her moods.

He secured his boat at the Grove House pier and after passing through the small iron gate, headed up the short path of packed earth that led to the bottom of the garden. There he saw at once that Lady Wetherell was working at an easel set up in the shade of a linden tree. She was wearing pale yellow, like a beam of sunlight captured and draped about her person. He might have enjoyed simply watching her work, but as soon as he reached the wider, formal paths of the garden itself, the crunch of gravel under his feet gave him away.

"Ah, Lord Ramsdale," she said, looking up.

"Good morning, Lady Wetherell. And a lovely morning it is. I see you are already thoroughly engaged. Please do not disturb yourself." Coming closer, he asked, "Do you mind if I look at your work?"

"It is nothing more than a paint sketch of flowers with the house behind them," she said in a dismissive tone, but she set aside her brush and wiped her hands on a rag beside her chair.

The gesture made him think instantly of the paint he had discovered on her hands the first time they had met. Was she thinking of that moment, too? He rather hoped so. However, when he approached to see what she had rendered on the canvas, she rose from her seat and moved aside. If she remembered that vivid moment from their first meeting, she clearly intended not to risk repeating it.

He liked what he saw. She had chosen an unusual angle from which to sketch the house, and the flowers standing large in the foreground were mostly masses of color where she had not yet worked in the details. The picture seemed full of light. The concept and the composition defied any traditional approach to what still was, in the end, a landscape.

"I can see you are not a follower of the classical school," he commented, keeping his voice neutral. He wanted to see how she would react.

"I dabble to amuse myself," she said in a rather lofty tone. "As the musician who composes a ditty for his own amusement may not concern himself with great themes or rules of harmony, neither do I feel constricted by convention when I merely experiment with paint."

"Well, I applaud your efforts, and I think you are far too humble. I think it is quite lovely, even unfinished." *Like you,* he wished he could add. "I suspect you are an admirer of Turner's work. Perhaps you are even a bit influenced by him?"

They launched into a discussion of Turner's unorthodox ideas and the effect he was having upon the staid Royal Academy. A full ten minutes went by as they stood on either side of her easel before Lady Wetherell suddenly interrupted herself.

"Oh, heavens, what am I doing? You will need to set off with Robbie, who does not even know you have arrived! And I have not yet spoken to you about the matter that is most on my mind—the very reason I asked you to come."

You do not have to have a reason, he wanted to say, but he held it back.

She rubbed the bridge of her nose, leaving a faint smudge of color there, to his amusement. She turned and began to pace along the walkway. Since she seemed hardly aware of this, he followed.

"I—oh, bother, this is most awkward," she murmured. "Right then, I'll just plunge in." Without warning, she wheeled around to address him—only, of course, he was right behind her.

As she careened into his chest it was only natural that his arms came up to steady her. Instinctive reflex, purely. The trouble was, once he had his arms around her, the devil if he could manage to release her. It was a wrong move—he knew it was a wrong move—yet she felt absolutely right there, as if she belonged there and always had. They were barely acquainted yet he had never experienced such a strong sense of rightness with any woman before now.

The absolute surprise of that reaction along with her

somewhat delayed attempt to push away combined to bring him back to his senses, and he set her back on her feet. For a moment they just stared at each other.

"I do beg your pardon," he said wonderingly.

"No, no, my fault entirely," she assured him.

Had she merely been so startled that she did not react for that long moment before she pushed away? Or did he dare to hope that perhaps despite her distrust she actually found herself attracted to him? He should not refine on it, as what happened had been purely accidental. He forced his attention back to the moment when she had whirled around.

"Is there a new problem? You said yesterday that I might be of some service with this business about Lord Ainshaw. I hope you know I am more than willing to do whatever I can. I feel as if I should have known Lord Wetherell was already in over his head. I did not guess that his losses were quite so extensive."

She seemed to recover her balance. "May I speak frankly, perhaps even bluntly?"

He nodded, offering his arm. "Perhaps if we walk along together, it will be easier." He knew, of course, that anything so difficult to say could not be good, yet he felt absurdly pleased when she slipped her hand into the crook of his elbow and they began to walk.

"You already know I had doubts about the Van de Velde painting I saw at your home yesterday," she said slowly. "Something about it did not look right."

"Yes."

She stopped and turned to look at him intently. "You said you bought it at the Beaufort Galleries?"

"Yes. I bought that painting from Galton Meregill himself. He has been dealing in artworks for years." Archer could barely keep his mind on answering her. He noticed that the sherry color of her eyes was flecked with gold and tiny bits of darker brown. "His reputation is spotless. I have bought many pictures from him."

She nodded, an odd expression on her face. "I know him. When did you buy this one?"

"Before I went to the islands. Maybe four years ago. Are you saying you truly think it is not genuine?"

"I am hesitant to say so, but I have questions. And now

I have questions about my husband's picture as well. I've learned that he also bought his from the Beaufort Gallery. Do you know where or how Mr. Meregill acquired yours? Did he give you any history of the prior ownership?"

It was deuced hard to think while staring into her eyes. "I am trying to remember what he told me. I believe he said he purchased it at an estate auction. The family did not know the history of how it had come into their own collection, only that it had been there for generations."

"Hm."

Her one syllable reply did more to gain his attention than her questions had done. "What is wrong with it? Why do you suspect it might not be genuine? I fancy myself somewhat knowledgeable about marine art, and I am certain Meregill is considered an expert. Neither of us saw anything amiss."

She sighed and began walking again, without benefit of his escort. Two long steps brought him beside her again. They rounded a corner of the garden and started down another path.

"Let us just say it is something technical about the color palette, a very small matter that I have no doubt would escape almost anyone else's notice, especially to the naked eye. It may shock you to learn that my father taught more than the occasional student. He ran an art academy. He saw to it that I was schooled very early in the techniques of producing pigments and paint. You might say I am on a very intimate basis with most colors."

Which was, Archer guessed, a skewed way of saying her father had put her to work grinding and mixing his colors when she still should have been in the schoolroom.

"It would have been easy to verify my doubts by comparing your Van de Velde to my husband's, but now—well, of course, that has become complicated. What I wondered was, could you manage to be invited to view Lord Ainshaw's collection? And if—if you could, would you be willing to bring me along? I am loath to ask this of you, but it is of the utmost importance that I be able to see that painting again, and I could think of no other way."

"So you can decide if mine is counterfeit?"

"Yes, although you force me to tell you, I have very little doubt. I am sorry. I have begun to worry now that my husband's could be, also. Can you imagine if Lord Ainshaw were to discover it? What if he thought Robbie and I had deliberately tried to swindle him?"

"I see. This could become a very serious matter."

"I would not ask you to be seen with me otherwise. There will be gossip—there always is." She sounded weary. "Perhaps you can make certain it is a private viewing? We could meet somewhere away from the house and go in a hackney with the curtains drawn."

"Such secrecy!"

"You have already been very kind to me and to Robbie. I should hate to see you subjected to the kind of talk that will circulate if we are seen together."

He rounded on her and seized her by the elbows, startling her. Patience suddenly deserted him. "And what would you think if I said I did not care about the gossip?" he said, staring into the brown depths of her eyes. "What if I said I would be perfectly content to be seen in your company—that I would be delighted to take you to see Lord Ainshaw's collection and anywhere else you wished to go?"

He had to admire how quickly she rallied from her surprise. Raising her chin a fraction, she replied, "Then I would have to say either you are a candidate for Bedlam or you have no idea what you would be getting yourself into."

He could not have released her then if ten thousand horses had been bearing down upon them. "It must be Bedlam for me, then," he said, drawing her closer and slipping his arms around her waist. "I have been lashed by the vicious tongues before, and I still have every intention of being seen with you."

His gaze locked with hers, and what he did next should have qualified him for Bedlam quite easily. Slowly, slowly he lowered his head to claim her lips, expertly avoiding the broad brim of her hat, intending to show her that perhaps she did not know what *she* was getting into. He watched for any sign of unwillingness on her part, and allowed her time to turn away if she did not wish his kiss. She stared back at him and moved not a muscle.

Her mouth was supple, yielding, her taste as intoxicating as wine. He tightened his embrace and deepened the kiss, exploring her lips with his. With every sweet taste of her he wanted more, and wanted her to want him. He closed his eyes, lost to a flood of sensation—the velvet of her mouth, her scent, the feel of her slender form in his arms.

Sensing the moment her lips parted under his, he slipped his tongue inside to meet hers. He felt the shock go through her and heard her faint intake of breath. His eyes flew open to see hers staring back at him, huge dark pools. Had she never been kissed so before? That he could not believe.

A kind of fierce possessiveness crept over him, and he pulled her fully against his hard body. *Mine,* he wanted to shout. He could not bear the idea of other men having this intimacy with her. Holding her firmly, he eased one hand up her back and caressed the nape of her neck. Then finally he slid his fingers up into her hair, rewarding himself with a touch of the silky softness he had imagined from the first day he'd seen her. He broke off the kiss and trailed his mouth along her jaw past her hat ribbon to her ear, kissing her there and then again beneath her ear, nuzzling her neck and reveling in the softness of her skin and a scent that was neither roses nor jasmine, but simply, purely hers.

With a gasp she pushed against him, breaking the moment. He released her with the greatest reluctance, as if he had barely the strength to drag his hands from her.

Had he made a mistake? Rushed his fences? "I refuse to skulk about in the shadows and be reduced to hiring hackneys and meeting in secret, just to escape from the gossips," he declared, searching her eyes. "We will go to Lord Ainshaw's, and we will go other places as well, as we please. Openly. You and I are entitled to live our lives as we see fit." He felt ready to defy anyone and anything, but she looked stunned. Would she refuse him now?

She closed her eyes, then opened them again, seeming to recover. She shook her head. "Fine words," she said, "but the truth of the matter is that while we may be entitled to, we cannot." She spoke with controlled dignity that he could not help but admire. "I will go with you to Lord Ainshaw's, and I thank you. But I will not go elsewhere."

"I beg your forgiveness if I have offended. I am but a man. You are the most exquisite, irresistible woman I have ever seen. I could not help myself."

She did not answer him immediately. "It is not so easy to ignore how cruel people can be," she said slowly, as if he had not spoken again. "I have had to endure the way they treat me for many years, although I have never deserved such harsh judgment. It has cost me much, and could still cost me even more. You might think that it would not hurt me anymore, I am grown so accustomed," she added with a bitter little laugh, "but it still does."

She looked so tortured, he wanted to take her back into his arms and kiss away her pain. He even raised his hands, but she turned and walked away a few steps.

From that safer distance, she faced him again and asked, "Mere helpless male that you claim to be, would you have behaved in this way with a woman you considered marriageable? If you are honest and a gentleman, I think we both know the answer to that."

She was right. He was a selfish clod. He also had never considered that the secrecy she proposed would protect her as much as him. He wanted only to love her, but she wanted respect. What a conundrum!

Heart in throat, he pursued his own defense. "Can you say with equal honesty that my embrace repelled you and that you did not enjoy my kiss?" He advanced toward her, shortening the space between them by a cautious single step. "Can you say you would not wish me to ever touch you in that way again?"

In all honesty, she could not. Daphne watched him move toward her again, knowing she was sinking into quicksand from which she might never escape. As shocked as she had been by his boldness, she had not been repelled. A part of her craved more of his touch; a part of her was spellbound by what he was able to make her feel. More men than she cared to remember had tried to press their attentions on her in the past, starting with the insidious Morgan Laybrook right under her father's nose. With all of them she had always felt revulsion, but not with Lord Ramsdale. With him it had felt so right! God help her, he was going to kiss her again, and she could make no move to stop him.

"Hey ho! So you have arrived, Ramsdale! Are we sailing?" Robbie's voice cut across the garden, and she clutched at it as if it were a lifeline tossed from shore.

"Here, Robbie! We're over here," she said stupidly, waving and forcing a cheery brightness into her voice. Of course, he must have already seen them.

"Oh, I say," Robbie said as he came up to them, his steps crunching on the gravel path. She could hear the dismay in his tone. "I have timed that rather badly, haven't I? Shall I go back in and wait to be summoned? I don't mind. . . ."

Dear Lord! Could Robbie tell that Lord Ramsdale had kissed her? Was her hat crooked? Was her state of confusion so evident? Was her heartbeat so loud?

"We are just talking," she fibbed, mortified yet thoroughly grateful for the interruption. "Planning how to see the Van de Velde at Lord Ainshaw's. Lord Ramsdale has agreed to escort me."

"Splendid! Absolutely capital!" Robbie responded with what she thought was rather an overabundance of enthusiasm. She slanted a suspicious look at him and he sobered immediately. "That is to say, very sensible, I mean."

She was not at all certain it was. The kiss had been dangerously revealing. She had nearly lost herself and everything she was striving for in that single, powerful moment. And now that the attraction between her and the baron had been exposed, the fine line she must tread seemed more treacherous than ever. She still needed his help, but at what price would he give it? Was he honorable enough not to press his advantage over her, now that he knew he had one? Was she strong enough to resist?

All of London would assume she was his mistress as soon as they were seen together. Rumor would be taken for fact. However, if she succumbed to the temptation of her attraction to Lord Ramsdale, she would lose the last defense that she had, the knowledge of her own innocence. She would never again be able to look anyone in the eye, not even herself. Yet, not to go with him could prove far more costly, risking a far bigger scandal that would cost her all her dreams and ruin Robbie as well.

She must proceed with the plan, although surely she was the one who should be locked up in Bedlam. If she somehow came through this heart-whole and unscathed, she would hire out to Astley's to perform with the ropewalkers.

Chapter Ten

Daphne was greatly relieved when Robbie and the baron went off to sail. The kiss stood between her and Lord Ramsdale now like a door left ajar—a door she had meant to keep firmly closed. How had he managed it on this, only the third time they'd been together? Since she could not avoid being with him, she would have to be stronger, more vigilant, more resistant.

Her relief turned to concern, however, when the morning's weather did not hold. Dark clouds gathered and the wind increased, driving her from the garden up to her studio. She became quite anxious for the two sailors to return as she began preliminary sketches for the Westwater painting. By the time Wilson came to tell her the men were back, it was noon and rain was slashing hard against the windows.

She hurried down to find them in the leather-covered chairs in the library, already sipping from cups of steaming tea. Their cravats and damp coats were spread before the fire to dry. Lord Ramsdale looked not the slightest out of countenance. In truth, he looked more appealing than ever with his dark hair tousled by the wind and his shirt open at the throat.

Sternly, Daphne fixed her attention on Robbie, who looked far less comfortable. He sat huddled in his chair, hunched over and staring down into his cup.

"Gentlemen, please do not get up. How did your session go?" she said upon entering the room.

For a moment, neither of them answered. They sipped, exchanging looks.

"Apart from the weather, Robbie, did you not find sailing to be wondrous?"

Lord Ramsdale set down his cup and stood up, despite her dispensation, clearing his throat. "Ah, um, do you recall my mentioning that some people are susceptible to becoming ill from the motion of the water?"

Daphne's enthusiasm faltered. "Oh, dear. I thought that was only after they had eaten. You do not mean to say . . .?"

The baron nodded. "I am afraid so. Of course, we had a stiff breeze today. He might do better on another day in much calmer conditions."

"Or not," Robbie said unhappily.

Daphne's heart sank with dismay. What would become of Lord Ramsdale's excellent plan to help Robbie, if the boy could not sail? Was this, then, the end of their scheme?

She bit her lip with disappointment. Turning back to the baron she asked, "What of your race? How will you practice? You said your new boat will need two people to handle it."

"I will have to find someone else." Clasping his hands behind his back, he moved to the window, looking out between the streaks of rain as if there might be an answer there. "It will not be easy at this point, but I must."

"I will do it." The words popped out of her mouth before she had time to think.

"No!" The response came from both men in chorus. It only echoed the appalled response in her own head. Lord Ramsdale wheeled away from the window and approached her. "It is unthinkable," he said, his brows drawn together.

"Why?" His reasons could not possibly match her own.

"You have commendable aptitude and enthusiasm. If only you were not a woman."

"Not a—?" Daphne clenched her fists, her pride stung. "You men think we are such a useless lot! I'll have you know I could do anything that Robbie would be able to do—haul on ropes, watch out for other boats, even—as you say—'man' the tiller. I could do anything that I saw you do just yesterday, sir!"

The baron smiled down at her. "I'll have you know that

I, for one, have never, ever, thought that women were useless." The way he looked at her made her blush to her toes. But he had more to say.

"Nevertheless, most gentle females have hands too soft to handle the ropes even with gloves, nor have they adequate strength to raise or lower sails quickly as is often the crewman's task. The sails and spars can be exceedingly heavy."

"I am stronger than I look."

"We could debate at length or even try out whether or not you have the physical strength, but that is not the only point to consider. Female dress is not conducive to leaping about with agility on a boat, you must admit, and any alternative to it would be an invitation to scandal. Furthermore, while the rules of the Thames River Fleet do not address the question of women as crew, I believe it is only because the very idea is inconceivable. It would not be allowed."

"But . . ."

"Daphne, I will do it."

Daphne and the baron both turned to Robbie in surprise. He still appeared a bit green about the gills, but he was sitting up and looked more alert than he had minutes ago.

"I want to do it, despite what happened today. I can overcome this seasickness. I think I simply must become accustomed, and besides, as Ramsdale said, we might not have such foul weather the next time."

"Ah, that's the rallying spirit, lad! You'll do well." Lord Ramsdale turned toward Daphne again, and his tone softened and became serious. "Please know that I do appreciate the spirit of your offer, Lady Wetherell. I am touched that you should care so much for me to be able to race."

Oh, heavens. What would her unguarded tongue betray next? She must not allow him to read more into her offer than was there. Her enthusiasm for sailing and her concern for changing Robbie's social circle had, merely for a thoughtless moment, eclipsed her need to stay out of the baron's company as much as possible.

"It is clearly important to you," she said. "As you are doing a great deal to help us, it seems only fair that we should try to offer something in return."

"It means a great deal to me that you care," he replied with an unsettling smile. "Never fear. There is much else you could offer, and I have the greatest faith in your generosity."

Archer had several errands to run that afternoon. He left the *Ariadne* at Grove House and allowed Lord Wetherell to drive him into town because of the inclement weather.

At Fitzwarren Place, he found his mother at his great-uncle's huge walnut desk up to her elbows in lists—lists of guests, tradesmen, food, furnishings, and decorations—all for Winnie's come-out ball. The event, delayed originally for Archer's return from the West Indies, had now been put off again because Lord Huntington was unwell and no one was quite certain when he would be ready to travel to Town.

"There is only one good thing I can think of about having to hold it so near to the end of the Season," Lady Ramsdale said with a discouraged sigh. "At least it gives us more time to make all the arrangements."

Archer bent to kiss her cheek and chuckled as he did so. "I can think of at least two more, Mother. First, consider the anticipation that will have built up by the time we actually hold this event, after people have had to wait all Season. Second, if Winnie should prove to be such a resounding success that some poor fellow comes up to scratch in her very first Season, you can save the expense of a betrothal ball by combining them both in one."

He grinned and moved away as she slapped at his arm.

"I plan to invite Sir Peter," she said. "Will he come? Will he be courteous enough to stay in the ballroom and dance with the young ladies, or will he spend the whole evening playing cards?"

Archer felt a little guilty for neglecting Holly. The truth was, knowing his friend disapproved of his pursuit of Lady Wetherell, Archer had very easily found himself too busy to find time for him.

"Holly is devoted to you, Mother. He would never disappoint you or be so discourteous. He knows what a special occasion this will be for Winnie. And I will personally wring his substantial neck if he hides in the card room all evening. What other gentlemen are on your list?"

"Archer, I am so happy you are taking an interest in this."

Archer had his own reasons for his interest in the list, although of course his sister's come-out was important to him. He peered over his mother's shoulder. "Hm, room enough to add a few more names, I see. I may have some suggestions. Let me think on it for a few days."

"Thank you, Archer. Do not take too long, however. The invitations must go out before everyone we wish to invite has made other commitments. Oh, it is such a shame our ball must be so late! It is much easier to be impressive early on, before everyone has been exposed to two dozen come-out balls with the same food, the same decorations, and the same people."

Archer smiled. He would be happy to remedy the last of those complaints, but he did not think his mother was quite ready to entertain his idea. There was still time left. He could wait.

He patted his mother's shoulder. "You are very creative when you wish to be, Mother. I know you will be up to this challenge."

He borrowed a carriage from his family's stables and headed for Southwark to check on the progress of his new boat at the shipyard. He needed to find out when the little sloop would be ready to go into the water so he could plan a celebration and make certain other arrangements. The sooner, the better. The date for the Duke's Cup Race was still several weeks off, but like everything else, it drew closer with each spent day.

His mind skipped ahead to the launching. The boat needed a name. To him she would always be the *Mistress,* permanently linked with an equally beautiful lady. To use that name officially, however, would be less than circumspect, especially if he managed to coax Lady Wetherell aboard! He had a feeling he had borrowed enough trouble already. But perhaps he would ask Lady Wetherell to christen the boat. That idea appealed to him immensely.

The rain had stopped by the time he had crossed the river to Southwark. Stepping around puddles in the busy boatyard, Archer found his shipwright supervising the delivery of a load of timber. A burly Scotsman of few words, John Forsyth quickly answered Archer's concerns and agreed to assist with a small matter.

Archer could not resist taking a look at his boat, still

cradled on stocks in a work shed, but then he closed their brief transaction by paying Forsyth another part of the small fortune the boat was costing and took his leave. He had two more errands, but the afternoon was growing short and he had another full evening ahead of him.

Daphne, in the meantime, had convinced Robbie upon his return to come up to her studio and look at her Royal Academy painting. She thought such a consultation might help her to put Lord Ramsdale and everything connected to him out of her mind. The picture sat in its corner on the largest of her wooden easels, an unfinished ship tossed in a stormy yet unfinished sea.

"It won't do," she declared, hoping Robbie understood her absolute certainty. Roquefort rubbed about her ankles, but she shooed him out of the way after giving him a quick, affectionate pat. "Only the most outstanding work is accepted by the Royal Academy. I know it won't do, but I don't know what is missing, or where I've gone wrong."

Robbie stared at the painting thoughtfully. "As always, I think your technique is brilliant. Not every artist can manage to make the water look so real, with depth and translucence and that subtle shift of colors." He tapped his lips with one finger, as if to hush a child. Daphne had seen his father do the same a thousand times.

The gesture triggered a rush of sadness. "Your father was a wonderful critic," she said, shaking her head. "He could spot flawed composition or a mistake in perspective or a color choice that did not work, every time."

"You still miss him very much, don't you?" Robbie asked, turning to her.

"Yes, I do." She wanted him to know he was not alone in continuing such feelings, even after their official mourning was over. "He was always good to me. He rescued me from an appalling future and was always, well, generous and kind." She had almost said a generous friend and mentor, but something stopped her—some sense that Robbie needed to believe her relationship with his father had been more than that.

Robbie paused, seeming to study her. "Did you love him?"

Her surprise and dismay at his words must have shown

on her face, for almost instantly he retracted the question. "Forgive me! I should never have asked you that." He turned back to stare at the painting again. "You saved him from many years of loneliness, you know. I always thought you were kind, generous, and patient with him in return."

"I did try to make him happy. I was the age you are now when I married him," she added, somewhat surprised to think of it. The old viscount had saved her from far worse than years of loneliness, at the time she was grieving for the loss of her own father. "I know you miss your father, too, Robbie. I hope you know what a good man he was."

Robbie nodded silently and kept his face turned toward her painting.

Our loss unites us, she thought, giving him time to compose himself. A moment later he steered the conversation back to the more comfortable subject of her painting.

"I agree that even though it is lovely to look at, it fails in some way to spark excitement," he said with honest candor. He sounded just like his father. "I don't suppose that helps much. Had you considered asking Lord Ramsdale for his opinion?"

Daphne stared. That was an abrupt turn she had not expected.

"As he is a collector and a connoisseur of marine art," Robbie continued, "might he not have a good idea of what to look for, or what might be lacking? You could ask him tomorrow when he comes to take me sailing again! I may be my father's son, but I definitely lack his eye and wisdom in these matters."

Robbie's suggestion filled Daphne with dismay even though it made a great deal of sense. So soon was Lord Ramsdale back again, in name if not in physical presence! How had this man, this total stranger, so quickly invaded every part of her life? Daphne did not want to invite the baron's opinion, but Robbie was altogether too inquisitive in nature not to ask why if she refused the idea outright.

"Your answer shows a different sort of wisdom, Robbie," she said, avoiding a direct response. "Many people twice your age do not recognize the limits of their own expertise, nor have they the tact to express themselves so gently. You could be a diplomat. You are your father's son in so many ways! Always be proud of that."

She hoped Robbie would not press her about Lord Ramsdale. Her studio was her sanctuary, the one place that was very personally hers and very private. She did not yet feel ready to share so much of herself with the man.

Yet? Mentally she shook herself, wondering how any inkling that she ever might or could afford to had crept into her head. On the other hand, perhaps she was foolish to think she could keep the baron out. He seemed to have quite thoroughly invaded the place already without once having actually set foot in it.

Chapter Eleven

"Are you mad?"

Sir Peter Hollyfield stared at Archer in horror. "One might almost suspect you were falling in love with the woman. They say that can make a man do idiotic things."

The two men were sitting in Holly's comfortable study in the wee hours of that night, drinks in hand. They had run into each other at the coming-out ball for the Hartdales' third fashionably frivolous daughter, and had decided to escape together after a decent interval of doing their duty. Holly had been quite miserable after a particular young beauty he fancied had spent the entire evening ignoring him. That was no mean feat given Holly's considerable size. Archer had been doing a great deal of thinking, and had just confided to his friend his newest strategy in pursuing Lady Wetherell.

"Do you think it is so idiotic? I want your true opinion, after you stop to consider." Archer looked up from the swirling contents of his glass and studied Holly's face. "Suppose—just suppose, all right?—that all of the tales you've heard about her were false. How would you set about restoring the reputation of someone like that?"

"I would try to track down where the rumors had come from, for one thing, but that is a nearly impossible task." Holly got up to refill his glass of port and topped off Archer's without asking. "Beyond that, I suppose brazening it out in the face of the *ton* would be an option, although a difficult one."

"If I could count on your support, that would be helpful," Archer said.

"Do you really believe you could pull it off? Look me in the eye and tell me she is not your mistress. She may not be—yet—but you cannot deny that is what you want. Or wanted." Holly paused in the act of replacing the decanter on his desk. "Please do not tell me your purpose has changed!" he said with a look of true distress. "You might manage to have her received again, but she could never become eligible."

"She is not my mistress," Archer stated flatly, standing up to look Holly in the eye. A staring contest ensued for a moment, until Holly turned and resumed his seat. The leather upholstery creaked in protest under his large frame.

"What makes you think she is innocent of those rumors?" he asked. "If she did none of the things attributed to her, what gave rise to the rumors in the first place? I grant you that she may have had far fewer lovers than have been said, but that would not make her innocent."

"I kissed her."

"What? What?" Holly sputtered and choked on his wine. "When? I would not let that get about—that hardly would help your effort to salvage her reputation."

Archer sat down again. "I know my confidences are safe with you. It was none of her doing—I caught her by surprise. You can tell a great deal from the way a woman kisses, and I am telling you, she is innocent."

"Or the most expert seductress you have ever encountered, and that is saying something."

"Will you not accept my word on it? I need your support in this, Holly. If I am to be seen with her about town—if I am going to include her in upcoming events—I must not be the only one who accepts her right to be there and treats her with respect. If we are convincing, people who do not know her or her reputation will take their cue from us, not from those who scorn her."

"It is not going to be easy."

"True. If it were, I would not need to ask for your assistance."

Holly took a large swig of his drink and cleared his throat, looking down into his glass instead of at Archer. "Have you considered that if you are successful in this campaign, you may well ruin any chance you had of forming a liaison with her? She may like her new respectability too well."

"I have considered that." Archer didn't believe that would happen. She was clearly not indifferent to him, and she would be grateful to him on yet another account besides his aid to her stepson. They would wait a bit, and then they would be utterly discreet. He wanted to do this for her. It was worth a small risk.

"We will have to confront those who judge her or try to pass along rumors," Holly said.

"Yes." Archer could see that the stubborn look on his friend's face was softening.

"Well, I've been known to stand up against a bully or three in my time. You are certain this is what you want? I've no aversion to championing a lady—assuming she is one." Holly leaned forward and raised his glass to Archer, offering a toast. "Here's to challenging endeavors—may we always succeed at them."

Two glasses clinked, and both men downed the remains of their drinks. Fixing an intent blue eye upon Archer, the baronet added, "If you prove to be wrong about her, Drake, there will be hell to pay, and I'll not be shy about demanding my share."

In the morning Daphne was safely in her studio applying herself to the sketches of Westwater, so she did not see Lord Ramsdale when he arrived to take Robbie out sailing again. Perhaps it was for the best, as she was abysmally out of sorts. Anxieties over the Van de Velde paintings and even the baron himself had plagued her sleep with dreams and haunted her waking moments all night.

The sketches were not progressing well. She knew the reason was not only that she had not slept well during the night—she needed to work with the view before her eyes. Capturing the light and the exact angle of the building in relation to the riverbank was proving impossible from memory alone.

Despite this, she felt it was more important than ever to paint the picture. Her art was one gift—perhaps the only gift—she could willingly offer to the baron in return for his help. She still suspected that what he really wanted from her was something she was not—and would never be—willing to give.

Once fully engrossed in the challenge she had set for herself, she failed to notice the passing hours. She was surprised when Wilson came to tell her that Lord Ramsdale and Robbie had returned from their sail and that the baron requested a word with her. With a sigh of frustration, she set aside her materials and untied the fastenings of her smock. She hated interruptions. Besides, she was wearing a faded old lavender muslin and her hair hung down her back in a simple braid—comfortable for work but no state in which to be seen by visitors. However, she had no business wanting to appear attractive to the baron. Was it not better that she should look her worst?

When she came down she found him studying the paintings in the drawing room, just as he had been on the morning of their sail.

"You seem to prefer the hard seat of a sailboat to the upholstered cushions of a drawing-room chair, my lord," she observed as she entered.

The rich, mellow sound of his laugh rewarded her as he turned to greet her with a smile that made her breath catch. Today he was dressed casually, wearing a loose brown jacket over a blue waistcoat patterned with thin red stripes. His white collar points rose above a dark red neckcloth knotted at his throat instead of a snowy cravat. How could she forget how thoroughly splendid he was when she had not even been apart from him the length of a full day? How easily he penetrated her armor and dispelled her bad mood with so small a thing as a smile.

"Good morning. Forgive me for disturbing you. How does your painting progress? Young Wetherell tells me you have begun to work on the picture of Westwater."

She was loath to admit that she needed to go out on the river again, after making her opposite intention so clear just two days ago. "Well enough," she hedged. "In truth, it is too soon to tell."

"I don't doubt that another look at the view could be helpful. It just happens I have come to spirit you away for an hour. The last time we were out in the *Ariadne* I promised you a picnic, and so you shall have it. There is a lovely spot for one on the river not far from Westwater, just on the opposite bank."

"Oh, but I—"

"Will not be allowed to say no. I will wait while you fetch a wrap of some sort and a bonnet. There is no need for high fashion on the river."

Daphne was inclined to bristle at his high-handedness, but she bit her tongue. The lovely day beckoned to her. A chance to make some notes and rough sketches of the Westwater view would be helpful. A sail and a picnic sounded so irresistible, despite her firm resolutions. She half feared she had fallen in love—not with Lord Ramsdale, but with sailing. Botheration!

"My dress—"

"Is perfect. You would not want to wear your best on such an outing. Besides, I have some news, and you shall not learn it unless you come."

She sighed. "All right. If I may bring sketch paper and pencils to make some visual notes of the Westwater view."

"Of course. I would be happy to watch you work."

Of course. More reason why she should not go.

Fighting the impulse to make herself more presentable, Daphne quickly gathered the art supplies she needed, a tunic-length pelisse, and a small bonnet, and set off with Lord Ramsdale. As they walked out through the garden and down the path to the pier together, Daphne remembered the problem she had had boarding the boat the first time they'd gone out in it.

If the sensation of Lord Ramsdale's body against hers had not already been indelibly etched into her mind, his embrace and kiss in the garden yesterday would have revived the memory. She was not willing to risk what might happen if she had to repeat that original boarding maneuver. Her attraction to Lord Ramsdale was beginning to loom as the greatest of her problems. He had invaded her dreams last night the way he had already invaded her days. Now, wearing a low-crowned hat and dressed as he was, he looked more roguish than ever, although perhaps more like a highwayman than a pirate. Taking his arm was one thing. She was afraid if she touched anything beyond the mere crook of his elbow she would melt.

Unfortunately, the boat was no more accessible from either steps or pier today than it had been their first time out. Their later departure offset the difference in the tide gained by the intervening day. To her relief, what looked like a wide piece of shelving from the kitchen larder lay beside the path at the top of the stone steps. She thought it should span the distance from the steps to the deck of the boat quite nicely.

"I suppose you would rather 'walk the plank' than trust your person to my strong arms," Ramsdale teased. "Your stepson intends to have a ladder built for the pier, but in the meantime he settled for this." Was there a hint of disappointment beneath his joking?

He picked up the board as if it weighed nothing and easily swung it into place, one end on the boat and the other propped against the highest step it could reach.

The plank was not as steady as she had expected. As the boat bobbed up and down in the water, the board rose and fell with it and at the same time rubbed forward and back where it rested on the deck rail. It looked much narrower now that it was set in place.

"Do you care to go aboard first, Captain?" she asked.

"After you, madam. Perhaps you would like a steadying hand?" He flashed a quirky smile of amusement—really an infuriating smirk.

She knew what would happen. Even with her gloves on, she would feel the strength in his hand and the warmth of the contact between them. It would spread through her and rekindle feelings she had not fully shaken off from her unsettling dreams. She shook her head. The trick was to make certain she was balanced, then to move quickly across without looking at the part that was moving up and down, forward and back.

Swallowing, she mounted the plank. After teetering for a moment and hoping she did not look as nervous as she felt, she crossed quickly and, grabbing the nearest support, stepped carefully off onto the nodding deck of the boat.

Once she had safely settled into the cockpit, she turned to watch Lord Ramsdale. She could not help wishing that he might fall off when it was his turn. However, he only grinned at her and walked across the board with perfect ease, even when it bowed under his greater weight.

His less-fitted clothing did not hide his muscular shoulders and thighs, only gave him a freer range of motion as he bent to his tasks. She watched him ready the boat to get underway, admiring his powerful strength. He explained what he was doing as he worked. Today the cockpit seemed infinitely smaller than it had before. She could not seem to stay out of his way or keep any distance between them.

"Why do they not simply say right and left instead of 'starboard' and 'larboard' or especially 'port'?" she asked at length, after moving out of his way for the third time. "Port is a wine, or a city on the coast, or such a number of other things already."

"Has not every discipline, be it fencing, boxing, horse racing, or archery, its own special terms and usages?" he replied. "Sailing is no different in that regard."

"But such names!" she said, laughing despite her best intentions not to do so. "So many of these already have other meanings. Thimbles and shackles and—and shrouds. Did no one ever consider it bad luck to name a part of the rigging 'shrouds'? Then there is the sheet—do you not think that this great canvas sail more resembles a sheet than does a rope?"

He raised an eyebrow and surveyed her with a cocky expression. "I'd wager sails have served as sheets of the more familiar variety on certain occasions," he said in a slow, suggestive drawl. An impish smile played about his mouth. "Now stays—surely you can see the similarity there."

She felt a blush creep up her neck but steadfastly refused to answer. He was delighting in teasing her. Odious man!

"Stays are strong cables that hold up the mast," he explained with a positively devilish grin. "That is not so different a purpose than a woman's stays, now is it?"

He was not being the perfect gentleman now, to speak of such things, yet she could not help laughing, quite improperly. She supposed she must bear some of the blame, for she was the one who had brought up the topic of words with extra meanings.

Once all was ready and the sail raised, the *Ariadne* swooped out into the river and began her battle against the tide.

"We would have an easier time of it were we to head

downriver," Ramsdale said, "but there are few picnic spots closer to the bustle of Town, and we would have to shoot Battersea Bridge. That is an experience for which I doubt very much you are quite ready."

She nodded, recalling newspaper accounts of accidents and drownings that had occurred while people tried to shoot one of the more notorious Thames River bridges. "I think I prefer a nice, quiet picnic, thank you."

They settled into the easy rhythms of sailing the boat and tacking back and forth up the river. The bright contrast between the sun and the summer blues and greens of the landscape seemed to feed her soul while the gentle lap of the water against the hull soothed it. The deep contentment she had felt during the first sail came back over her and she relaxed.

"I do have some news to report," Ramsdale said after a few minutes. "I have been invited to view Lord Ainshaw's art collection. I mentioned that I would bring a friend."

"So soon? Oh, that is *splendid!* I am terribly impressed." Daphne could not imagine how he had accomplished the task so quickly, but she was grateful. She did not know how many anxious nights like the last one she could bear. "Thank you so much. How soon do you think we can go?"

He laughed again—that deep baritone laugh that affected her so strongly. "I like it when you do not hide what you are thinking," he said. "We can go tomorrow afternoon, if that would suit you."

This was good news indeed. "Oh, yes, please! Going tomorrow would be wonderful. However did you manage it?"

"I had an interesting afternoon after I left you yesterday," he said. "Among my several errands I stopped in at White's. I found Lord Ainshaw there and spoke with him."

"Was it very awkward? What did you say?"

"He and I actually had a very civil conversation. After all, we have similar tastes in art, even if we are usually rivals. I believe he was flattered that I was interested in seeing his collection. Told him I knew that young Wetherell had recently sold him a Van de Velde. He seemed quite eager to show it off."

"You are more than clever. I hope some of your brilliance may rub off onto my stepson."

He had not finished surprising her, however. Raising an

eyebrow at her, he added, "I also visited the Beaufort Galleries yesterday."

She straightened up abruptly. "Did you? You were very busy. What did you do? Did you see Mr. Meregill?"

"Yes, he was there. I told him an astute and knowledgeable friend had questioned the validity of my early Van de Velde painting."

"Oh, dear. That was very direct." She had never expected Ramsdale to act so quickly on her unconfirmed suspicions.

"He was understandably upset and wanted to examine my painting again for himself. Although we discussed setting an appointment for another day, as it was closing time and I was headed home after that errand, he suggested he might accompany me to have a look at the picture right away. I returned my mother's carriage and simply accepted transport back to Westwater with him instead of hiring a hackney."

"What did he say?" Her attention was riveted to Lord Ramsdale now.

He, in return, fastened his gray eyes upon her. "He agreed with your assessment. He was shocked and apologetic and quite curious to know how I discovered it."

"Oh, dear. I am sorry. Somehow, I had still hoped I might be mistaken." *Hoped?* She had prayed for a miracle.

"I daresay he was as impressed with your eye as he was upset about the discovery. I did not identify you to him without your permission, of course, although he did ask. He also offered to buy the painting back."

"Oh." Daphne was shaken. She had not considered that something of this sort could happen. If there was anyone in London besides herself who might recognize her father's color in the baron's Van de Velde painting, it was Galton Meregill. The art dealer had been well acquainted with her father and had handled the sale of many a painting that had kept food on their table and supplies on the shelves of the D'Avernett Academy.

Had the dealer recognized the anachronistic pigment? If so, what would he do now? She hoped she could trust him to say nothing until all the facts could be discovered. As the seller of the counterfeit, his reputation could be at risk now, too.

Holding her breath, she asked, "Did you accept his offer?"

The baron fixed his gray eyes upon her. "No, I did not. I reserved the right to think it over. Told him I was fond enough of the picture to perhaps settle for a partial refund and keep it."

Daphne suppressed her sigh of relief. "That may be just as well," she said, concealing the importance she attached to his decision. "It will make any comparisons we wish to do easier if you still have the picture in your possession."

Chapter Twelve

The baron's picnic spot was an inviting grassy knoll under elm trees that grew close to the river. The bank along this section was high and dropped off with a straight sheer, unlike other parts where marshes or mudflats prevented easy access to solid ground. Daphne watched with admiration as Ramsdale sailed up beyond the landing point, turned the boat, and allowed the current to bring them in close as he lowered the sail and put the fenders out. At the most precise moment, he leaped from the boat, painter in hand, and walked along the bank to secure the boat to an exposed root as big as his arm.

"If you would toss me that other line from the stern, we shall be set quite nicely," he called to her, pointing to the rope he meant. Secured at both ends, the *Ariadne* snuggled up neatly to the steep edge of the bank.

At the baron's instruction, Daphne dragged the hamper of food from the underdeck and managed to pass it to him. Setting it aside, he turned back to her.

"Your turn," he said cheerfully, holding out his arms. "Clamber up onto the deck and jump."

Well, there really was no other way, but she was not about to put herself into his arms again.

"I don't need assistance; just give me some space," she said, waving him away.

He stepped back a little, and she jumped, wobbling as she landed. He quickly took her arm to steady her and led her up the slope, then returned for the hamper.

He had thought of everything. There was a blanket to sit on and a tablecloth to spread under the food. In the basket was a substantial veal-and-ham pie, cold chicken, pickles, potted meat, cheese, hard-boiled eggs, fruit, a bottle of wine, and plum duff, which particularly delighted her.

"Plum duff! I have not had it in ages," she exclaimed. "I feel like a little child again. This is a feast." She could not imagine how they would eat even half of what was there, but they did surprising justice to it all.

When he had finished, Lord Ramsdale lay back on the grass with a great sigh of contentment and stared up at the sky. Daphne licked the crumbs from her fingers after she finished her wedge of plum duff, checking first to see that he was not watching. She was not enough at ease to copy his action, but she did uncurl her legs and after carefully arranging her skirts assumed a semireclined position with her weight resting on her arm.

"Robbie tells me he is doing better with his sailing," she said. "Do you feel he will be able to learn all that he must know in time for your race?"

"He is doing very well—better than I hoped. He's a good lad, and very capable."

"I think I already see an improvement in him, since you began to be involved. I am very grateful to you."

Gratitude, she realized, might be a dangerous topic for them to pursue. *How grateful are you?* Before he could reply or even ask something she desperately did not want to hear, she quickly spoke again.

"Tell me more about the Duke's Cup race, and about your boat. Who else will be competing for the Cup? On what part of the river will the course be set?"

He turned on his side so he could face her. "You have many questions all of a sudden. Is that what comes of feeding you too many currants? Or keeping you out in the sun and fresh air?"

She blushed. "Forgive me if I am overly inquisitive."

That he paused and looked at her intently made her wonder if he knew she had purposely redirected their conversation. However, he said, "No, no, you have good reason to want to know these things. Your stepson, after all, will be racing with me."

He launched into an explanation of the history of the

Duke's Cup, one of the last sailing races still tried on the Thames. The last Vauxhall Cup had been sailed for seven years earlier, although subscription cups continued to be offered by various organizations. The course would not be decided until just prior to the day of the race.

"We could be racing right out here," he said, gesturing toward the river sliding past them, "or we could be shooting London Bridge with vast crowds watching and cheering us on."

"Is it dangerous?"

He hesitated and she pressed him to answer. "Tell me the truth, please. I have some right to know, as you said."

"The bridges can be dangerous, if we have to shoot Battersea or London Bridge. The others have wider arches and are not so bad."

"But there is something else." She could tell from the look on his face and an odd note in his voice.

"Some people will tell you that young Wetherell is putting himself into danger simply to sail with me."

"Are you so dangerous?" Dangerous to her, she could believe—nay, did believe—but surely not dangerous to Robbie. She couldn't help smiling. "I thought you assured me you were merely eccentric."

He answered her with a warm smile of his own, and suddenly the air between them was charged again. "Quite harmless. I did not say these people were right, now, did I?"

She thought it best if she busied herself packing away the remains of their picnic. Wrapping a cloth around slices of chicken, she said, "No, indeed. But what is the basis of their belief?"

He sighed. "In sailing there is always the danger of a rogue wind coming up out of nowhere. The idea that we ever have complete control over the elements is a fool's illusion. But that is not their concern. My boat is not being built to a proven design, and there is great skepticism about my design ideas. Remember the books and plans you saw in the Westwater library? Those represent just a fraction of what I have studied, and that's not to mention my exposure to American ideas I saw in use in the West Indies. Even so, many expect my boat to be unsafe. That is one reason, besides the late season, that I have difficulty in finding someone to crew for me."

"Is my stepson aware of all this?"

"Yes. He seems to think of unpredictability and the unorthodox adds excitement. He is fearless."

She had to laugh. "That I can well believe. He is young."

"So are you."

She let the comment pass. Sobering, she asked, "Has this all to do with your friend—the one who drowned?"

"You are as perceptive as you are beautiful. Haverthorpe was trying out some similar ideas, but we will never know exactly what happened to cause his boat to capsize." He looked off at the river. "I wish I had been here then. Perhaps it never would have happened if I had been the one sailing with him."

His pain was palpable, but she did not think he should blame himself. "Perhaps. On the other hand, perhaps you both would have drowned. Furthermore, you would never have had the opportunity to learn from those American boats you saw in the islands. Regrets are pointless, are they not?"

"True. Not only are you young, beautiful, and perceptive, but you are also wise—a prize beyond value."

"Heady flattery, sir. Perhaps it is you who has eaten too many currants or stayed out in the sun too long." Safer to make light of them than to accept such compliments. Still, she hoped she was wise to trust Robbie to this man. Somehow she felt instinctively that he would never put her stepson at risk.

She had finished packing up the basket. "If I am to make any sketches of the Westwater view before we head back, we should go now, while the light is similar to what it was the other day," she said.

"I am at your disposal, dear lady. I just want you to rest assured that your stepson is and will continue to be perfectly safe with me."

If only she believed the same could be said in her own case.

Before Lord Ramsdale left her, he and Daphne had agreed upon a time to visit Lord Ainshaw's the following afternoon. Inspired by the beauty of the river and their picnic spot, Daphne worked in her studio for most of the hours until she needed to dress for that outing. She found it extremely difficult to concentrate. All she produced were more unfinished pieces, which of late seemed to fill the studio wherever she looked. What was wrong with her?

During a break for a light nuncheon, she had decided to sort through a small pile of mail in her sitting room. Most of the mail consisted of bills or invitations for Robbie, but with a sinking feeling she spied a familiar scrawl on a franked letter addressed to her. Lord Pasmore again. So soon! Perhaps she should have read the letter he had sent a few weeks ago instead of tearing it up unopened. The man was a nuisance.

She slid the blade of a silver letter opener under his wax seal to loosen it and spread open the folded sheet.

Lady Wetherell, it began without so much as the courtesy of a greeting, *several new matters have come to my attention regarding young Robert and your most recent scandalous behavior.*

What followed was a litany of accusations of the wildest nature, only alarming by virtue of the faint relationship they bore to her actual life. He knew, for instance, that Lord Thornhurst had been to see her, but of course he assumed she was welcoming the old earl's attentions. He also "knew" Lord Ramsdale was calling on her and accused her of turning her stepson's home into a "stable" for multiple lovers of all ages. Scandalous indeed! And also thoroughly ridiculous.

What distressed her more was that the matters concerning Robbie appeared to be far more accurate, and Daphne wondered, not for the first time, where and how Robbie's uncle got his information. He seemed to have very specific knowledge of the people Robbie had been spending so much of his time with and the seriousness of his debts, something Daphne herself had not known until Lord Ramsdale had told her. Lord Pasmore's information seemed to go well beyond ordinary gossip, yet the man was not even in London.

Perhaps if he learns Lord Ramsdale is escorting me to the private homes of the haut monde, *he will be so shocked he*

will keel over with apoplexy and never be a bother again.
The thought was vindictive, but Daphne felt only a slight
twinge of remorse for thinking it. From the moment her
husband had wed her, Lord Pasmore, the brother of Robbie's mother, had made his hatred no secret. He resented
Daphne's right to be called Lady Wetherell in his sister's
place. She did not know if he had also resented her youth-
fulness, but his simmering jealousy over her relationship
with Robbie had become crystal clear when she had been
named the boy's guardian in her husband's will.

If Robbie's uncle had been in London to spread his evil
thoughts about Town, she might have been ruined even if
she had never done anything wrong. She could not prove
any connection between him and the constant gossip about
her, however. As far as she knew, he only vented his
twisted imaginings in letters he posted to her, all the while
dreaming of having his revenge on her in court. Clearly
there were enough other people in London who were
happy to spread rumors about her.

She had decided that the baron was right in one regard—
if she was going to make an appearance anywhere at all,
she should make an effective one and not skulk about secretly as if she had no right to be where she was. She could
not help the unfortunate consequences to his reputation,
but if she acted the coward or did not appear at her best,
she might only make matters worse.

Accordingly, she chose to wear her most elegant corded
silk pelisse over an expensive embroidered muslin gown.
Her feet would be shod in slippers to match the pelisse,
both in a very fashionable shade of sea green. Mattie restored some curls around her face and arranged the rest of
her hair loosely in a becoming and fashionable upswept
style. With the addition of a white beaded reticule and a
narrow-brimmed white chip hat that accommodated the
pile of hair on her head, Daphne looked very much like an
Ackerman's fashion plate come to life by the time she was
ready and waiting in the drawing room downstairs.

Her heart leaped when she heard the front knocker followed by the deep rumble of Lord Ramsdale's voice in the
entry hall. Surely the reason was only her nervousness over
the consequences of what they were going to do. The

amazed look on the baron's face when he walked into the room and saw her was almost comical. She stood still, hands folded primly, while he inspected her.

For some reason it did not feel at all the same as being inspected by students preparing to sketch her at the art academy. She realized she was holding her breath, waiting for him to pass judgment, and it was dismaying to realize, too, how much she craved his approval. Such a small thing! Should it matter so much? It made her uneasy. She could not—must not—fall in love with anything more than the sailing.

She smiled, pretending a confidence she did not feel.

"I am ready," she announced, watching as his reaction lit his face. His obvious admiration warmed her—the very laws of nature decreed that response, despite what her brain might wish to tell her. She tried to wrap that pleasant feeling around her like armor to see her through the rest of this afternoon. Pride and a bright, brittle carelessness would serve as her other means of defense.

She tossed her head slightly and raised her chin, as if to shake the proper attitude into place. Then she accepted Lord Ramsdale's arm, marveling at the way such an ordinary action triggered a response in her.

"You are magnificent," he whispered as they turned to go. A shiver of both ice and fire slid down her spine.

Lord Ainshaw's London residence was a large Palladian-style mansion of beige stone situated in Piccadilly, across from Green Park. Daphne was very grateful that Archer had provided his closed town coach to transport them there, for they would have been very much on display in his curricle. She secretly hoped Lord Ainshaw might have left them to the care of his servants to see his collection, but that hope was dashed as soon as they were admitted. The liveried footman who took the baron's card conducted them into an elegantly furnished saloon, saying that they were expected and that the earl would join them soon.

Lord Ainshaw did not keep them waiting long. A distinguished-looking older man, lean and long-limbed, he hurried into the room with an air of gracious hospitality until he recognized Daphne. The slight check in his step and the sudden chill in the air between them betrayed the moment he did so.

"Ah, Lord Ramsdale," the earl said, apparently deciding that a cut direct to Daphne was the only way to deal with the unexpected situation. "I am pleased by your interest in my humble collection. I am forgoing the pleasures of my club this afternoon to take you through personally."

"You are too kind," the baron replied. "Such a sacrifice! You honor us. Altogether quite unnecessary but extremely generous, and of course we do appreciate the gesture." The edge under his words was clearly audible to Daphne, but the earl did not seem to notice it. Perhaps he thought obsequiousness was merely his due.

"Please allow me to present Lady Wetherell, although perhaps you are already acquainted?"

Thus did her companion champion her cause, smoothly and politely refusing to allow the earl to continue to ignore her. Would the man be so rude as to try? To do so now would be a direct affront to Lord Ramsdale. The thing was neatly done. Daphne tried not to smile.

"Ah, yes, Lady Wetherell," the earl said uncomfortably, giving her the smallest possible nod of acknowledgment.

She made the smallest possible curtsy in return, and fixed a dazzling, empty smile on the earl.

"The gallery is this way," he said, falling back a step.

Daphne remained quiet, satisfied to look about and study the paintings as the earl took them through his collection. There was much on her mind. She trailed along a few steps behind the men, allowing them to become engrossed in their common interest and forget her. Ramsdale diverted their host, recalling auctions where the two had bid against each other but cleverly including only the ones when the earl had won.

The earl's art collection was eclectic and included much more than old masters. Silently she prayed that they would not encounter any paintings of her staring out from a frame. She still had not told Lord Ramsdale the details of her scandalous past and did not want him to encounter such blazing proof of it, even if he already knew. She feared the tentative alliance they had formed could crumble instantly should he come across such evidence.

To her relief, they reached the opposite end of the huge room without seeing any paintings she had posed for. However, they also had not seen the Van de Velde from her husband's study.

"The Van de Velde your stepson sold me is a particularly fine piece," the earl said, turning to her with a sudden, cruel smile. "I have made a special place for it in the salon through here."

He led them through a doorway and into a smaller room furnished with an overabundance of ornate French pieces but well lit by three large windows along the outside wall. Prominently displayed above the marble fireplace mantel was the Van de Velde they sought.

"There are few paintings from his first visit to England," the earl said, "but I believe this to be one. These nonmilitary paintings are rare. His son was far more prolific, of course, but that only adds to the value, as far as I am concerned."

He continued to talk, but Daphne was not listening, for her attention was focused entirely on the painting. What she needed to see was not easy to discern without a lens to magnify it, but she did not want to draw attention by asking for one.

Fortunately Lord Ramsdale seemed to have anticipated her need. In response to some comment of the earl's he withdrew his quizzing glass and peered at the painting. "Yes, I quite see what you mean," he said vaguely and handed the little lens to her. "Do have a look, Lady Wetherell. I daresay you may never have noticed such a thing when the picture hung at your house."

"I must admit I never paid it much attention at all," she said, accepting the glass and keeping her face expressionless. She had no idea what particular point they had been discussing, but she knew a cue when she heard one and was happy to play along. She refused to give the earl the satisfaction of thinking he had deprived her of a treasured keepsake, nor did she want to arouse any special notice of her inspection.

She carefully looked at the spot Lord Ramsdale had studied on the painting, and then quickly examined several other spots before handing back the glass with a shrug. "I am certain the painting brought my husband great pleasure. I am happy if it does the same for you, Lord Ainshaw."

It was the best portrayal of polite disinterest she could muster, given the despair in her heart. This painting showed the same traces of D'Avernett blue she had discovered in Lord Ramsdale's. Both pictures had been painted by the same hand, she was certain, and it was not Van de Velde the Elder's, nor a Van de Velde of any generation. But who then? Her father? One of his students? Only someone with great skill and talent could have matched the artistry of the great Dutch master.

She had to calm her racing pulse and put aside these thoughts, for the earl was not finished with her, as it happened.

"I have another painting over here that may interest you, Ramsdale," he said, leading them to the far wall. "It is not a marine painting, of course, but I imagine you'll agree that it does have a certain charm about it."

Daphne's heart, already full of dismay, sank all the way to her toes.

The picture was a highly romanticized landscape of Greek ruins, complete with a Grecian-garbed nymph who was a younger but unmistakable version of Daphne, posed with one arm draped casually over a giant urn. She remembered the painting, done by one of her father's more talented students. She had been fifteen years old at the time it was painted, mortified by her budding sexuality and fervently hoping no one would notice it. While the Grecian attire she had worn covered her decently, the artist had still managed to suggest her youthful curves and a seductive, sultry innocence.

For a moment, Daphne thought she would be sick. Looking away, she struggled for composure, not wanting to give the earl the satisfaction of seeing her do anything more than flinch. She was as mortified now as she had been when she posed.

"It has a fine mythic quality, has it not?" Lord Ramsdale said without a trace of emotion—indeed, as if he were perfectly unperturbed. "Very romantic, well executed. As you say, charming. Not quite in your usual taste, however, is it? Perhaps you are a patron of the artist?"

The baron's questions drew the earl's attention away from Daphne, and she could have kissed him for it. By the time the older man's regard returned to her, her pride was back in place, ready to deflect his arrows of petty disdain.

No matter what happened between her and Lord Ramsdale when they left this place, she would always be grateful for the way he handled this.

"My father was a gifted teacher," she said, smiling sweetly and burying her shame deep in her heart. "I am proud to see a painting by one of his students in the collection of a connoisseur like you, Lord Ainshaw."

Take that, she thought. He could hardly deny the picture's merit without injuring his own vanity.

"I am a connoisseur of many things besides paintings," the earl replied, his voice turning oily. "Another trait Lord Ramsdale appears to share with me." He regarded Daphne now with what could only be described as a leer. "I happen to find the subject of that painting quite—enjoyable—to look upon."

His tone and lecherous expression made her feel defiled, not admired. She fought the urge to slap him, holding her arms as rigid as sticks. One could not assault an earl, even if he deserved it.

Apparently the earl's manner displeased Lord Ramsdale also, for he ended their visit quickly. As the front door closed behind them, Daphne breathed in deeply, as if the very air in the house had turned foul while they were there.

"I can see the earl has not improved in the three years I have been away," the baron said as they went down the steps to the street. "He is as insufferable as ever."

"He is so quick to judge me from his position of power," she said with a note of bitterness in her voice. "He, and everyone else. Now you know the worst—my father made me model for the students in his school. It saved an expense. We could seldom spare two farthings to rub together."

"And I suppose such a thing could not be kept secret for long."

"Unfortunately for me. Does it shock you? Do you see now why I had concern for your reputation? Multiply the earl's attitude by as many people as you know," she continued. "Add in the fact that evidence of my offense hangs in rooms all over London, continually under the noses of the *haut monde,* and you begin to see what I am up against. Some scandals are allowed to die away, but not mine."

The baron's carriage moved forward to meet them from down the block, and they walked toward it.

"All I saw was a painting of a very beautiful young girl," he said stubbornly. "I begin to understand that your father did the world a great service in seeing that such beauty should be captured on canvas and preserved and shared."

She blushed, wishing that had been her father's motive. "You are unusually open-minded to take such a view. Most people do not. I fear that some—like the earl—see the pictures as a form of advertising. What harlot would object to having her face and form displayed in houses all around the city?"

"But you are not a harlot."

"Are you so certain? Still, you can see that no man wants to find his wife's image hanging in another man's hall."

Unfairness never failed to make Archer angry. "The more fool that man is then, if his wife should be so beautiful. Did Lord Wetherell mind? He married you. Had I such a wife, I would be proud to find her so admired."

Suddenly aware that he was treading on dangerous ground, Archer stopped. Words like those he had just uttered might certainly give a wrong impression. He thought Daphne was far too intelligent to mistake him, but it would be cruel indeed to accidentally create any expectations in her mind. Holly's words echoed back to him. *You wanted her for your mistress. Please don't tell me your purpose has changed. She can never be eligible, you know.*

"I think if you actually had a wife, you would feel differently," she said quietly, as if she saw the struggle in his mind.

Archer handed her up into the carriage. Her hand and arm seemed so fragile compared to his. Another surge of protectiveness welled up within him, and he knew an immediate change of subject would be advisable.

Climbing in behind her he asked, "Were you able to make any judgment about the Van de Velde? I know it was hung too high for you to put much of it under the lens."

She studied him for a moment before she answered. He saw sadness and wisdom in the depths of her brown eyes, as if she knew exactly why he had changed the subject of their conversation so abruptly. He felt like a fraud and a coward.

"Yes," she replied finally. "It is no more genuine than yours. Did I not dissemble nicely?" She shook her head slowly. "I am baffled by it, and I do not know what to do now. I think it might be helpful to speak with Mr. Meregill."

Chapter Thirteen

Lord Ramsdale rapped on the carriage wall to alert his coachman and, as he gave the man new instructions, Daphne silently cursed her impulsive tongue. She had not meant that she wanted the baron to accompany her to the art gallery. Now she wondered exactly what she would say to Galton Meregill. The man had known her father well, but she had not seen him in many years. There were questions she simply did not want to ask in front of Lord Ramsdale.

In the meantime, she wondered about him, too. She had revealed her worst shame to him, yet he had seemed to take it completely in stride. Had he already known? Or had she found the one man in London to whom it truly made no difference? Could she afford to risk allowing hope into her heart?

The Beaufort Galleries were empty of customers when the pair arrived there, just as Lord Ramsdale had suggested might be the case so near to closing time. As Daphne entered, still holding his elbow, a frisson of apprehension ran through her. Was pursuing this a huge mistake? Perhaps she should never have raised the issue of the fraudulent paintings.

Too late, said the little voice in her head as Mr. Meregill hurried out from a back room.

The art dealer reminded Daphne of an egg. He was broad about the middle and tapered at each end, with thin legs and a narrow head set on a thick neck. She had always suspected he was bald as he affected to wear an old-fashioned wig, although a few elderly men still clung to the custom. As soon as he saw them his sagging face drew up into a grin.

"Lord Ramsdale! And my heavens, do my eyes deceive me? Miss D'Avernett, upon my stars. What a long time it has been. Of course, I mean Lady Wetherell. I do beg your pardon, but of course I haven't seen you in all these years since your father passed on, bless his soul."

He paused for breath and seemed unable to take his eyes off her. "You are every bit as beautiful as ever, my dear—no, even more beautiful. Things did not work out too badly for you, did they?"

He coughed, as if suddenly aware of the tactlessness of his last remark. "I mean to say, considering how things stood with your father, and all. Oh, dear." His pale face turned red as he glanced at the baron and then turned to him.

"Have you come about the business we discussed day before yesterday, my lord?" he asked Ramsdale. Before he received a word of reply, realization appeared to dawn in him. "Oh, by George! Is Miss D'Avernett—you said a friend—is it . . . ?"

The baron raised his eyebrows at Daphne, questioning. She rescued Meregill from his floundering. "I had an opportunity to view Lord Ramsdale's fine collection of paintings," she said, choosing her words carefully to mask the indiscretion of her visit there. "It is very unfortunate that I happened to notice the problem with his Van de Velde."

"I might have guessed it would be you—of course it would be you," Mr. Meregill murmured, nodding his head sagely. In a stronger voice he added, "Very embarrassing, this all is, and a terrible shock, as you might imagine. Beaufort Galleries stands behind the works it sells. I simply cannot imagine how we were taken in."

"We have come today with more bad news," Lord Ramsdale said.

Daphne moved forward and took the older man's arm, concerned about the way he would handle a second shock. Very gently she told him the news about her late husband's painting.

"What, did you see the same exact problem?"

"Yes, the same blue that should not be there. I did wonder if they might both have come from the same source, although they were sold several years apart, and that some years ago. I hope your records are not kept by date?"

She did not want to dwell on the color issue, afraid that Lord Ramsdale would take an interest in and pursue the topic. Unfortunately, it was Mr. Meregill she should have worried about.

"Miss D'Avernett—Lady Wetherell that is—would be the most likely expert to have discovered this, my lord. She has a trained eye for color that is unsurpassed." He sounded as proud as if he had trained her himself. "Of course, it helps that the particular shade of blue we are talking about was formulated by her own father."

Daphne's hands flew halfway up in exasperation, then dropped to her sides. *Men!*

Oblivious, Mr. Meregill continued. "He called it D'Avernett blue. Might have become quite popular if the colorists hadn't introduced cobalt blue so soon afterward."

"I see," said Ramsdale.

She could well imagine what he thought he saw.

"My father had hoped to license his formula for D'Avernett blue to the colorists and earn some money from it, but like most of his schemes, fortune did not favor it," she explained quickly. "Even so, many people had access to the color—all of his students, for instance. Mr. Meregill, might it not be possible that these two paintings were copies made by a student, sold as genuine by mistake?" She knew she was grasping at straws, for the expertise shown in the two paintings was not likely the work of a mere student.

"Mistake? Well, always possible I suppose . . ."

"I do not see that a mistake is likely, Lady Wetherell," the baron said with a pointed look at the art dealer. "There is the ownership history to consider."

"Yes, quite right." Mr. Meregill seemed truly flustered by the disaster that had arrived at his door. Daphne could not help feeling sorry for the man. "We always check the background of each work very thoroughly. Someone would have had to lie."

"You keep the records, do you not?" The look on Lord Ramsdale's face was not exactly cordial.

"Yes, yes, indeed. I shall look into this thoroughly. Can't always remember the source for every painting we handle."

A momentary silence fell. As the dealer made no move toward his office, Daphne prompted him. "Can you not check the records now, Mr. Meregill? What information can we give you that would help?"

He gave her an odd look. "Nothing, no, nothing at all. I have a file for each of my customers. It should show me what pictures they bought and when, and any other information about the paintings, including the provenance. I am afraid it will take me some time, however. My clerk has already gone home for the night."

"Perhaps we could come back tomorrow," Daphne suggested, but Lord Ramsdale had moved close to her and now took hold of her hand.

"We will wait," he said, signaling her with a quick squeeze. "It is no trouble to us."

With a bow that did not quite conceal his sigh of resignation, the dealer excused himself and headed for the office. At the doorway he turned back to them. "While I am digging in the files, perhaps you would like to take a look around, my lord. Perhaps you'll see something new that catches your fancy. And my dear," he added to Daphne, "please do let me know if you see any more counterfeits. Very bad for business!" He did not sound very jovial at all, but at least he winked.

Daphne's mind was spinning, struggling to fathom how the counterfeit paintings could have come to pass through this well-respected gallery. "Someone would have needed a strong motive as well as the artistic talent to carry out a fraud like this," she said, thinking out loud. "The consequences would be catastrophic to the artist if they were caught."

"No one wants to think ill of their own father," Lord Ramsdale said very gently, "but you told me yourself that there was never a farthing to spare in his school. Given such need, is it inconceivable that he might have succumbed to temptation? His talent would yield more profit used that way than he could gain in any other. Perhaps he tired of fortune's lack of favor."

"My father did not do this." She had known he would think this way. The very blood in her veins felt like ice.

"Perhaps he was more desperate than you knew. A man has his pride. He would not have wanted you to know. Is it also why you did not want me to know? You could have told me about the blue."

She moved away from him, striding angrily. "You don't know the first thing about my father. How dare you to presume! What makes you think you have any idea of what it was like for us?"

"Perhaps the fact that my father, too, could not keep two coins in his pocket. I have seen firsthand what a desperate man will do to hide his secrets from his family."

Daphne was certain her father had not hidden secrets from her. Obviously, Ramsdale was speaking from that hidden pain of his own.

"If you knew anything at all about my father, you would know he could never have done this," she insisted in a rising voice. She turned back to face the baron, her hands fisted. "The whole idea is so ludicrous, I hardly know where to begin to show you."

"The beginning is always good."

She was in no mood for flippancy. She frowned, but he seemed determined to condemn her father.

"You said that he was so desperate for blunt to run his academy that he put his own daughter to work! Do you now deny that?"

"If he had made money from counterfeit paintings, do you not think he would have hired models instead of using me?"

"Perhaps not."

"Why not? Why do you insist on judging him so harshly? You never knew him!"

The intensity and anger in Daphne's voice had reached a high level. Ramsdale moved back to her and took hold of her rigid arm. "Did you wish for this to be more than a private discussion?" he said quietly, nodding his head toward the office doorway.

Daphne pulled her arm away, subdued but still angry.

"Listen to me," he said, "even if just for a moment. Your father was a gifted artist, was he not? He had plenty of students for his academy, did he not? Did you never wonder why he was always under the hatches anyway? Was the cost of running an art academy so exorbitant that no amount of students could make it turn a profit?"

Daphne had wondered that, sometimes, especially when creditors were hounding her father. He had never allowed her to look at or help with his bookkeeping. Yet she knew very well they had run a frugal home and school, as much of the managing had fallen to her. She had assumed they must be doing the best that could be done. "My father was an artist, not a businessman."

"What of the years before your father opened his art academy?"

"We lived comfortably before my mother died. She had a small estate, Summerwood, in Hertfordshire. She was a Mortmain—the Earl of Melden was my great-grandfather. Summerwood had been a gift to her. But the family cut all connections after she married my father against their wishes."

"And when she died?"

"I do not know the details. I was eight years old, overwhelmed by grief. There was no money left. The house was sold, along with everything in it. We moved to London, to the house in St. Martin's Lane."

"That must have been very hard for you."

"Do not pity me, and do not patronize me! None of this makes my father a criminal."

He would not give it up. "Daphne, who else but your father had the expertise to paint those Van de Velde pictures? They fooled Mr. Meregill; they fooled me; they fooled your husband. All of us would have noticed an inferior attempt."

She was too upset to notice his use of her given name.

"My father fought for recognition of his talent all of his life. To paint a masterpiece and put someone else's name to it would have been utterly foreign to him. He would not do it. What is more, if my father had painted those pictures, why would he be so foolish as to include a color he knew could be traced directly to him?"

"Ah. Now you have raised a point for which I have no argument. Why, indeed?"

"Well, he would not have done so, that is all." Daphne folded her arms, clearly satisfied that she had won her point.

She was so beautiful, impassioned by her anger, that Archer could not help thinking of how she would look impassioned by a lover's caress instead. He was loath to have words with her—hated the tension that had sprung up between them. He conceded the argument to her for now.

"Let us try to think, then. If not your father, who could have painted the pictures? Were there any among his students who had such prodigious talent? Did they all study marine art? Who had access to your father's color, a strong enough need, and no qualms about passing his own talent off as that of someone more famous?"

"I do not know. I do not. I shall have to think upon it, perhaps try to draw up lists from my memory of who his students were. I have nothing left of his records."

"That is an excellent idea." Archer wished to heal the rift between them, but her expression did not soften at his praise.

Galton Meregill emerged from his office at that moment, waving a sheet of paper. "I have the information," he said with some excitement. Daphne and Archer approached the broad counter that filled the space between two support columns. Mr. Meregill put the paper there with a flourish.

"I found that both paintings did come from the same source," he said, "even though the sales were three years apart. We bought them from a French émigré, a count, who was living in Islington. To maintain his style, he would sell off a painting or other treasure every year or so. This is his name and address."

"Have you bought anything from him more recently than the Van de Velde you sold me?" Archer asked. "Much can change in four years."

"I don't recall, but I do not think so. I do not know if he is still alive—he was quite elderly, if I am remembering the right person. He may also have returned to France after Boney lost his second try. You know how eagerly so many of them hurried home once he was shipped off for good."

"Yes." Archer was thinking hard. "Well, we do not know where he obtained the paintings, do we? It seems we are at an impasse. You will be happy to know, Mr. Meregill, that we said nothing of all this to the current owner of the late Lord Wetherell's painting. Perhaps, if we have no recourse, it is best to leave matters as they stand. He is happy in his ignorance of the truth, while we must remain frustrated in our knowledge of it."

"It is late in the day for philosophy, my lord. But rest assured that we will investigate this further."

"We will take our leave. I do not see what more can be done. At least you are unlikely to fall victim to the same fellow again."

Archer could see by Daphne's stubborn expression that she was not ready to leave. He moved to offer her his arm and tried to signal her with a sharp look.

"And if I have questions about a piece, perhaps Miss D—Lady Wetherell, that is—will allow me to call upon her expertise?"

"You were a good friend to my father, Mr. Meregill. You must know I should be happy to help."

Archer hustled her out of the gallery before she could say anything more.

Outside the gallery, Daphne turned to him indignantly. "Why did you—?"

Archer hushed her with a finger upon her lips. "Once we are in the carriage," he said, glancing back at the gallery. He helped her in and climbed in after her, closing the door behind him. Once the carriage began to move, he nodded.

"We are *not* finished with this matter," she said.

"I am aware of that," Archer replied calmly. "However, I think it best for now if we do not include Mr. Meregill or the Beaufort Galleries in our plans."

"But why? They have a stake in discovering the perpetrator of the fraud. They have been made victims, too."

"I will feel more comfortable when I am sure of that." Archer pulled from his waistcoat the same piece of paper, now creased, that Mr. Meregill had brought out from his office.

Daphne started. "I did not see him give that to you."

"He did not. I picked it up as we started to leave." He smoothed it out and looked again at the name written there. "The history of ownership he gave us today is quite different from what I remember him telling me at the time I bought my painting."

"He is old—no doubt he simply told you the wrong information at the time of your purchase."

"Or perhaps neither story is the truth. Perhaps he is involved in this. Why bring out to us a name written on a piece of paper? The ink was not even dry. Why not show us the information actually contained in his files?"

"Perhaps there was too much paper, or perhaps there was other information we did not need to see."

"Perhaps."

"You are as quick to find guilt in him as in my father." Anger was building in her voice again. "But of course, that would be the easy solution, would it not? Settle for the first likely culprits you come across? Then there is no need to investigate further."

Archer did not answer for a moment while he reined in all impulses other than that to stay perfectly calm. The squeak of the carriage springs and the rumble of its wheels filled the pause. He hoped she could hear the unfairness of her words as they hung in the air between them.

"I have every intention of investigating further," he then said quietly. "However, I did not feel it would be to our advantage for Mr. Meregill to know. Let us think on these matters, and when I call at Grove House in the morning we can decide our next step."

They sat in silence for the rest of the drive back to Chelsea.

Chapter Fourteen

In the morning, flowers arrived at Grove House instead of the baron.

"From Lord Ramsdale, my lady," Wilson told her. "Fellow says there's a card attached."

The heavenly scented lilies were exquisite and expensive. Were they meant as a peace offering? After admiring them Daphne directed the footman to have them placed in a vase on the pianoforte in the drawing room and sat down warily on the matching bench to read the message.

The baron's hand was elegant, steeply slanted but not difficult to read. His note, however, said only that business matters had detained him and that he would be unable to call or to take Robbie sailing that morning.

Drat the man! Daphne swallowed the lump of disappointment that formed in her throat. He had offered no apology for his accusations. Given his attitude about her father, she ought not to feel so disheartened at the prospect of not seeing him. She ought to feel every bit as angry as she had when they parted yesterday. For that matter, she didn't know why she even cared so much what he thought. Hadn't she just yesterday resolved that she should stay away from him as much as possible? Yet the day suddenly seemed to stretch ahead of her offering endless, empty hours without him. It was troubling in the extreme.

A clattering outside the door interrupted her musings. A moment later a smiling Robbie bounced into the room, dressed in the informal clothes he wore for sailing.

"What, no Ramsdale?" he asked. "I quite thought we were to go out in the boat again this morning."

"No," she replied. "He has sent a note with his regrets."

Robbie's face fell, his enthusiasm extinguished like a pinched candle. "Just when I have begun to show some real promise," he grumbled.

Guilt swept over Daphne as she looked at him. What if she had irretrievably offended Lord Ramsdale yesterday? She had railed at him like a fishwife. She might have felt hurt and angry, but Robbie still needed his friendship. The man had only been accommodating her request to visit Lord Ainshaw, after all. Certainly he had discovered enough about her history to give most people a thorough disdain for her without the added consideration of her father's possible sins. The thought caused a most unsettling pain in her heart, which she quickly endeavored to hide.

"I am certain he has not abandoned you, Robbie," she said brightly. "Perhaps he will take you out later on today, or most certainly tomorrow if the weather holds. Come and sit, and tell me how you find the sailing now."

She had not had an opportunity to talk at length with her stepson in several days, but she thought she had already begun to detect a change in him—a healthier color in his face and fewer nights spent out till all hours, as if already he was both drinking and gambling less. She hoped she had not ruined that now. For the next little while she listened as he described sailing with Lord Ramsdale by day and meeting the baron's associates at various social functions in the evenings. She had to admit to herself that her relief and happiness at these excellent results were tinged with at least a small measure of envy.

After their conversation Robbie went off to change his clothes and attend to some correspondence, leaving Daphne to face her empty day. She retreated to her studio, seeking distraction and determined to accomplish something useful. Lord Ramsdale had wanted a list of her father's students who could have painted the counterfeit Van de Velde pictures. What better way to mend their rift than to prove that his suspicions of her father were unfounded? He had been so open-minded about her own situation, it had felt like a betrayal when he could not be that way about her father, too.

Setting paper and pencil before her, she began to roam back through her memories of the years at her father's academy. Who among his students had shown the most talent, the best aptitude, especially for marine art? Who besides her father could have painted the counterfeit pictures? All of her father's students had been wealthy and idle enough to buy private art instruction. What motive could they have had, even assuming they had the expertise?

The process dredged up heartaches she had long since buried and memories of people she had tried hard to forget. Those had been years of struggle in which she had often felt she had lost not only mother but father, too. *If only her father could have been as devoted to his daughter as he had been to his art.*

Her list, when she finished it, was very short. She doubted it would be much help—of the three people she had written down, none had any possible motive that she could imagine. Lord Edward Aylesworth, the son of an earl, was wealthy enough to buy a dozen Van de Velde originals of his own. Harlan Jeffries had had enough of a wild streak to paint the counterfeits as a lark, but he had married and settled down quite respectably after only a short term of study at the academy. Gordon Morris-Marley, heir to a baronet, had such an inflated sense of position and duty, he would never have risked any sort of scandal. She would have gladly put Morgan Laybrook's name down had he possessed the necessary talent, but he did not.

Stymied, she pondered Lord Ramsdale's questions, trying to examine them with objective honesty. Could her father have kept secrets from her? It was possible, although it hurt to admit it. But had he painted the pictures? No. He had the talent, and few others did. But she could not believe that either her father's pride or his integrity would have allowed him to stoop to commit a criminal act. Moreover, if by some unimaginable possibility he had, surely she would have known. Such expert paintings took time to produce. Finally, however, she did not believe her father had any more motive than his students. His biggest problem had always been that he did not care about money.

She took her list down and put it in the desk in the library, to give to Lord Ramsdale later. She would have to find some other way to convince him of her father's innocence, if his suspicions remained when she saw him next. *If* she saw him next. Oh, dear!

The thought of not seeing him drove her back to the studio to work on the preliminary layout of the painting of Westwater. He wanted the painting. He would have to see her again if he was ever going to have it.

The studio offered comfort in its warmth and personal familiarity. Her mother gazed down from the only framed painting in the room, keeping watch over the sanctuary. Roquefort, a boneless puddle of fur draped on the window seat, lifted his head to acknowledge her return, blinking yellow eyes at her and settling back into his nap with a small sigh of contentment.

She had been that content with her life before Lord Ramsdale barged into it, had she not? Yet another annoyance she could put to his account, along with occupying her mind to the point of madness. For the last several days, her hours, her thoughts, her every feeling seemed linked to him.

She had only accepted his friendship for Robbie's sake. How had things progressed so quickly? Surely she had not been so foolish as to fall in love with him. Could that explain why she'd become so angry when he cast suspicion on her father? She must have expected him to blindly support her view merely because it was hers. In hindsight she had to concede his questions were not unreasonable. It had been his clear-eyed objectivity that hurt. Was love like this?

I do not know, she realized with some surprise. She was nearly twenty-five years old, a widow, and had never been in love.

As she laid out her rough sketches on the worktable, the baron continued to intrude where he was not wanted. Had he truly believed what he had said yesterday? Where was he today, and what was he doing? Why had he sent the flowers, when he might have sent simply the note? If this was love, no one had ever warned her that it could be so utterly confusing or could hurt so much.

A short while later she was staring at the prepared canvas she had chosen with her materials neatly laid out in readiness to begin the Westwater painting when Robbie knocked and entered, surprising her.

"Lord Ramsdale is here."

"What? But he sent flowers," she said, as if that made his subsequent arrival impossible.

"I took the liberty of telling Wilson to show him up. You can ask his opinion of your Royal Academy painting."

"Oh, no. I did not expect . . . I do not really want . . ." The brightening of her spirit was at odds with her reluctance to let the baron into her sanctuary. "Robbie, why are you so eager to have the man see my painting?"

The man in question poked his head in around the doorframe at that moment. His smile grabbed at her heart so strongly she sank back onto her work stool. Hurt and anger melted away, at least for the moment.

"I dismissed your footman myself," he said. "May I not come in? Your stepson wants me to see how talented you are."

"Exactly," said Robbie.

Trapped, thought Daphne. Once again she wondered if she had been the victim of some sort of conspiracy. How could she keep the baron out now?

Ramsdale came to her, and she felt a momentary panic over what he intended to do with Robbie standing right there watching. However, he merely bowed over her hand politely. He straightened and looked about the room with apparent interest.

She felt as if she had been stripped naked as he walked about, looking at sketches left in piles and watercolors still pinned up where she had left them to dry. He appeared to take in every detail of the room, eyeing her few treasures and nodding thoughtfully when he saw the portrait of her mother.

"Your mother, of course. A stunning beauty—the resemblance is quite marked. Did your father paint it?"

She nodded, unable to speak.

When he came to the window seat he stopped to scratch Roquefort behind the ears. The traitorous cat did not seem the least disturbed by this stranger's invasion—he rolled over to expose his furry underside for more scratching.

"Roquefort, my heavens," she managed to protest faintly. "Where is your dignity?"

Lord Ramsdale smiled and moved on. He looked at her sketches laid out on the table, giving her no clue to his thoughts. Finally he moved to the big easel in the corner and stood before her unfinished marine, studying it in silence.

"Is this the problem painting?" he asked at length. After what seemed like an eternity, he announced, "Your technical skill is superb. I suppose that is not so surprising."

By then Daphne trusted her knees enough to relinquish the stool and move over to join him. She found that she wanted his opinion. *He is here. I may as well ask.*

"It is not finished," she began. "I had hoped to submit it to the Royal Academy to earn my acceptance as a student there, but, well, even I can see that something is lacking. I cannot seem to pinpoint what. Robbie suggested that you might know."

Archer looked at her then with a very peculiar smile. He looked at the painting, and then looked back at her again.

"What do you love about this picture?" he asked.

She thought for a second. "Well, I enjoy the challenge of capturing the water's fluid quality, its translucence, its movement. But also the ship—"

"No, not what you enjoy painting, what do you love about the picture itself? Why paint *this* picture, of *this* ship, in this particular moment, this scene?"

She looked at him, unsure how to answer.

"Hm," he said, nodding wisely. "As I suspected."

"What?"

"As I look about here, I see so much variety in your work, so much talent. Much that is unfinished, too. But many of these small pieces, these informal studies, have something that is missing from the one picture you would show the world. *Passion.*"

"Passion?" She was dumbfounded. She did not know what she had expected him to say, but surely this was not it.

"Let me ask you again why you chose that scene to paint."

"I thought it would be pleasing to the Academy members. They are very conservative, you know."

"Ah, but the problem is, it is not a scene that has meaning to *you*. Is it not, in fact, the sort of scene your father would have chosen? Your passion is directed at the goal—of being accepted into the Academy, rather than into the picture itself. I may be wrong, but I'll warrant that despite your obvious talent, that picture would not make the cut.

You chose what you thought was safe, but in avoiding any risks, you lost the excitement, the interest, that the best art evokes."

He raised an eyebrow. "Perhaps I can illustrate the lesson. There is something I would like to show to both of you. It is the reason I came, in point of fact. But it may also help to answer you. Will you go with me up into Town?"

Daphne was becoming accustomed to Lord Ramsdale's tendency to catch her by surprise. With Mattie's help it took her very little time to change into more respectable and fashionable clothes—her pale blue India muslin and dark blue spencer, topped off with the hat she had bought at Madame Michaud's in May. Robbie had changed out of his sailing clothes earlier, so as soon as she was ready, the trio set off in the baron's glossy town coach.

Ramsdale refused to reveal where they were going. Daphne wondered if this was their next step in investigating the counterfeit paintings, but if so, then why had Robbie been invited along? She had decided to keep her stepson informed of only the minimal facts that were uncovered. She could not bear it if he should agree with the baron's suspicions about her father.

At the pace required in London's busy thoroughfares, it took an hour to cover the five miles from Chelsea across the river to John Forsyth's shipyard in Southwark. Daphne's heart beat faster as soon as she realized where they were.

"We have come to see your boat!" she exclaimed, hardly able to wait to get out of the carriage. From the window she saw piles of timber waiting to be cut in one corner of the yard and an odd assortment of work sheds and other small buildings scattered about the space. The unfinished hull of a huge vessel stood in stocks by the water's edge, dominating the scene like some sort of giant whale skeleton on stilts. Some smaller vessels in various stages of completion could be seen around the yard. She breathed in the scents of freshly cut wood, varnish, and pine tar.

Ramsdale turned to assist her after he and Robbie had climbed down. A boyish sparkle of excited enthusiasm lit his eyes.

"More than seeing," he replied. "She is ready to go into the water. Once she's afloat, the yard will put her mast and rigging in place. She'll be ready for sailing in a matter of days—and not a moment too soon. We've only a couple of weeks to become accustomed to her before the race."

They found his builder, John Forsyth, in his shirtsleeves supervising his workmen in the shed closest to the riverbank. Both ends of the building were open, and the fresh breeze blew through, catching up little drifts of sawdust and twirling them in spirals. Motioning over the noise of saws and hammers, the fair-haired Scotsman beckoned them to follow him and led the way across the yard to his small, cluttered office.

He welcomed them as they crowded into the one-room shed and the baron performed introductions. Then, reaching up to the shelf behind him, Forsyth took down a mysterious shape draped in black flannel. He removed the cloth with a flourish, revealing a finely crafted model of Lord Ramsdale's small sloop. In shape and line it was quite different from any sailing boat Daphne had ever seen.

"She's a beauty, arright," Forsyth said to the baron, grinning. His speech wasn't Highland thick, but his r's rolled with a typical burr. "I had to mak' some changes amidships, as the model was showin' a consistent tendency to roll to the left, e'en w' the sliding keels. She's balanced out nice an' tight now, though, an' she slips through the water like a knife cuts butter. She'll do, an' I think she'll show them other gents a thing or two." His face reflected as much pride as if the boat were his own and had already won races.

Ramsdale brought Daphne and Robbie closer so they could have a good look at the model. "The Americans have learned a great deal about sailing craft that we have yet to accept over here," he said. "In the islands I had a chance to see some of these features in practice."

He explained some of the boat's special features, including the long, hollow "knife" bow and the keel boards that could be raised and lowered, running his hands along the model and pointing here and there. The sleek, graceful curves delighted Daphne. Standing so close to him she shivered, almost as if he had touched her instead.

"Now, John here is a master at his trade," the baron said, handing the model back so it could be draped in secrecy again. "He happens to share my curiosity about the shape and design of boats and the natural forces at work on them. It was his criticism of some of the Thames yachts that first brought him to my attention. He was the obvious choice when I was ready to commission my own."

He grinned at the builder and shook his hand. "Are we ready to float her out?"

"Aye, that we are, sir."

Forsyth took his brown frock coat and high-crowned beaver from his office chair and, putting them on as he went, led his guests back out through the busy yard. At the head of a dock slip behind the huge ship skeleton, Lord Ramsdale's new boat, minus mast and rigging, stood poised in a cradle on rollers ready to be lowered stern first into the water. A wooden pole stood in place of its mast, flying the British colors, which snapped and fluttered in the breeze.

"It is beautiful," Daphne whispered.

The baron took her hand and looked into her eyes. The moment felt strangely intimate. "Many will laugh when they see this boat," he admitted. "They will say John and I are fools or touched in the head. But this boat is more than beautiful. It is a true masterpiece. Do you know why?"

Daphne shook her head. "Passion?"

"Yes," he answered simply. "Mine. John's. Our passion for excellence and for advancing science. For proving to others what we believe is true. Passion that makes us willing to take risks, that gives the work meaning. That is what is missing from your seascape, and present in your other work."

When she started to speak he put a gentle finger against her lips. "Let us talk more about it later."

The warm touch of his finger was gone all too quickly. No one else seemed to have noticed.

The yard workers had set aside their tools and followed the procession. Now they formed a small crowd around the boat, bantering with each other and waiting expectantly. Behind them a small cart bearing a punch bowl and cups had been drawn up. Seemingly out of nowhere John Forsyth produced a bottle of wine.

"I've been savin' this fine old Madeira for a special occasion, my lady," he said gruffly, handing the bottle to her. "His lordship says you're to do the honors today."

Dumbfounded, Daphne turned to Lord Ramsdale. "*I* am to christen her? Today? Should not that honor go to your sisters, or your mother? Should there not be a grand gathering of your friends?"

He smiled. "'Tis a small boat, and one whose attributes I do not wish to advertise, as yet. It would please me greatly if you would perform the task."

The look on his face was so warm and full of affection she could not say no. "What name have you chosen?"

"*Mistr*—" He stopped abruptly and coughed as if something were stuck in his throat.

"*Mist?* Oh, I think that is lovely! It calls up images of the river at early morning."

He smiled brightly, apparently recovered. "Yes, *Mist.* You just christen her by name and break the bottle against the heel of the bowsprit as she slides into the water. John will give you the signal." He offered his arm and escorted her to the position where she would need to stand to perform the ceremony.

The bottle of wine was smooth and heavy in Daphne's hand. She looked at John Forsyth expectantly, feeling suddenly a little nervous. Cups of punch were passed around to all the men gathered there, and toasts were made to the new boat, the races she would win, and the glory she would earn. The baron looked deeply moved.

After a second round of toasts, to John Forsyth, to the yard, and to Lord Ramsdale, a crew of men began to move the boat, some operating a winch that played out the line and others helping to push the cradle. The mood became solemn briefly when John offered up a prayer asking for the blessings of both speed and safety, and then, just as boat and cradle slid into the water, he nodded to Daphne. She swung the bottle hard, clutching the neck with both hands. "I christen thee *Mist!*"

The bottle broke with a satisfying crash, and a great cheer went up from the yard workers. Red wine sheeted down the smooth side of the bow into the river.

Archer Everett Drake, Lord Ramsdale, was happy. His boat was launched and his campaign to win the lovely Lady Wetherell did not seem to have suffered any setback from the previous day's contretemps. If there was one tiny wrinkle in the smooth path of his present contentment, it was that he had no opportunity to talk with Daphne during the drive back to Chelsea from the shipyard. Young Wetherell, entirely enthused by what he had seen there, was full of questions about the boat's design and the improvements it featured.

Archer had encouraged the boy's interest and had loaned him books about the scientific principles of ship design during the past week, so he could not with any fairness curtail the discussion of those matters now. What he needed was a chance to speak with Daphne alone. She was very quiet now, and he had no idea what she might be thinking.

He finally had his chance after they arrived back at Grove House. The boy bid him a happy adieu and went off to look up a point of discussion in one of the books Archer had loaned him. Standing in the carriage drive in front of her house, Daphne looked up at him.

"I have drawn up a list of my father's students who might have been capable of painting the Van de Velde pictures. If you will step into the house for a moment, I will give it to you. I suppose I should warn you, it is very short—only three names."

"That is more than we had before."

"Yes, although I doubt it will help." With a sigh she turned and began to walk toward the house. "I think I do understand what you meant when you said passion was missing from my painting," she said. "I have put nothing of myself into that picture. It is a showcase of technique, but lacks the heart that brings it to life. You and John Forsyth have both put your hearts into the *Mist*."

"Just so." He was so delighted that she understood, he wanted to hug her, but if he did so the footman on duty at the door would have been rightfully shocked. "It takes courage to put oneself onto a canvas for others to see. I know you have no lack of that quality."

"Well, certainly no lack of experience."

He caught her by the elbow and made her face him. "You know that is not what I meant. Perhaps one of the other pictures you have already begun would make a suitable substitute?"

"Perhaps. Thank you for your insight. I will need to consider what I should do."

He wanted to ask if her specific interest in the Royal Academy was really for her own sake or her father's, but to do so would reveal how much of her story he had learned from other sources and also might risk offending her further than he had already done yesterday.

She was not finished, although her manner became increasingly formal. "In the meantime, I feel honored that you wanted us at the boat launching today. I can understand that you might want Robbie to feel a connection to the *Mist*, since he will be sailing her with you. Thank you for that, too."

So, she had it all reasoned out. If she wanted to believe that was his motive, he would not naysay her. He knew his motives were not nearly so clear and neat as that, but now was not the time to admit it to her.

They entered the house and he followed her to the library, where she retrieved the list from a drawer in the desk and handed it to him.

He glanced down at the list, knowing she was ready to dismiss him. "We did not have a chance to discuss our other plans," he said, hoping to postpone the imminent moment. "I have put some things in motion that you should know about. One is that I have managed to have myself invited to a soiree at the home of Lord Ordham tomorrow evening. I am allowed to bring a guest. Will you attend with me?"

He could see her refusal coming before he had even finished. He raised his hand. "Ordham is a frequent patron of the Beaufort Galleries and he has a fine collection of marine art. If any of his pictures are not genuine, you would be the only person who can spot it. Do you not think it wise on our part to determine if there are more of these counterfeit Van de Velde paintings among the collectors of the *ton*?"

She was plainly torn. He could see the struggle in her brown eyes until she looked away.

"The Ordhams would likely be appalled to discover you had brought me. Are you seeking to be excluded from their guest lists in future?"

"Not at all. They are friends, and I can assure you they will accept my judgment in this. Do you feel you have no right to go among the members of the *ton*?"

As he expected, the challenge ruffled her. "Of course not! It is they who condemn me."

"Well, then. Think of this as an opportunity to throw their prejudice back in their faces." In a softer voice he added, "I will stand by you every minute."

She did not look quite convinced. "You said you've put other things in motion. What are they?"

He smiled. "There is so much that we need to know. I would rather wait and tell you when there is information to report. Will you trust me?"

That was the key question, of course. He could see the doubt remaining in her eyes, even as she nodded.

Chapter Fifteen

Between that afternoon and the following morning, the heavens opened. Worst of all, they seemed inclined to remain that way. Lying in her bed with the bedclothes drawn up to her chin, Daphne listened to the steady drumming of a heavy downpour. There would be no sailing for anyone this day. She could almost believe it was a sign of celestial disapproval—of her choice to attend the Ordhams' soiree, or of her continuing involvement with Lord Ramsdale.

Barely more than a week had passed since she'd first met the man, and for the past five days she had been with him every day. She would be with him again tonight. She needed to reclaim her life! In encouraging a friendship for Robbie's sake she had never expected such an impact on her own.

By next month this interlude would be over—the Duke's Cup won or lost, Parliament closed, another London Season ended. The baron would go off to wherever it was he would spend his next few months, and life would return to normal. If she tried, she could not devise a more direct route to heartbreak than falling in love with him. She could not afford it; she could not allow it.

Accordingly, she set about having a normal day with great determination. If knowing she would see Ramsdale that evening helped the hours to pass, she did not acknowledge it. The unpleasantness that was bound to accompany her attendance at a social event would no doubt prove eye-opening for him. She could only pray that she would not cross the path of disaster while she was there.

The rain continued all day. By evening it had let up to a fine mist that glowed around carriage and streetlamps and illuminated windows, softening the look of the night. Carefully attired in her best evening dress of azure blue gauze, Daphne admired the effect from the carriage window as she and the baron waited in line to approach the entrance of Lord Ordham's town house. A few intrepid couples walked along the pavement trying to avoid the puddles, but most sat in their vehicles, wanting to be as close as possible before alighting.

"We could walk up," Daphne offered, aware that she had been unduly quiet during the drive from Chelsea. She felt as though she should apologize in advance for the debacle they were about to endure.

"Are you so eager to get there, then?"

"No. I only thought you might not like this waiting, and wanted you to know I was willing to wet my shoes."

He chuckled. She was going to miss that deep rumbling sound when all of this was over.

"Thank you, but no. Your sacrifice is not necessary." He gave her one of those unsettling, warm looks that always seemed to rattle her. "I am quite content to sit here as long as necessary. After all, I have with me the most beautiful lady in attendance this evening. What could possibly compete with that? If we had no specific task to perform, I daresay I could be persuaded not to go in at all."

She was afraid he might be perfectly serious. It would do neither of them any good if she took it that way, however, so she laughed. "You put me to the blush, sir, with such fulsome compliments. I must protest! However, if you truly do not mind waiting, then it will definitely benefit my shoes to do so."

"Only your shoes?"

What answer did he want? It definitely did *not* benefit her heart, sitting in this close space with him, alone, pulse racing, fighting the attraction to him for all this time already. He was looking at her intently, leaning forward in his seat, waiting for her response.

"Oh, certainly my shawl as well," she replied lightly.

"Some silks do not do well in the rain, you know, but it is my best evening wrap for such warm weather."

"Ah, I see. Your shawl."

She didn't know what he was about. As he said the words, he reached across and seized one end of her shawl between his fingers. It was white silk shot with stripes of metallic silver thread. The fringed ends were bordered with bands of floral embroidery. "Very lovely," he said, drawing it slowly toward him for inspection. The same motion began to slide it off her shoulders. The silk slipping across her back felt incredibly sensuous.

Panicked, she clutched the other end before it disappeared behind her. "What are you doing?"

"Only this," he said innocently. He pulled a little harder on the shawl, now firmly anchored by her grip on the other end. His action drew her toward him. In an instant he closed the distance between them, claiming her lips in a kiss.

He had caught her too much off guard for her to resist, and once the kiss began, she was too lost to resist. She didn't know exactly when his arms closed around her, or when he actually shifted himself to the seat beside her; she only knew the kiss began sweet and warm and intensified with each passing moment until her whole being felt on fire. The deeper the kiss became, the more she wanted his arms around her, holding her tight against him. The tighter he held her, the more she craved his touch.

How easy not to fight it—to give in to mindless passion. She might have been lost entirely had not the carriage just then jolted and started forward, moving up in the line. She struggled back to sanity like a swimmer coming up for air. Indeed, she broke from his embrace with a gasp.

"No. Oh, please, no. We cannot do this. Perhaps we had better get out and walk after all."

He looked hurt and a little dazed.

"Why? What is wrong? I did think you were enjoying it as much as I was."

Daphne could no more lie to him about this than she could have stayed silent when she discovered the first counterfeit painting. "My lord, I like you, and I did enjoy it. But we mustn't indulge in such behavior. I simply cannot."

He truly did not understand—she could see that by the

look on his face. She swallowed, trying to get rid of the lump in her throat. If only the whole world were different! "I think you'll understand it better in a few minutes," she said, "after we have been inside."

The soiree was a mad crush, which meant it was so crowded it would be considered a huge success. Once Archer and Daphne finally got into Lord Ordham's home, they squeezed through people to find the room being used for cloaks and wraps and then squeezed out again in search of their host and hostess. A harpist played in one room, barely audible over the chatting crowd. A refreshment table was laid out in another room under a huge glass chandelier blazing with dozens of candles. In all the rooms people stood elbow to elbow, making dutiful contributions to the overall noise. A small ripple of reaction ran through them, however, wherever Archer and Daphne passed.

Archer discovered that he had not fully understood until now what Daphne had tried to explain to him more than once. People who turned to him with a pleasant look of greeting froze in place when their eyes traveled beyond him to see the lady who had accompanied him. Others broke off in midsentence to stare, and everywhere whispers and glances followed in their wake. As they made their way through the throng, he could feel Daphne's arm become stiffer and stiffer, her hand like ice. She held her head high, however, as determinedly proud as royalty, meeting the gaze of every person bold enough to stare at her directly.

An alarming collection of emotions welled up in Archer, threatening his calm facade. Anger, protectiveness, and pride made him want to simultaneously strike out at those around them and fold Daphne into his arms. But something more was there, too—something he had never felt before, something he couldn't name, or wouldn't—filling his heart and trying to burst out of it. That was the most alarming of all.

He refused to be ruled by emotion. He continued the search and at length found Lord and Lady Ordham receiving their guests in another handsome room upstairs.

People made way for Archer and Daphne, perhaps to avoid the necessity of conversing with them. Archer could see their middle-aged hosts clearly, like a matched pair of figurines at the end of a tunnel. He saw Lord Ordham's face turn three shades of red, and saw Lady Ordham search for her partner's hand and take hold of it. She smiled, not exactly graciously, but with a fixed determination not dissimilar to Daphne's. *And these are my friends,* Archer thought, approaching.

He introduced Daphne and had to give credit to Lady Ordham. Her smile never faltered, and when Archer had finished, she said in a clear voice loud enough for all those nearby to hear, "I am pleased to meet you, Lady Wetherell. Any relation of the Earl of Melden is welcome here. Was your mother not Helena Mortmain, one of his granddaughters? I believe she attended school with my elder sister."

Apparently satisfied that she had achieved her purpose, she turned to Archer and added in a much softer voice, "Perhaps she would like to see my husband's collection while she is here, Lord Ramsdale. I've no doubt she must share your interest in art."

Lord Ordham, whose color was slowly returning to normal, nodded in agreement as if he still did not trust himself to speak.

Grateful, Archer bowed over his hostess's hand and after making a courteous reply, guided Daphne away. By pretending she had no objection to having Daphne as her guest, Lady Ordham had been protecting her own reputation and trying to control the gossip, he had no doubt. Regardless of the reason behind it, her approval would help his campaign.

The lively strains of an English country dance could be heard in the adjoining salon where people were dancing. "Do you care to dance a set before we seek out the gallery, madam?" he asked. "I suspect it might cause more talk if we fail to mingle now that we are here. And after our hostess has publicly suggested we visit her gallery, slinking off right away will be bound to cause notice."

"I know only a few dances, ones I learned when Robbie was studying with his dancing master. I think—I know it would be better if we did not. We cannot dance only one dance. And you cannot dance only with me."

He had not thought of that. Damnation! If only he could guarantee that someone else would ask her to dance, and would treat her as kindly as she deserved. Had Holly planned to attend this event?

Archer quickly scanned the salon. Holly was so tall, he

was never difficult to spot in a roomful of people, even in such a crush as this. If the young lady who had recently snared his interest was here tonight, there was a good chance he would not even be hiding in the card room. But he was not evident among the dancers.

"All right, then, let us simply wander slowly among the rooms, and make our way to the gallery by an indirect route." Surely he would come across some other friends he could depend on to be courteous. "Remember, you have every right to be here. You told me so yourself."

She swallowed, then nodded, clearly ill at ease.

They managed to have several polite conversations, including one with Sir Ellison Tolley, who asked about Archer's new boat and was full of gossip about the current odds on the Duke's Cup participants. He was gracious to Daphne, and Archer made a mental note to be sure to invite the fellow when he celebrated the *Mist*'s formal debut. They had made the circuit back to the stairway hall when Holly appeared, making his way toward them.

Archer made the introductions and Holly bowed graciously. Then, with apologies to Daphne, he pulled Archer aside. "By Jove, Drake, I have never given so many setdowns in one evening in my life," he reported, keeping his voice low. "I have firmly disabused several people of the notion you are anything more to the lady than a family friend. But I think your bringing her here tonight may be doing a bit of good. Some people seem to be reviewing and revising their opinions of her social category."

"I am heartily glad to hear that," Archer replied, hoping the depth of his gratitude came across in his voice. "I will catch up with you later."

He returned to Daphne's side and took her arm, guiding her expertly past one knot of people, only to have her pull away a moment later. "Give me a moment," she said. "There is one thing I simply must do, even though it is probably most unwise."

To Archer's amazement, she headed off toward a rather loud woman at the edge of another little knot of people nearby. As Archer looked more closely, he recognized the ample proportions of Lady Brumborough, the woman Holly had pointed out to him at the milliner's shop that day when Archer had first seen Daphne.

"Why, my dear Lady B.," exclaimed Daphne, assuming a cheery and familiar tone. "Imagine chancing across you here. I hope you have been well?"

The other woman blanched. Daphne showed no mercy, however. "Have you been pleased with the purchase you made in Madame Michaud's that lovely day last month when we saw each other? I've been thinking of you, you see."

With a strangled cry that Archer could not have described to anyone, Lady Brumborough fled, elbowing innocent people out of her way in her haste. As Daphne returned to his side he fixed her with a questioning look.

She smiled a beautiful, mischievous smile, but offered him no explanation. "I am ready now. Let us go to the gallery and proceed with our purpose in coming."

Lord Ordham had no counterfeit paintings in his collection as far as Daphne could see. The few Van de Velde works he owned were by the younger of that name—tall marine compositions with skies full of colored clouds. To her relief, Daphne detected not a stroke of D'Avernett blue among them.

She was also immensely relieved that there were no pictures for which she had posed, ready to throw her past in her face and remind all other onlookers. Perhaps best of all, she and the baron had managed not to run into a single one of her father's former students—neither friend nor foe—despite the large number of people in attendance at the soiree. However, the evening did not prove to be entirely free of problems. Lord Ramsdale pulled her into his arms the moment they were alone in the gallery.

"You are a magnificent creature," he whispered into her ear just before he claimed her lips. "What am I to do about you?"

Daphne felt herself melting and fought the response. How could she both want and not want something with such equal intensity?

She managed to push him away after only a brief kiss. "What you are to do is simply teach my stepson to sail your boat, help me to solve this puzzle about the paintings, and then—well, nothing. We go our separate ways."

She looked at him reproachfully. "More to the question

is what am I to do about *you*? If you insist on this behavior I cannot continue."

"Why? Do you not think passion is as important in life as in art? We are neither of us married; we harm no one. . . ."

He still did not understand. She sighed in frustration. "Did you not see the way they all look at me? They are making assumptions about us just from having seen us together here. It will get worse as soon as the gossip mills get hold of it. Are you prepared to deal with that? Do you think I could look those people in the eye if I knew what they were thinking was true?"

Daphne didn't dare to tell him she was also afraid. If she revealed her true feelings for him, how much sooner he would break her heart! She could easily become as accustomed to his kisses as she had already become to his company—as accustomed as she was to breathing. That was dangerous to her indeed.

He looked like a small boy chastised by his nanny. "So, no kisses?"

"No kisses," she said firmly. "No embraces. We will attend strictly to business."

He sighed. "You are heartless, madam. However, I give you my word that I will *try*."

Chapter Sixteen

In a matter of days most of London was abuzz with the word that Lord Ramsdale and the notorious Lady Wetherell were "an item." Despite a certain resistance and skepticism on the lady's part, Archer had convinced her that such gossip and speculation helped to conceal their true intention of investigating the paintings fraud.

He thought it certainly helped his strategy to salvage her reputation and spent time with her on each of the following several days. He persuaded her to go driving in Hyde Park and to attend some exhibitions and even a small musicale given by friends who happened to have a fine art collection for her to examine. She had drawn the line, however, at accompanying him to the theater, saying there was no possible connection to their investigation and that their other activities provided quite enough of an appearance for the gossips.

In truth, Daphne went because she could not resist being with him for some part of each day, not because she was convinced by his arguments. She knew in a few more weeks she would return to her solitary existence and the gossips would become vicious again, gloating over how she had tried to step out of her place and had been justly used and cast aside. It was a price she was willing to pay.

Young Robbie did not seem to mind that his new friend was suddenly more occupied than ever, as long as there was still time for sailing. However, the same could not be said of Archer's mother. On the following Sunday afternoon Archer answered her summons to present himself at Fitzwarren Place.

"What can you be thinking, Archer?" was how his distraught mother greeted him the moment he stepped through the double doors of the blue salon. It was not a good sign that neither of his sisters was present.

He opened his mouth to reply after dutifully planting a kiss on her cheek, but got no further.

"You are *not* thinking, that is the answer." Taking his arm, she walked him into the center of the room. "Going about with Lady Wetherell so openly—why, people think you must be courting her, those who know better than to think something worse. They'll soon be laying wagers on your betrothal date! That is no way to attract an eligible parti. I have already sensed a distinct cooling of interest among many of the ladies of my acquaintance."

"Truly?" Archer brightened. He had concentrated so much on Daphne he had not considered this bonus to their activities.

"What exactly are your intentions toward her, my son? A man does not take his mistress about publicly, but you cannot be thinking of her as marriage material. So I am completely flummoxed. Pray do enlighten me."

Lady Ramsdale released his elbow and sat down, looking up at him expectantly.

Archer smiled at his mother. "Is it not permitted for a man and a woman to be merely friends?" It was the answer Daphne would have liked to hear, he knew. "Her stepson has become rather like a protégé to me, and she and I happen to enjoy some similar interests. Providing her an escort is a simple courtesy."

In his heart he knew things were not so simple, but how could he explain what he had not yet sorted out for himself?

"I doubt there is anyone in London who would believe that possible, especially with this particular woman," said his mother, folding her arms and looking at him sharply. He met her gaze, wondering how much she could read in his face. Could his mother sense his confusion?

Taking a deep breath, she finally said, "If that is truly the case, Archer, we have some counter measures to perform. It is imperative that you be seen at least *some* of the

time around town without her at your side. That has not
been the case since Wednesday. What are people expected
to think? You must offer a bone of hope to the younger
ladies who are suitable, my dear."

She was not finished. "The Dunnetts are hosting a dinner
tomorrow night in honor of their daughter's birthday. I
would like you to accompany me and Winnie. Tuesday you
had already agreed to attend the Willmots' ball, so that is
all right. Wednesday is the grand opening of the new
bridge. I should have liked you to join us for that, but our
plans are already made with the Bridleys and I declined on
your behalf as I assumed you would be out on the river in
a boat."

"You are infinitely wise, Mother." He would have to
unmake some of his plans with Daphne, but at least they
could keep that one. He had invited her to observe the
Waterloo Bridge festivities from the *Ariadne*, assuming the
weather proved favorable. The river would be alive with
watercraft of all sorts, including the elaborate state barges
and the personal barge of the Prince Regent. He did not
want to expose the *Mist* to public scrutiny so soon, and had
actually postponed taking delivery of her until the following day.

"On Thursday you could join us—we have tickets for
Kean's *Othello* at Drury Lane. Then on Saturday there is
a breakfast at the Longvilliers' out in Clapham. . . ."

Archer could see where this was heading, and realized
he could turn it to his advantage. "There is something you
could do for me in return," he said quietly. "Add Lady
Wetherell and her stepson to the guest list for Winnie's
come-out ball."

His normally unflappable mother gaped at him, bereft of
speech for perhaps a full twenty seconds.

"Archer, you know how important Winnie's ball is to
her—to all of us! Furthermore, it appears it is to be one
of the last big events of the Season. Would you turn it into
gossip-fodder that will linger all the way to winter?"

"Mother—"

"I have never even met your Lady Wetherell, although
I believe I have met her stepson. He is quite unobjectionable, as far as I can see, but she—"

"Mother!" It was time to assert himself. "You know you

will not mind at all if Winnie's ball becomes fodder for gossip that is complimentary. You'd revel in it. And you told me yourself you were hoping to have something that would be different from everyone else's event! I can assure you that Lady Wetherell, like her stepson, is quite 'unobjectionable'—even charming—when given a chance. And finally, you will be meeting her before then. I am planning a sailing party and picnic at Westwater, and she will be among my guests. I fully expect you to attend with Winnie and to bring Caro, too, even though she is not yet out. They will both enjoy it."

His mother blanched. "When is this party to be held, Archer? Our schedule is already very full."

"A week from Saturday," Archer replied, making the decision that instant. He had been vaguely making plans for some time now, but with the date of the Duke's Cup approaching quickly, it was time to settle the details. "I apologize if you will have to send regrets for something else. I know I am thoughtless. But the party is important to me. You could think of it as a coming-out event of sorts—for my new boat."

He gave his mother a winning smile he knew she could not resist. He would have slightly more than a week to test the *Mist* in private before her debut at the party. He would send out the invitations tomorrow.

Like a dutiful son, Archer adjusted his plans to accommodate his mother. At dinner the following evening, Miss Dunnett, a lovely young woman with stunning blue eyes, attractive wheat-colored curls, and lively, intelligent conversation, tried her best to entertain him. She was an appealing young woman, and he did his best not to offend her, but he just could not make himself interested. The image of Daphne glowing with delight during their afternoon excursion to Kensington Gardens ruled his mind.

In the same way, the Willmots' ball the next evening seemed a very dull affair without Daphne there, as if no other woman in the world existed for him but her. He could not wait to leave. His sister Winnie had a splendid time, danced nearly every dance, and was annoyingly determined to stay to the very end. At least her bubbling enthusiasm afterward in the carriage ride back to Fitzwarren Place served to cover his persistent ill humor.

He had remarked upon this strange new phenomenon to Holly when he ran into him during the ball, shaking his head in consternation. "I have never felt this, this *craving* before. She agreed to go to the opening of the bridge with me tomorrow, but refuses to accompany me to Vauxhall for the gala in the evening. My mother has all sorts of other plans for me. What am I to do?"

Holly had merely looked at him sadly. "You are lost, my friend," he pronounced. "Truly lost."

More than a week had passed since Archer and Daphne had visited the Beaufort Galleries and argued over her father's possible involvement in the art fraud. Since then, social engagements both with and without Daphne, sailing practice with young Wetherell, attendance at some key sessions of Parliament, and paying calls and making arrangements for his party had left Archer little time to work on the problem beyond checking other collections for more evidence of fraud and making a few inquiries. It was most fortunate, then, that he had arranged for someone else to work on it in his stead.

He had hired a Bow Street Runner the morning after he and Daphne had been to the Beaufort Galleries. The flowers he'd sent her that morning had come from a seller just a few blocks from the Bow Street magistrate's office. Loath to argue with her again about her father's possible involvement, Archer had decided not to tell her what he was about until he had more information. He had given the agent the name and address of the French émigré who Galton Meregill had claimed was the source of the counterfeit paintings and had asked the man to learn what he could.

Very early on June eighteenth a plain black gig stood outside the front entrance to Westwater. Inside, ensconced in a fine leather chair in Archer's study, a stocky, thick-necked Mr. Joseph Allardice gave Archer his report.

"There's nary a trace of the fellow to be found, m'lord," the agent said apologetically. With heavy jowls framing his square face, he put Archer in mind of a bulldog. If the man had the same toughness and tenacity, Archer thought he would do very well as an officer at Bow Street.

"E'en if he'd gone back to France, there'd be some trace left behind," Allardice continued. "Folks don't live without leavin' a trail—they eat and move about and they interact with other folks. No Frenchie ever lived at that address you give me. 'Tis my professional opinion that the fellow didn't never exist, sir, that's what."

"I appreciate your hard work on this," Archer said. He was prepared—he had almost expected this. "I'm going to require your services for a similar task, then, and also we may need some extra help."

He pulled a sheaf of papers out of a pile on his desk and extracted a page. "This is the information I was originally given about the ownership of the painting I own. Now that we know the other information was incorrect, I'd like you to check this. The job may be as much of a wild goose chase as the other, but at present I have only suspicions. I need facts."

If the agent came back empty-handed again, the next step would have to be a midnight raid on the art gallery's records. Archer did not know where else to turn. But that last was such a drastic step he was not ready to take it until the other information was thoroughly checked. Daphne might still be livid at the idea, but at least then he would have some justification to offer in his own defense.

In the meantime, he had learned nothing helpful about any of the former students on Daphne's list. None had been in financial difficulties, or any other sort of trouble that he had been able to ferret out by subtle inquiries.

"I would like you to do some checking on these three gentlemen, also," he said, handing the agent a second sheet from the pile. "Very quietly, you understand. My own inquiries have turned up nothing questionable at all."

He was concerned about Daphne. Her loyalty was endearing, but if it was misplaced, might it not eventually prove dangerous to her? If anyone connected with the fraud was still alive, still in London, and realized she had uncovered the trouble, they might consider her a threat. Perhaps he worried overmuch because he cared about her, but he could afford to indulge himself. Old family friend or not, the art dealer had given wrong information once. Archer was not willing to wait to see if that proved to be an honest mistake.

He leaned forward, clasping his hands in front of him on the rosewood desk. "I would like to hire another runner, Mr. Allardice, to keep watch over someone whose safety might possibly be at risk. Can you make the arrangements for me?"

The Bow Street man nodded. "Happens we do that sort of thing all the time, though I say most of the so-called cases are just an excuse by some jealous nob to keep tabs on his lady."

"It is not amorous rivals that concern me in this case, although the subject is a lady. Discretion will be required, for I do not wish her to know anything about it. No sense in alarming her if it turns out there is no danger, would you not agree?"

Allardice nodded again. Archer gave him the details and outlined the payment arrangements for both agents. "I would rather be a poor fool than a sorry one," he said, rising from his desk. The men shook hands, and he walked Allardice to the door. "I hope to hear back from you as soon as possible. The faster we can clear up this matter, the happier I will be."

No more than two hours later, Daphne could be found perched on the stone end of the Grove House pier with her legs dangling over the water. The day was unseasonably warm, even for mid-June. A breeze ruffled the surface of the river and broke the reflected sunlight into sparkles. For someone who had undoubtedly lost her mind, she felt remarkably calm.

She was waiting for Archer. He was due to come by and pick her up in the *Ariadne* so they could watch the Waterloo Bridge proceedings from an advantageous viewpoint on the Thames. They had more than four miles of river and three other bridges to pass through to get there, so Archer had wanted to start early with a favorable tide.

Daphne looked forward to the outing. The river was one place where no reminders of her past might lurk in ambush—one place where she felt she could be herself without the risk of approbation. That is how she knew that she had become a prime candidate for Bedlam. She had allowed Archer to persuade her to go to all sorts of other places with him in the two weeks since she had first met him.

What was she doing? Her firm resolutions to stand against him evaporated like wisps of morning fog each time she was with him. He made her forget all that was at risk, all her fears and reluctance. At least she had had sense enough to refuse to go to Vauxhall—she could never have enforced her "no kissing" rule under the fireworks in those softly lit walkways. But now he had asked her to attend his sailing party at the end of the following week, and his sister's coming-out ball, too.

She thought she had finally begun to recognize what he was trying to do, and it meant he was even more ridiculously insane than she was. The fact that in all the past days she had not come across one of her father's students gave a false sense of hope that she could continue to escape that. She knew in her heart such luck could not last.

She scanned the river, looking for the *Ariadne*. Few watermen plied their trade this far from the center of London, but river barges and fishing boats were always to be seen along with other small craft. How much she had learned in the space of half a month! Archer had opened her eyes to a world she had never known. She would always be grateful for that in the bleak days that lay ahead.

A sail detached itself from an indistinct group of vessels upriver and soon she could tell it must be Archer's. As it came closer, she waved and stood up, prepared to climb down the wooden ladder Robbie had seen installed on the pier. After her first two boarding attempts, this would be a huge improvement.

There was not a hint of impropriety when Lord Ramsdale took her hand and helped her to her seat in the cockpit, discounting the eager gleam of pleasure that showed clearly in his eyes. Daphne could not fault him for that as she did not doubt her own face betrayed a similar glow of anticipation.

Minutes later they were on their way. "Are you nervous about shooting Battersea Bridge?" Ramsdale asked her.

"Not at all. Robbie has described it to me in the most exciting terms." Brave words. She thought she might have been less nervous if no one had told her of the danger, but she was not about to admit any weakness. "Besides, I have the utmost faith in your skills."

He raised an impish eyebrow. "As you should. However, you will get your wish to be a crewman after all, for I will need your assistance."

The smile he gave her flooded her with warmth. At the

same time, it reassured her that he was perfectly confident about the maneuver they would shortly perform. "You will need to do exactly as I say, exactly when I tell you, and must not be frightened. Can you do that?"

"Of course! I am no milk-and-water miss. Just explain it to me beforehand, so I will have no questions at the last second."

Daphne had second thoughts when she saw the bridge looming ahead of them. Battersea seen from the water could intimidate the stoutest of hearts. Unlike the elegant stone bridges in the heart of London, this was a primitive wooden structure. Clusters of blackened piles caged in by rough, rather haphazardly placed boards supported it instead of handsome arches and columns. The openings between the supports were narrower and considerably shorter than those of the bigger bridges. The water that gushed through those constricted openings foamed and twisted like a live thing.

"We haven't the wind power to make more than one try," Ramsdale said to her, "although I am going to set the jib to get as much power and control as I can."

She nodded. "I suppose you know from experience that the mast is not too tall," she said with only a small note of doubt in her voice. Her job was to drop the peak of the sail by lowering the gaff. If she dropped it too far, the throat would break and the boat would be disabled.

"We are less than two hours from ebb tide, which should leave enough room. I grant you that from here there is an illusion that the mast will prove too high. You will see."

Perhaps it was just as well if she concentrated on her task, she reflected. She understood the true problem was making sure the boat was centered in the space and held steady as it swept through and that no sail, lines, or rigging could catch on the bridge supports. If the boat turned sideways it could capsize or be smashed to pieces against the bridge.

The jib was in place none too soon. Archer quickly reclaimed the helm and steered toward the center span of the bridge. Daphne took up her position at the front of the cockpit, ready to lower the peak of the gaff.

"Do you know, the bridge would look less forbidding if

it were not so dark," she said thoughtfully. "For instance, if the boards were painted white."

Archer laughed. "Leave it to an artist to think of that. Of course, they would not stay that color for long."

The bridge was coming up quickly. He issued her orders: "Uncleat that line now, but hold it steady. Brace your feet if need be. Whatever you do, do not get up or try to move while we are going through. Here we go."

Even as he spoke the boat was picking up speed. "Drop the peak now, but no lower than the top of the mast," he said. "You've only to hold it there until we get through. Use the cleat to help relieve the pressure."

She did exactly as he bid her, although she found it difficult indeed. The gaff and canvas sail weighed far more than she had expected, and she strained to keep control of them. The *Ariadne* rose up on the swell of water racing through the bridge opening and then shot through like a thing pursued, swept along by the current. The moment they were clear, Daphne restored the gaff peak to its former position. Her arms shook with the effort. As soon as she had refastened the halyard, she sat down again abruptly in the cockpit.

"We did it!" she exclaimed, letting her breath out in a rush and fixing him with a rather shaky grin. Her own pulse was pounding and she could well imagine his must be, too.

"We did indeed," he replied, grinning back at her. "We've earned more than two miles of clear sailing to Vauxhall Bridge, and I can assure you shooting that one is much easier. Well done."

Chapter Seventeen

The rest of the morning passed pleasantly as they cruised down the river. The pastoral landscape of marshes and windmills along Chelsea Reach gave way to the more developed urban shoreline once they passed through Vauxhall Bridge. By noon the banks of the Thames beyond Westminster Bridge were crowded with spectators on both sides of the river, in the gardens, on the rooftops and in stands that had been constructed on wharves and in many of the yards. Huge barges that normally carried corn and coal were loaded this one day with human curiosity instead. A flotilla of sailboats similar to the *Ariadne* milled about in midriver, weaving in and out of an even larger assemblage of rowed vessels—excursion boats, private barges, watermen's wherries, and the like.

Many of these vessels carried flags that snapped and fluttered smartly in the breeze. Buildings and even several church steeples were similarly adorned, while eighteen standards flew upon the bridge itself. Ramsdale furled the sail and anchored the *Ariadne* close enough so that as he and Daphne delved into the contents of their picnic hamper, they could listen to the footguards band that was among the military detachments stationed on the bridge.

"You have not given me an answer yet about coming to my sailing party next week," he said, neatly slicing off a piece of cheese and passing it to her.

Daphne paused, regarding him intently.

"I do not believe I should attend. I have been tempting

fate and behaving very unwisely this week, going into society with you. I believe you have misled me about one aspect of your character."

"Have I?"

"You are much more of a gambler than I realized."

He looked both astonished and chagrined. "How can you
say so? Have I made a single wager in the time you have
known me?"

She sighed. "No. Instead you have been risking your reputation in an effort to salvage mine. That is a huge gam-
ble—one I should not permit you to try."

"I think it is too late now to alter course, my dear. To
use your terms, the wager has already been placed."

"We have both been exceedingly lucky in escaping people who have been a part of my past. Such luck will run
out and all your efforts will be undone."

"Not if these people have the courtesy and common
sense to leave the past where it belongs—in the past."

She scoffed. "And do you believe courtesy and common
sense are the foundation of society?"

"For most people, yes. Malicious gossip may titillate
some—all right, even many—but I would not condemn everyone as subject to that failing. Those who do indulge in
it are not worthy to know, in my opinion."

She threw a grape at him. "The patronesses of Almack's
are not worthy to know? I'd no idea you were so high in
the instep!"

He captured and ate the grape, giving her a teasing smile.
"There is still a great deal you do not know about me, my
dear. All the more reason for you to attend my little
gathering."

"It is one thing to have you help my stepson. Please do
not think I have not appreciated your efforts on his behalf."

"Why not allow me to help you as well?"

Daphne looked off at the crowd of faces lining the riverbank. Was there anyone among them who knew and recognized her? Would there next be gossip about her being
out on the river with the baron? She could imagine how
Robbie's uncle would delight in that. Or was Ramsdale
right? Was there truly a chance her life could be changed
simply by facing up to it?

She sighed again, this time in capitulation. "Do not

blame me later if it all blows up into the greatest scandal you have ever seen."

Predictably, the encounter that Daphne had been dreading the most happened just when she finally stopped worrying that it might. Another week had passed, in which Ramsdale had taken delivery of the *Mist* and begun to sail her with Robbie upriver where she would be least noticed. He had continued to divide his time between all the demands upon it, managing to spend some of it with Daphne almost every day.

In such a large city with so many choices of activities, what were the chances that she would end up in the same place, at precisely the same time, as her particular old nemesis? In three weeks she had been to more places with Lord Ramsdale than she and her late husband would have been in three months, all without encountering more than one or two of her father's former students and without encountering Morgan Laybrook at all. The people she had met bore out the baron's faith in them, treating her with a courtesy she had not expected.

Still, the circles of the *beau monde* were relatively small, so the fact that she had not run into Laybrook could have meant that the man was not even in London. The reasons he had been dismissed from her father's academy had never been made public, but he had not suffered the speculation and gossip about it gracefully. He was the one man among her father's students who had pressed his attentions on her so ruthlessly and taken the consequences so badly that she knew he would delight in an opportunity to shame her.

Ramsdale, with his inimitable charm, had convinced her to go with him to Leicester Square to see the new panorama of the Battle of Waterloo. Except for two small receptions they had attended to look at art collections, most of their excursions had been in the afternoons following his sailing practice with Robbie each day. Most evenings he escorted his mother and sister, which Daphne found commendable. It also lessened her own public exposure, for the exhibitions and other daytime entertainments were not as crowded with the cream of society as the evening events.

She had gone to see the panorama convinced that doing

so would be harmless enough—every hour she spent with the baron put her heart more at risk, but she no longer counted that. An urgent need to be with him and to store up memories of their time together before it all came to an inevitable end had overcome her other concerns.

The panoramic view of the battle seemed breathtakingly realistic—perhaps too much so. Ramsdale, who had been away in the West Indies when Napoleon had his Hundred Days, was fascinated. While Daphne was content to stand in the central viewing area and have an overview of the surrounding painting, the baron kept going back to the rail at various points in the circle, studying the work in detail. As Daphne stood alone in the center, intent on watching him, suddenly there was a hand at her waist and a man spoke close to her ear.

"So, Miss D'Avernett, or I should say, Lady Wetherell."

Startled, Daphne instinctively tried to step away, only to find that the man prevented it by the firm grip and positioning of his hand. She tried to turn to see him, opening her mouth to protest, again to find her intention thwarted. From behind her he placed a finger against her lips, a shockingly intimate position to take, indeed.

"Miss Sketch-me Paint-me dares to mix with the gentry these days, does she, then?"

It was Morgan Laybrook. She would know his low-pitched drawl in any setting, even though she had not heard it in eight years. A sharp elbow to his ribs was the only reply he deserved, but he was probably counting on her to cause a scene. With Ramsdale there, she dared not call attention to what was happening. All his efforts to redeem her place in society would be undone as would his own reputation along with them.

"Unhand me, sir!" she hissed through her teeth, hoping they would not attract notice.

"Do you not know your old friend?" His voice was teasing, every bit so confident that she knew exactly who was accosting her. "But then again, you never did *know* me, exactly, did you? Your father saw to that."

Moving his hand to her arm, he turned her to face him, standing so close there was hardly a hand's width between them. It was grossly improper. Daphne wished the floor would open and swallow them both before anyone else took notice, but at least now she was able to step back from him. He stepped forward.

"I am crushed that you have no welcome for me after we have not seen each other in all these years." He raised his voice enough so that people near them could not help but hear. "But of course, you have been a very busy lady, haven't you? So many, er, admirers! No time for an old friend?"

From the corner of her eye, she saw Ramsdale take notice and start toward them. She sent up a prayer that no one in the viewing room knew who she was. She was usually resourceful, but at this moment she could not think what to do. It seemed a gossip's delight was inevitable.

What happened next could have been heaven sent. Before the baron ever reached them, another man walked by and stumbled against Mr. Laybrook. This, of course, required that the clumsy man then stop and apologize profusely. While Laybrook was occupied trying to get free of him, Daphne and Ramsdale slipped out the exit.

As soon as they were outside, Daphne urged Archer to get them away quickly. "I believe he had every intention of creating a scene. I am afraid he will come after us and try it again here in the street."

"Who is he?" Archer asked, hurrying her along the pavement toward his waiting carriage. True enough, behind them came a shout from the fellow, hailing them in vain.

Slightly out of breath, she did not answer until Archer had handed her up into his town coach and climbed in after her. She shuddered. "Morgan Laybrook. He was a student of my father's. Yes, another one. However, he was the least like a gentleman of any that ever studied at the academy. I could not get him to stay away from me, and finally had to convince my father to dismiss him. He already resented me for not giving him what he wanted, and I'm afraid he resented me even more after that. But that was eight years ago!"

Archer nodded thoughtfully. He noticed that her color had risen as she explained, and she seemed very shaken. "You do not believe that you are to blame, do you?"

"No. It is just unfair that the woman is usually blamed, and even when nothing happens, she is tarnished by the attempt. Why is that? Men seem to be able to do whatever they please!"

Leaning toward her, he reached across and took her hand, enfolding it protectively between his. "It is not fair. That is why men should take all the more care of their ladies. Unfortunately, not all of them do." He could not help thinking of her father.

The incident with Mr. Laybrook raised a new possibility in Archer's mind. The name had not been on the list of potential suspects she had given him, but he wondered if the former student could somehow be involved in Daphne's troubles. Although she had not said so, she seemed to fear the man himself as much as the scandal he might cause. That left Archer wondering exactly what had happened between them during the days at her father's academy.

He was very glad he had taken the extra care of hiring a Bow Street man to watch over Daphne now—he suspected the man who had so fortuitously bumped into Laybrook might actually have been the agent guarding her. He thought he had glimpsed the fellow several times since last week when he'd arranged the hire. However, as of yet, he had not had any further report from Joseph Allardice.

The elaborate preparations and the schedule on the day of the Queen's Drawing Room meant that Archer could not see Daphne on the twenty-sixth. The day of a young woman's court presentation played a huge part in shaping her future, and accordingly Winnie and Lady Ramsdale were both in a frenzy of nerves. Archer could never picture Daphne falling into such a state and wished heartily that he could be with her.

It struck him as ironic that, while the queen may have been receiving visitors for the entire afternoon, most of the fabulously dressed presentees and their accompanying relatives or sponsors spent more time in their carriages progressing slowly through the streets and the park in line to reach the Queen's Palace, than actually inside it being seen once they got there.

At any rate, Winnie seemed to meet with the queen's approval. Archer was happy for her and proud, too, for she did indeed look very fine despite the ridiculous nodding plumes and old-fashioned style of the clothing required for court. The Prince Regent even favored Archer with a snippet of conversation. It was a moment of family triumph. Best of all, the thing was over. In two more days, guests would be descending upon Westwater for the sailing party and picnic.

Saturday dawned tentatively with mist rising on the river, but by late morning the sun had burned that away and promised a fair afternoon. The guests began to arrive at one o'clock, gradually congregating on the broad parterre behind the house. A few wandered on the lawn or took shelter from the sun under the huge striped pavilion that had been erected for the day's festivities. An interesting collection of pleasure boats tied up at the Westwater dock, more varied in size and type than the collection of carriages delivering other arrivals at the front of the house.

Daphne and Robbie were among those who came by carriage, arriving in her maroon vis-à-vis. Daphne had tried to convince Robbie to go separately from her, but he would not hear of it.

"Many of these people are my new friends," her stepson had explained patiently. "They are Ramsdale's sailing friends. They won't prejudge you. I am proud to arrive with you on my arm, and if anyone thinks ill of it, or you, then I say they don't belong at this gathering!"

Hoping he was right, Daphne walked in with her hand on Robbie's arm and her head high, her armor firmly in place. She had avoided public places in the last few days since the incident with Morgan Laybrook, but this was a private event. She did not see Archer. As she and Robbie made their way through to the parterre, she thought that this time, the house was full of laughter and activity, the way it should be. The thought brightened her smile.

The parterre at first seemed to be awash with only strangers. Then Daphne began to pick out faces she recognized, some from recent days and a few who were former acquaintances from the days of her marriage. Robbie stopped and introduced her to several people, who all responded politely enough. Perhaps it would be all right after all. The tension in Daphne's shoulders eased slightly.

People were talking about the Duke's Cup, their boats, other people's boats, who had the best chance of winning and why. No one seemed to expect the women to take part in these conversations or to notice if Daphne did not. But no one excluded her or made a special point of avoiding her, either, as far as she could tell.

Robbie introduced her to a Mrs. Haverthorpe, and Daphne realized this must be the mother of Archer's lost friend. Her heart went out to the woman in sympathy, her nervousness forgotten.

"I have heard Lord Ramsdale speak of your son with great respect and affection," she told the woman. "He was obviously special—a good friend and an inspiring one. And a great loss."

The other woman smiled and began to talk about her son. As she did, Daphne gained more insight into Archer's character as she learned about their friendship. Robbie drifted away to talk to other people, then came back to her to point out Archer at the edge of the lawn.

Explaining that she and Robbie had not yet greeted their host, Daphne excused herself with a promise to talk with Mrs. Haverthorpe again. She began to make her way through the crowd to where Archer was standing.

He was talking to Sir Peter Hollyfield, whom she had met at the Ordhams' soiree. Daphne did not know why, but there was something familiar about the juxtaposition of the two men, one tall in a blue coat and the other even taller, dressed in brown. Before she could think about it any further, however, they noticed her approaching with Robbie and broke off their conversation.

The smile the baron turned on her was heart-stopping. She knew, in that moment, that she was irretrievably lost— that there was no chance left that she might save her heart from breaking. She loved that smile and everything else about him. She loved him.

"Lady Wetherell," he said, taking her hand. The glance that accompanied his formal words was much warmer and more intimate, a secret glance just between them. "You'll remember my good friend, Sir Peter Hollyfield."

The baronet bowed graciously. "It is my great pleasure to see you again, madam," he said. "And I know how happy you have made my friend here just by gracing us with your presence."

Daphne curtsied, glad that she had heard a little bit about Archer's friend Holly so she was able to make polite conversation in return. But underneath her courteous demeanor, she was beginning to feel uneasy, wondering if she were not in a dream. This would not last, this pleasantness and this love, and when it ended would it not then seem like the prelude to a nightmare?

Ramsdale took her hand again and tucked it under his arm, comfortingly real. After excusing himself to Robbie and Sir Peter, he said, "Come with me, my dear. There are some other important people I would like you to meet."

He led her to a corner of the parterre where a distinguished-looking dark-haired woman was conversing in a group of people that included two young women, one dark-haired like she was and one a comely blonde. "My mother and my sisters," he explained with a nod toward the group. Daphne did not have time to react to this or panic before he approached them and made the introductions.

They were courteous and proper, his family. Daphne sensed a great deal of curiosity in his sisters and a kind of dignified reserve in his mother. As they carried on a carefully circumscribed conversation about the weather and the party, a manservant approached Ramsdale and spoke to him in a harried undertone.

"What? Now? Oh, no. No, no." The baron turned back to them with a look both pained and apologetic. "It seems my great-uncle has chosen this moment to make known his arrival in town. He is in the library waiting for me to attend him."

In what was not exactly a quiet aside, he said to Lady Ramsdale, "Mother, did you know of this? It is the height of discourtesy to demand that I leave my guests in the middle of my event. Does he do this on purpose? But I cannot simply leave him waiting, either."

"Do not worry," Lady Ramsdale assured him smoothly. "You may leave Lady Wetherell with us. We will keep an eye on things while you speak with the marquess."

Daphne was not a coward, but she did not relish the prospect of being forced to stay with Lady Ramsdale for too long without him. "I have met a number of people here and can always seek out my stepson again," she said gamely. "I also promised to speak again with Mrs. Haverthorpe. Please do not worry about me."

"I won't be long—I hope," Ramsdale said. With a quick bow he took his leave.

Lady Ramsdale linked her arm through Daphne's before Daphne could escape. "This is not so bad, then, is it? We have the chance for a comfortable coze. We might have had no such occasion if Lord Huntington had not decided to be so importunate."

Chapter Eighteen

At eighty-two, Archer's great-uncle no longer cut such a fine figure as he had as a younger man. Stooped with age, he now used a cane not for fashion but to help him shuffle from one place to another. All that remained of his once-fine head of hair was a long white fringe that encircled the bald dome of his head.

Standing, Archer loomed over his wizened relation. Sitting put them on an equal level, but only in a physical sense. The autocratic Marquess of Huntington, who still possessed a sharp eye and keen wit, retained a great deal of power and influence over everything in which he was involved, from family matters and managing his substantial estates to matters of government and the social affairs of London. He stared at his great-nephew with an authoritarian air and gave him leave to be seated in the library chair that faced him.

Archer was not in a proper frame of mind to have this interview. Not only had his great-uncle called him away from his guests in the midst of a large party, but the man was sitting in Archer's favorite chair, granting him permission to take another in what Archer had come to consider his own home.

"My lord, I must protest—" he began bravely, only to be silenced when the marquess raised his hand.

"I know what you are going to say, Archer. I am a selfish old man and rude besides. That's true enough—I am. Should you happen to reach my age, then you can be, also, with my blessing. In the meantime, I am still the head of this family. What in blazes are you about with this Lady Wetherell business? The rumors I have heard offer every variation you can think of, casting the chit as anything from your ladybird to your betrothed. I haven't had a sensible answer from your mother, so now I am asking you."

Archer had expected to be summarily raked over the coals for what he'd been doing. "I can assure you that neither of those instances is true, my lord."

"Well?"

"Well, welcome to London, sir. I hope your journey will not put you at risk for a relapse of your illness. Did you have a chance to rest or did you come straight here?"

"Kind of you to be concerned. You have not given me the information I want, young man."

A dog with a bone was nothing compared to his great-uncle. "What can I say? She is not my mistress; we are not betrothed—we have simply been spending some time together."

"Hmph. Simply? Doing what?"

"Oh, excursions to exhibits and events, a few outings on the river. We are friends. I've been teaching her stepson to sail."

"Few men would settle for mere friendship with the likes of her, my boy. Sounds suspiciously innocent to me. Exhibits and sailing, eh?" The old man looked intrigued.

Intrigued was a better reaction than Archer had been hoping for. He explained about Daphne's artistic talent. Encouraged and happy for the diversion, he then launched into a description of what he had been teaching young Wetherell and finally an admission that the lad would be his crew for the Duke's Cup. As his great-uncle seemed inclined to listen, he also told him about the *Mist*, her unusual features and his high hopes for her performance in the upcoming race.

When he finished, Lord Huntington steepled his fingers and looked over them at Archer thoughtfully. "How like you, Archer, to go for the unorthodox. You have never been one to follow the beaten path. Just like your father and grandfather, although of course that trait helped earn my brother his title.

"It didn't end so well for your father, God rest him. But

like them, you never look ahead to see where you will end up. I don't know whether to wager on the boat or the woman," he said. "You seem equally ensnared by them both."

He waved his hand vaguely in the direction of the back of the house. "Go back to your guests. We will talk again. I'll want to hear your impressions of affairs in the islands, and we will see where this other matter is heading. Be a good lad and send your mother in to me.

Archer was astonished to have gotten off so lightly.

Rescuing Daphne from his mother's clutches was an easy task for Archer since Lady Ramsdale's presence had been requested in the library. However, he had little time just then to learn what had transpired between the women. The guests had to be sorted into groups: those who wished to go out on the river and those who would stay behind relaxing at Westwater; then among the sailors, those who would captain their own vessels and those who wished to be merely passengers, which passengers wanted to sail, and which preferred to be rowed. Archer had hired two private barges to accommodate extra guests on the river.

Picnic boxes had to be distributed once the groups were established, and the course laid out for those who wished to make the entire circuit. Time mattered; the incoming tide would reach its peak by midafternoon and then begin the ebb flow. The course Archer had chosen, upriver toward Putney and back again, was planned to coincide with the shift in the tidal current. The idea was to make the excursion a pleasant exercise rather than work.

Daphne was surprised that Archer's friend Holly was among those who chose to stay ashore. "He is not a sailor? I expected that such a close friend would share your passion."

"His passion is cards, I am sorry to say, at least until he finds something better one day. He seems to feel his great size would sink ships, despite all the reassurances I have given him over the years."

"Did he know your friend Haverthorpe? Perhaps his loss has made Sir Peter extra wary."

"I am certain that did not help. Knowing how difficult I found that time from four thousand miles away, I cannot imagine how hard it had to have been to be here. But Holly has always felt this way about sailing, as far as I can remember."

Archer had, of course, made certain that Daphne would sail with him. As the guests went to their assigned stations, he guided her along the narrow plank walkway to the slip where the *Mist* was tethered, off to the side among the reeds where she had not yet attracted much notice.

"There should be some interesting reactions when we get out into the river with the sails up," Archer said as he climbed aboard and turned to help Daphne. His eager anticipation was obvious in his face and his voice.

The *Mist* was only slightly larger overall than the *Ariadne*, but she was shaped very differently—narrow at the bow and broad at the stern, quite the opposite of the usual "codfish"-shaped sailing crafts. That her cockpit was larger was immediately evident as Daphne clambered aboard, but there was less room to move in it, for the boxes enclosing the sliding keels took up space that had been open on the other boat. She could not help brushing against Archer as she moved to take her seat. Only firm resolution and the need to duck under the substantial boom on this boat kept her from glancing at him. Somehow she knew he would be looking right at her.

The *Mist*'s other most noticeable strangeness was that the foot of her sail was laced to the boom along its entire length, fixed just the way the head of the sail was laced to the gaff. Many small boats like the *Ariadne* had loose-footed sails, with no boom at all. On boats that had booms, the foot of the sail still was anchored only at the outer end.

"Just wait until you see what a difference the fixed sail makes," Archer said. "You'll have to get used to ducking the boom when we come about. But the inconvenience is worthwhile. When we get underway you will think we are flying!"

Warmth tinged with sadness filled Daphne's heart. She loved that boyish enthusiasm in him, so thoroughly mixed with the mature capability he also possessed. But this day she must banish those tinges of sadness or any thoughts about what lay ahead for her after the Duke's Cup was over. She knew his mother was right—if she was truly the baron's friend, she must accept that their friendship in the long run would harm his chances of marrying a suitable bride. Although Lady Ramsdale had worded her message with exquisite tact, she had essentially given Daphne the responsibility to make sure the friendship ended. Today and in the coming week she must treasure every minute they had together.

"Can I help with that?" she asked, watching him begin to unfurl the sails.

"You will soil your gloves," Archer said, moving close to her and reaching for the strap in front of her. She caught her breath and for a moment did not trust herself to move.

"Mmm." Diverted, Archer's hands slid around behind her instead. "You smell so good. Devil take it." His lips sought hers with soft entreaty. The kiss, while gentle, revealed to her all the desire he had held at bay since she had set her "no kissing" rule more than two weeks ago. How foolish she had been then, to think she could avoid falling in love by the imposition of rules! She suspected now that it had been too late even then.

The sweetness of his kiss sent a wave of fire through her and threatened to overwhelm all common sense as she responded. Fortunately, a sudden puff of wind caught at the partially unfurled sail that screened them and set it rippling in protest, almost as if the *Mist* herself were chaperoning them. They broke apart with palpable reluctance.

"You are not supposed to do that, my lord," Daphne said, trying hard to make her protest sound sincere. "You promised."

"I never promised more than to try."

Silently they finished preparing the boat. Pushing against the pilings with a boat hook and paddling from the bow, the baron backed the *Mist* out of the slip and into open water beyond the dock. Once clear, he raised the sail. She felt the boat lift as the wind filled the sails, and again the little thrill of excitement she always experienced at that moment rippled through her.

"Is this what you intend to race against us for the Duke's Cup, Ramsdale?" called the captain from one of the other boats.

"Does the lady know you'll wet her lovely dress in that thing, Ramsdale?" called another. "Shall we stand by to rescue her when you go over?"

"What's the matter with your sail, Ramsdale? Afraid it was going to fly away?"

Archer only grinned. The more they tried to bait and tease him, the bigger his grin became. "You'll see," he said finally. "You'll see."

The group of vessels leisurely milling about began to form some sort of order, heading up the river with the sailboats leading the way and the barges following at their slower pace. Surprisingly, Robbie had chosen to take the river cruise onboard one of the barges, and Daphne waved to him. Only when she saw that he was with the baron's younger sister, Caro, did the reason for his choice become quite clear.

Once Ramsdale maneuvered the *Mist* into a space where she could get clear air, she did indeed seem to fly. Daphne and the baron waved merrily as they passed other boats and smiled at each other as they saw those captains suddenly start to adjust their vessels to improve their speed. It was not officially a race, but a competition had begun, nevertheless.

Nine days of practice had given Ramsdale a good idea of what the *Mist* could do. She gradually left the other boats behind, but she could go no farther than the bridge at Putney. They dropped anchor and waited for the others to catch up. Daphne got out the box containing their picnic and exclaimed with delight as she discovered each item— an elegant collation of cold marinated chicken, hot house fruit, and tea cakes, with a delightful assortment of treats from Fortnum and Mason: figs, almonds, and dried pears. A bottle each of Sauterne and fine Madeira were provided along with glasses wrapped in linen tied with ribbon and a nosegay of flowers. She realized Archer had spent a small fortune on this part of his event alone.

"It is wonderful! What lovely choices you made!"

As they ate, he finally asked, "How did you get on with my mother? I knew she would like you if I could just arrange for you to meet."

"Oh, she is lovely," Daphne said with some truth. "I could see much of you in her. We chatted at some length. Your sisters, too, are delightful young women." She would not say more.

They saluted the other boats with glasses of wine when

they arrived, and afterward all sailed back down the river past Westwater. The last leg of the cruise was back up to Westwater against the tide, but only for a short distance. The wind had freshened and clouds were rolling in from the west by then, making one and all very happy to have used the sunny hours when they had.

As the baron and Daphne put the *Mist* back in her berth and prepared her for the night, curious guests came to watch them and study this odd new boat from the shore.

"Damnedest lines I've ever seen on a pleasure craft," one fellow was heard to say. "Looks like a little helmsman boat."

Daphne felt an odd sort of relief. For once, the talk was not about her at all. No one had seemed troubled by her attendance at the party or her presence on Lord Ramsdale's boat. The *Mist* was now the subject on everyone's tongue.

There was also no more opportunity to speak privately with Ramsdale.

"Tomorrow?" he whispered as he handed her off the boat to other helping hands on the wooden walkway.

She nodded mutely, biting her lip. It seemed she lived for their moments together now. *One more week.*

Chapter Nineteen

July opened on the third day after Archer's party with pouring rain and a poorly attended levee given by the Prince Regent, which Archer attended with his great-uncle. The heavy rain had continued all day and all evening, preventing sailing and even the outing with Daphne that he had looked forward to earlier in the day.

On the day after the levee, just two days before the Duke's Cup Race was to be held, Archer received another visit from Joseph Allardice. The man did not look exactly flushed with success as he entered Archer's study, hat in hand.

"I've put my findings into a report for you, m'lord," he said, handing Archer a folder with several pages inside it. "I'm right sorry to say I've little to show for what has been a good effort of work. Didn't want you to think you was being cheated."

Archer's heart sank. Preparations for the Cup race were going so well, he had wanted progress on the problem of the counterfeit paintings, too. He opened the folder and stared down at the top document as Mr. Allardice talked.

"I tracked down the family what was supposed to have owned that picture. The family exists, I can say that much, although it took me some time to find them. Drove all the way to Somerset, I did. But they didn't seem to know anythin' about an estate bein' sold off, nor especially any ship paintings. Seemed to think they still owned their family holdings. Sorry, sir."

Allardice had documented his travels and expenses as well as the time spent, the names of people he had interviewed, and the steps he had taken. But there were still more pages in the folder.

"Meanwhile, I'm to ask if you hired anyone else besides my fellow to look after your lady friend."

"What?" Archer looked up from the papers.

"You know, I hired a fellow, Mr. Brown, to keep an eye on your Lady Wetherell, like you asked me. Well, he says that sometimes he sees another fellow hanging around, not all the time, but it seems almost anytime she goes out in public. How he would know that we haven't figured out, but unless you hired another fellow, it seems curious all right."

Archer sat up very straight. "Curious indeed. I did not hire anyone else—I have every confidence in your services. I do not like the sound of this!"

"Well, it seems he never does anythin', just keeps an eye out, so to speak, pretty much the same as my fellow does."

Archer racked his brain to think if he could recall seeing any person hanging about when he and Daphne had gone out, but he realized if he had, he would have assumed it was the mysterious Mr. Brown. Remembering the day at the panorama, he quickly described the man who had bumped into Morgan Laybrook and confirmed that he had indeed been the Bow Street man. Could Morgan Laybrook have been following and spying on Daphne without them noticing? It seemed unlikely. To be sure, he described him also to Mr. Allardice, but the description did not match the fellow who had been spotted by Mr. Brown.

Archer propped his elbows on his desk and rubbed his face with both hands, releasing a huge sigh of frustration. "All right. We are not going to sit here and do nothing." He got up and went to the window.

"I understand that Bow Street officers are the arms of the magistrate," he said, staring out without seeing the view. "But unorthodox methods are sometimes necessary to achieve a lawful end, would you not agree, Mr. Allardice?"

"Yes, sir," Mr. Allardice confirmed. "Quite so."

"Could you arrange to, er, interview this other fellow who has been spying on Lady Wetherell? Find out what he is doing, who he reports to, if that fits the case, and if someone hired him, I want to know who. Also, how he gets his information."

"Yes, sir."

"Try not to hurt him, unless you find he's been up to worse mischief. Meanwhile, there is this other business."

He returned to the desk and sank back into his chair. It was time to determine what was really in the art dealer's files. Was Galton Meregill a victim here, or a culprit? Had Daphne's father and the dealer conspired together?

"I want a look at the Beaufort Galleries files. They were the source of both leads you chased after to no avail. Two mistakes? Possible. Do I think they were? No."

Daphne would be livid, he was certain, if she knew what he had in mind. Either that, or she would want to undertake the task herself, and that was far too dangerous. Her ruination would be complete if she was arrested for burglary.

Archer realized he would have to participate, but he certainly could not do it alone. He hadn't the slightest idea how to break into an office. "Do you know any 'clever tradesmen' who might be persuaded to help us out?"

It was risky—besides the danger of being caught, there was the possibility that the thief would later try to blackmail him with the knowledge of his involvement. But how else could he make certain that nothing was stolen and at the same time get a look at the records he needed?

"What I need is someone reliable who can get me into the place, stand watch, and get me out again when I am finished," he told the agent. "I will do the rest myself."

"Easy enough, m'lord. I can arrange it. All in the cause o' keepin' the laws, o' course."

"Very well then. I have a race to sail, and you will need time to make arrangements, I presume. Shall we plan for the night after the Duke's Cup?" At the man's blank look Archer realized just how far apart their worlds truly were. He added, "That would be Saturday. It gives us three days."

Daphne saw Lord Ramsdale every day during that final week before the race, except for the Tuesday when the rains poured down. Reluctant to risk another encounter with Morgan Laybrook by venturing out in public, she eagerly agreed to sail with Ramsdale in the *Mist* on those days instead. The baron practiced racing techniques with Robbie in the mornings, then in the afternoons cruised in a more leisurely fashion with Daphne, showing off the boat's capabilities like a proud father.

During all her other hours, Daphne worked feverishly on her painting of Westwater. The baron had more than fulfilled his promise to help Robbie. Who could have known she would lose her heart to him in the process? He had wanted her to put her heart into her artwork, so she had. It would be his, once she gave him the painting along with her gratitude, although he would never know it. But she could not give him the picture if it was not finished.

As she put the finishing touches on her canvas late on the day before the race, she received a note from Galton Meregill asking her to help him authenticate a painting he felt was suspicious. It was no more than she had offered to do for him, so on the morning of the race she set off in her vis-à-vis with her maid Mattie sitting across from her. The day was everything one could have wished for—brightly sunny, warm, and breezy enough to drive the boats without knocking off all the spectators' hats. In truth she was pleased to have something active to do to pass the morning hours, for despite her heartache at the approaching end of the relationship, she could hardly wait for the race.

It took close to an hour to reach the heart of the city. When her carriage pulled up outside the Beaufort Galleries, Daphne bade her coachman wait and sent Mattie down the street to buy flowers from a seller on the corner.

"I don't expect to be long," she informed them, and added that Mattie should meet her back in the carriage.

Galton Meregill greeted her warmly when she stepped inside the gallery. "My dear! Thank you so much for coming. I appreciate your offer to help so much, you know. You cannot imagine how upset I have been about the painting I sold to Lord Ramsdale. To learn that there was a second one was quite a shock, so of course I want to be certain that nothing like that ever happens again!"

She followed him now as he moved around the huge

display table to the office door. "Where is the picture you would like me to look at?"

"Wait here and I will fetch it from the back. I did not want it out where any patrons might chance across it. If they wished to purchase it, what could I have told them?"

He left Daphne standing there as he hurried off into the bowels of the building. She folded her arms and looked about, but curiosity was nibbling at her. There was no one in the office behind her. The cabinets full of files were, well, *right there*. How much harm could there be in taking a quick peek? If she saw with her own eyes what documentation was in the files for her husband's painting and Archer's, would that not help her prove to Archer that he was wrong about her father?

She was hesitant to simply ask Mr. Meregill—perhaps Archer, with his doubts and suspicions, had made her a little leery despite her conviction that the art dealer was an innocent dupe. If she spent too long thinking about it, however, she would lose this opportunity. With another quick look around, she ducked into the office and headed straight for the drawer marked "T–Z."

Her husband's file was thick with notes and records of sales to him. Daphne flicked through the pages with shaking fingers. Nowhere did she find the information about the Van de Velde he supposedly had bought a year before she'd married him.

She moved to the drawer marked "P–S" and looked for Archer's file. His, too, had many papers, although not as many as her husband's. After all, her husband had been collecting paintings for many years longer than Archer. But in neither file did she find any reference to the French emigré who had supposedly provided both of the counterfeit Van de Velde pictures. Was Archer right? Could Mr. Meregill be involved in the swindle? She could not believe it. Might he not have pulled out the information to give to them and not yet refiled it?

Her hands were sweating now as well as shaking. Hurriedly she closed the drawer and went to the one marked "A–F." The D'Avernett file was also fat with paper, but that was not surprising. Her father had done business for years with the gallery, arranging exhibitions and sales of pictures by his students as well as himself, and sometimes arranging purchases for patrons. She scanned the pages quickly, hoping the name Van de Velde would jump out at her if indeed there was any reference to it here and at the same time hoping not to find it.

She almost missed it—a small receipt slip caught between two other pages. In her father's hand she read, *Delivered, February 5, 1810,* The Mercury *and* Windmaiden Off Dover, *two yacht portraits after William van de Velde the elder.*

Her father *had* painted the pictures! But had he intended that they would be sold as genuine? The receipt seemed an indication that he had not. Her husband and her father had been friends as well as student and master. How could her husband have purchased one and not have known? Or had he?

More confused than ever, she knew now that Archer might be right—kind old Mr. Meregill might not be all that he seemed. She took the receipt slip and was just replacing the file when a harsh voice spoke behind her.

"Ah, Miss D'Avernett. So, you are a sneak as well as a slut. I suppose we should not be surprised."

Daphne had left Grove House just a short time before Archer arrived in the *Mist* to collect Robbie for the race. The starting positions would be assigned in the order in which the boats arrived, so there was no time to waste. The participating boats were to assemble near Blackfriars Bridge an hour before ebb tide, to allow for ceremonies and a band concert before the race. Competitors would start from their anchored positions around noon, after the tide had changed.

Archer had arranged for Daphne and Holly to watch the race from several vantage points along the riverfront, beginning at Hawkes Wharf by the Temple Gardens where he and young Wetherell were to meet them before the race began. The two sailors made good time during the morning hours covering the four miles from Chelsea, shooting the bridges without incident. After reporting to the race committee and receiving their starting position, they headed for the wharf. In a scene reminiscent of the opening of the Waterloo Bridge, crowds of spectators were already gathered along the riverbanks wherever there was access, as well as along Blackfriars Bridge.

Holly was waiting at the wharf. He told them there had been no sign of Lady Wetherell as yet. Archer checked his pocket watch with concern. The preliminary ceremonies would soon begin, at which time he must be at anchor. He thought he knew Daphne better than to mistake her lateness for a lack of consideration. After all these weeks of anticipation, he did not think she would have allowed anything to prevent her from watching the race.

"She'll be here," young Wetherell declared staunchly. "She would never miss this."

"You said she had gone off to do an errand this morning?"

"She would not allow anything to keep her. Wait just a few minutes more."

Archer nodded after a quick glance showed him only some of the boats had taken up their positions and no signal yet flew from the headstay of the race-committee boat. He realized that he was even more eager to see Daphne than her stepson was. His great-uncle was right—he had not looked ahead to see where he might end up when he had so lightly taken on the challenge of winning her. He had never expected to need her as much as a man needed air to breathe.

Two minutes later he knew they could wait no longer. "We must go," he said, but at that moment Daphne's vis-à-vis raced around the corner of the wharf building and slid to a stop by the wharf itself. He saw in an instant that Daphne was not in it.

"Help, oh, help—my lady's in trouble!" wailed the maid as she climbed from the carriage, waving frantically.

Daphne's coachman hurried to meet Archer. "She's been taken, my lord!" he exclaimed breathlessly. "Your Bow Street man sent us to fetch you." He stopped and wrung his hands in distress. "I drove her myself, right into the hands of them villains! If I had known . . ."

Archer fought to control his impatience. "All right, never mind. Tell me exactly what the runner said. What has happened? Where was she?"

" 'E sent this note," the man said, handing Archer a little folded paper.

Archer scanned the scribbled lines with some difficulty. It appeared that Mr. Brown had followed Daphne to the Beaufort Galleries. She had left her servants waiting out front, so Brown had lurked about the building. He had checked the back in time to see a man hauling Lady Wetherell into a hackney and setting off. Brown had quickly commandeered her carriage from out front and followed the hackney to a wharf near the Custom House. There the lady had been taken on board a charter packet, the *Persephone,* which looked to be making ready to sail. He was going to get aboard somehow, and implored Archer to bring help.

"How long did it take you to get here?" Archer asked, trying to think rationally.

"Twenty minutes," the coachman answered. "No one dared get in our way."

The Custom House was more than a mile downriver, on the other side of London Bridge. If the *Persephone* had left her wharf by now, the challenge would be not only to catch up to her, but also to find her among the maze of vessels that filled the Pool of London.

"Go to the Thames police and show this note," Archer said. "I will round up some other help and go after Lady Wetherell in the meantime."

Holly and young Robbie crowded him, both asking questions at once. Archer filled them in quickly and began to issue orders.

"Wetherell, climb aboard. Holly, give me that pistol you always carry."

"It isn't loaded.

"Give it to me anyway—I can bash someone with it or threaten them. If I don't have to shoot it, they'll never know."

"Take me," Holly said. "I'll be handier in a fight than young pigeon here."

"She's *my* stepmother," Robbie protested. "I have to go."

Archer appreciated the sacrifice Holly was offering, to come with him in the boat, but he shook his head. "I need the best speed I can get now. Less weight is better, plus the viscount's used to crewing. Holly, your job is to rally the troops—bring help! We may have to fight off an entire ship's crew to rescue her. Get one of these fellows to row you out so you can recruit my fellow racers. They'll put a woman's life ahead of the Duke's Cup today."

"Right. I'll do more than that!"

As Archer and Robbie raced back to the *Mist,* Archer heard Holly yelling to the spectators nearby. "There's been a kidnapping," he called. "The victim's aboard a packet called the *Persephone* and she's heading out from near the Custom House. Any able-bodied man with a boat who's inclined to help will be handsomely rewarded!"

Leaping aboard the *Mist* with the viscount close behind, Archer cast off and let the current start the boat downriver as he raised the sail.

"You'll never catch up!" someone shouted at Archer.

Archer only shook his head. "We can. We will. Whoever can come up behind us will be most appreciated!"

So it was that the *Mist* raced through the midst of the Duke's Cup participants instead of taking her place among them, heading straight for the arches of Blackfriars Bridge as the band played and the speeches began. Behind her, wherries, fishing boats, and lighters fanned out from the shore and went out to the tethered racers, who one by one pulled anchor, raised sail, and headed off in the same direction, leaving a stunned populace and race committee gaping behind them.

Once clear of Blackfriars Bridge, Archer strained the *Mist* to her limit, heeling her as sharply as he dared. Wetherell's face was as white as sea-foam, but he held on for dear life and did exactly what Archer told him as they closed the distance to London Bridge. Archer thanked God that the tide had not yet turned, for a small sailboat working against the current would have had no chance at all against the big packet boat they were pursuing.

The ancient, narrow arches of London Bridge were notoriously dangerous, but at least the tide was nearly at ebb. Archer glanced at the young viscount, grateful the lad had shot the other bridges in practice any number of times by now. "This will be no different than shooting Battersea," he reassured the boy. "Same procedure." He tried to project a calm confidence he was far from feeling.

Shooting London Bridge was like entering the gateway to a separate world. On the east side of it hundreds of

huge, ocean-going frigates and schooners were moored together in rows along both sides of the narrow channel, as
many as four or five deep, their masts and rigging crowding
the sky like some fantastic forest. Behind them barges and
freight boats lined the quays. On any day, vessels of all
sizes moved through the channel, and it was always amazing that there were not more accidents. Archer began to
ask for the *Persephone* as soon as they drew near the Custom House. Had any seamen seen her? Had she left her
berth?

In his head, he totaled the time elapsed since Daphne's
servants had left the Custom House area and come to find
him. *Too much time.* The *Persephone* had indeed set sail.
Had Mr. Brown managed to get aboard? Was Daphne all
right? How far downriver was the ship by now?

Chapter Twenty

The last thing Daphne remembered was an argument between Galton Meregill and the man she had not expected to see at the gallery, Morgan Laybrook. It was Laybrook who had found her with her hand in the files, still shocked and puzzled by the evidence of what her father had done.

Now her head throbbed, her vision was blurry, and she was lying in a ship's bunk with her hands tied. She hoped she would awake from this dream any minute. Surely reality would return if she tried to move.

She made an effort to roll onto her side, which only brought on greater pain and caused a little moan to escape from her lips. Morgan Laybrook's smiling face swam into view.

"I am quite certain you'll do better to lie still for the time being," he said. "You've a nasty bump on your head. I suppose I should apologize for inflicting it, but you gave me no choice, you know. We were going to use ether, but I couldn't allow you to escape just because Meregill was distracting me with his stupid second thoughts."

Slowly she collected the words to make a sentence. "What did you—where is he?"

"Oh, never mind about him. We've left him well behind. We are on our way out of London now and into our new life together."

The very pleasantness of his tone alarmed her. Focusing her wits, she realized the sense of motion she'd been feeling was not dizziness. She could hear the creaking of the timbers and the slap of the water in the bilges below. The ship was underway.

Panicked, she tried to move again—definitely a mistake. Laybrook came to sit on the edge of the bunk and put his hands on her, pushing her back. That was the moment she felt the bile rise in her throat. She swallowed it, knowing she did not dare to make him angry. She was in enough danger as it was.

Remain calm. How many times had Ramsdale said those words to her the first day they had sailed together? She clung to them now, but the thought of him brought tears into her eyes. And then she remembered the race. *Oh, God, the race.* It could last for most of the afternoon. He and Robbie might never know what happened to her. When she thought of them both, the tears spilled over, trickling down from the corners of her eyes. She would have to find some way out of this.

Laybrook was still smiling at her. "Always before, it was look but don't touch. How many men have you had, yet you wouldn't have me? But no more of that now." He stroked the side of her face, and brought away his finger with her tears upon it. Looking at it, he frowned.

"Tears won't work with me," he said harshly. "I'm not your father, to be swayed by them. It was your tears that convinced him to put me out of the school, away from you. Do you think I don't know that?"

She was remembering more now, of what had happened back at the gallery. Pure alarm chilled her to the point of numbness.

"You are mad," she whispered.

"If I am, you have driven me to it. For eight years I have waited for this. Or not exactly this, but something."

At the gallery, Laybrook had slammed the wooden file drawer shut, nearly catching Daphne's hand in it. "Those who snoop deserve whatever they find out," he had sneered. "Your father was not so hard to persuade, when he thought your ruination was at stake. He painted those two pictures. It was a brilliant scheme when I thought of it, and when I realized how greedy for money Galton Meregill was. I could have my revenge and make money from it. But then your dear papa wouldn't do any more. When we realized he had flawed the pictures by using his special color, he had to be punished even more." Meregill had come back into the room at that point and Laybrook had presented her like a prize.

"Not only did she come willingly, she thought she had a right to snoop," he'd told the art dealer.

"Oh, dear. I wish you had not done that," the older man said. "You have become quite a problem for us, my dear—an unexpected one. Now you know even more. . . ."

She had tried to explain that everything was still a puzzle, but the men would not listen. Laybrook said he was taking her with him, and Meregill had balked at that, saying that had not been their plan.

"Perhaps not your plan, old man, but it is mine," Laybrook had said. She had tried to slip out, and Laybrook had turned and struck her.

Now she thought it best to keep him talking. Maybe he would tire or leave and she would be able to think of some plan.

"What did you mean back at the gallery when you said my father had to be punished?"

"Forcing him to paint the pictures wasn't really enough, but when I found he had tricked us, I was furious. It was not difficult to cause the accident that killed him."

Daphne felt sick, but she could not give in to it. *Her father had been murdered.*

Laybrook continued. "Besides, I thought his death would put you out on the street. You might have been grateful to me if I'd rescued you. Instead that old fool Wetherell swooped in like a damned knight and married you. So all I could do was keep chipping away at you, trying to punish you."

"What do you mean?"

He looked immensely proud of himself. "Oh, rumor and innuendo can be such helpful tools. People are so willing to believe whatever is nasty. But when I learned about Lord Pasmore's agenda against you, that played into my hands exquisitely. He is so eager to believe, and he has been paying me handsomely for the very thing I was doing anyway—obtaining reports on you and spreading rumors whenever I could. It has been doubly delicious."

Daphne closed her eyes, barely able to grasp that one single demented man could have orchestrated so much of her misery, or that the rumors, the counterfeit paintings, and even her father's death were all connected.

Laybrook began to touch her again, running a finger along her jaw. "You are still as beautiful as ever, but now you belong to me. Finally I have what I wanted."

Twisting her head away, Daphne had to ask, "Did my husband know . . . about the paintings, or any of it?"

But before Laybrook could answer, the ship lurched suddenly, throwing Laybrook off the bunk and nearly throwing Daphne with him. There was a commotion above them on deck and the sound of shouts and running feet.

Hope bloomed in Daphne's heart.

"What the devil . . . ?" asked Laybrook, struggling to his feet.

In the busy Thames channel, a small boat like the *Mist* could maneuver far better than a large ship with only a minimum of its sails spread. Determined to follow all the way to the sea if necessary, Archer and Robbie had continued to pursue the *Persephone* down the river, racing against time until the heavy three-master hove into sight.

"We must find a way to delay or stop her until the others can catch up to us," Archer had said. "But we must also discover what has become of Daphne and Mr. Brown."

Archer knew they faced a considerable risk, having no idea of the size of the crew who would be aboard to receive them, or indeed, if that crew even knew a kidnapping had taken place.

He sent up a prayer for guidance to see Daphne home safely as he fastened a line from the *Mist* to the bottom of the *Persephone*'s rear starboard shrouds. He and young Wetherell then furled the sails and secured the boat as quietly and quickly as they could.

At Archer's signal Robbie hoisted himself up by the chain wales at the foot of the shrouds and began to climb. Archer followed, up and over the rail. The instant he dropped onto the deck, Archer pushed past Robbie, pulling Holly's pistol from his waistband as he went. The astonished fellow at the wheel did not have time to raise an alarm before the nose of the pistol was pushed roughly against his jaw.

"One noise and I'll blow your head off," Archer said

gruffly. "Where are your passengers and crew? Did you know that a woman was brought aboard against her will? If you're in league with the villains you'll rot in Newgate right along with them."

He watched the man turn pale at first, then flush. He looked suitably frightened. Archer moved the pistol down to the fellow's chest. "Where are they?" he repeated.

"I didn't know," stammered the man. "He said she was a doxy, that she'd drunk too much. Took 'er down to the fo'ard passenger quarters."

Archer shoved the pistol. "Are any of the crew in league with them?"

"H-hit's a charter, sir. We hire out to anyone."

"Then consider yourself under a new hire. I'll double what they paid you. And the new orders are to strike sail and stop this ship. Tell the crew while we rescue the lady."

Archer removed the pistol, but before he could turn away the helmsman gave the wheel a vicious spin. As the boat lurched, the man knocked the gun from Archer's hand. An uppercut to his jaw followed, and Archer fell backward with the impact, pain rocketing through his head.

The man yelled an alarm to his crewmates, then told Archer, "Only the captain can change the hire. How'm I to know what you say is true? You've snuck on board like thieves, and maybe that's all you are."

Robbie had scrambled to retrieve the gun and now turned it back on the man, but the noise had brought others running. Archer, recovering, took the gun back and held it against the helmsman again.

"Move any farther and he's a dead man," he threatened the others. "Where's your captain?"

"Here." A man stepped forward. Behind him Archer saw, to his surprise and chagrin, Morgan Laybrook. He had a pistol in his hand, pointed at Daphne, who looked dazed and whose hands were tied. And, Archer thought, no doubt Laybrook's pistol was loaded.

"Well, we seem to have struck something of an impasse," he said. "Is this the man you've been hired to, with his gun at a lady's head?"

He paused to let the thought sink in, but in that moment a cry went up. "Look out!"

The *Persephone*'s course had not been righted after the

helmsman had spun the wheel. Bearing off to starboard, she was making for a huge collier moored beside the channel. Sick at heart, Archer realized that even if the two big ships only grazed each other without major damage, the *Mist* was going to be crushed between them.

The helmsman lunged away from Archer and grabbed the wheel, hauling it back in the opposite direction. The ship lurched again, and Daphne used the moment to fling up Morgan Laybrook's arm, discharging the pistol into one of the sails. She fisted her tied hands and began to wield them like a club, striking anyone within range and ducking as Laybrook tried to strike her with the pistol. Half of the crew became embroiled in the fight while the other half ran to the side to see if the ship would miss hitting the collier. Shouts from the collier's crew added to the confusion. In the midst of it all, Mr. Brown emerged from hiding, waving his own pistol and trying to restore order.

Archer felt the impact all the way to his heart when the collier struck the *Mist*. The grinding shriek of her timbers as she tried to resist the pressure crushing her was like a human cry. The sickening crackle of breaking wood followed. He thought he would never forget that sound. But at that moment Daphne emerged from the fray, looking disheveled but more beautiful than Archer had ever seen her.

"What in heaven's name are you doing here?" she asked.

Robbie, who had been looking aft, turned around and shouted, "Sail ho! Or, er, sails!"

For sure enough, coming up behind the *Persephone* were sails, at least a dozen small sails, and behind them a host of other assorted vessels—apparently the entire Thames River Fleet along with half the spectators who had meant to watch a very different sort of race.

"Reinforcements," murmured Archer. "Not a moment too soon."

The crew of the *Persephone* cast their lot firmly with Archer once the little fleet of followers began to come alongside. Archer convinced Daphne to hide belowdecks until the *Persephone* was temporarily docked and all reinforcements and stray personnel had gone ashore or sailed away. He would have liked to stay with her, but he seemed to be in charge of operations on deck.

Morgan Laybrook was trussed securely and handed over to the River Police once they arrived. Mr. Brown went with them to give a statement, promising Archer that he would not divulge Daphne's name. Authorities were going to be dispatched to the art gallery to see what had become of Galton Meregill. Holly had kindly offered to see young Robbie home.

Archer hired another hackney to take Daphne home in anonymous and comforting privacy.

"Mr. Brown witnessed your abduction," he advised her, "so they can prosecute Laybrook without you. Let the scandal center around the art dealer and Laybrook and Bow Street. There's no need for our names to come into it, although the gossips will love the debacle I made of the race."

"What if Laybrook insists on naming me and my father? He could wreak more damage on us still."

"I think it can be made clear to him that doing so will only make his fate worse than ever. Rest now, and we'll discuss it all tomorrow," he said wisely.

"But—"

"Hush. I am serious. You have already been through too much for one day." He was holding her in his arms, and he decided kissing her was the best way to quiet her. He felt quite unwilling to ever let go of her again, although he would have to once they arrived at Grove House.

Daphne quite liked the comfort and security of being held in the baron's arms, but she was not willing to put off explanations. She'd had time to sort through the muddled information Laybrook had given her, but still did not understand how she had come to be rescued.

"Who is Mr. Brown? How did he come to be on the ship?"

Archer then had no choice but to explain how he had brought the Bow Street Runners into the investigation.

"You were right about my father," Daphne said. "He did have secrets. Laybrook blackmailed him into painting those pictures, and I never knew. But I was right, too. Father never intended to pass them as genuine. I think he may have planned to expose Laybrook and Mr. Meregill, and that is why he deliberately used the D'Avernett blue in the pictures, as evidence of sorts. I did not learn if my husband knew about it, but I suspect he did. He may have wanted to buy both of the paintings, to protect my father in the meantime."

"Except that one got away—the one I bought. And then, of course, I left for the West Indies, never knowing."

She nodded. To her dismay, tears threatened to return to her eyes. She sniffed them back. "Laybrook told me he caused the accident that killed my father. I suppose there is no way to ever prove it."

Archer drew her even closer and tenderly stroked her cheek. "Laybrook will pay a steep price for his misdeeds, nonetheless. Whatever possessed you to go the gallery this morning?"

"I did not believe Galton Meregill could be involved in the art fraud," she said, heaving a shaky sigh and leaning her head against his shoulder. "He asked me to come to authenticate a painting, but it was a trap. I walked right in. I should have trusted you, but I have known him far longer than I've known you."

"Do you not know by now that I am a very special man?"

Yes. She wanted to tell him just how special he was, how much she loved him. But even now, with things changed, she knew his mother was still right. Some people would always question Daphne's behavior and remember her past. He deserved a woman whose reputation was unblemished beyond question, and even friendship with Daphne would stand in the way of that.

"Oh, you are a veritable paragon," she replied, seeking a safe answer by teasing him. But she sobered again when she thought of what he had sacrificed this day for her.

"What about the race?" she asked. "What about the *Mist*? I am so very, very sorry." She was appalled to consider the sacrifice their friendship had cost him.

He smiled and took her hand gently between his. "The others will reschedule. They still have next week before Parliament closes. Today the *Mist* won a much more important race. I can build another boat. I could never find another *you*."

Chapter Twenty-one

Archer had insisted that Daphne rest for twenty-four hours, but he put a claim on her time for the following evening. Her headache had cleared by then and she felt better physically, but as Mattie arranged her hair after dinner, Daphne did not feel in the least like facing people. A quiet, private evening at home so she could savor his company and say goodbye was what she wanted.

A knock on her chamber door startled her just as Mattie placed the last ornament, a pearl-trimmed comb, into the twist of hair at the back of her head. Robbie's voice came through the door.

"When you are done, might I have a word, Daphne?"

"We are finished now, Robbie. Come in."

He had been unusually quiet and very solicitous of her all day, even at dinner. What could suddenly need to be said now, before Archer arrived? Daphne smiled bravely at her maid, who tactfully slipped from the room.

"You don't know how sorry I am," Robbie began.

"Except for the hundred apologies you've already given me." Daphne could not help trying to lighten his mood. Since the crisis he had become so sober, it nearly broke her heart.

"I keep thinking if only I had not sold the painting, if only I had not been gambling to begin with . . ."

"Robbie, we've had this conversation already. You cannot shoulder all the blame. There was far greater evil at work than your small share."

"I suppose. And you would not have met Lord Ramsdale if I had behaved more circumspectly," he added with a glimmer of his old good humor.

The prick of tears in her eyes made Daphne turn away from him. "True." If she had never met the baron, she would not have the pain of parting from him now. Yet, even after all she had been through since their meeting, she could not wish it. She would cling to the memories of her time with him in the empty days ahead.

"I have been thinking," Robbie continued, as if she might consider this a new occupation for him. "I realize there are changes ahead for us."

He rushed on, before she could react or even realize what he was saying. *What changes was he expecting?*

"Yesterday when I was riding home in the carriage with Sir Peter, he was telling me all about the adventures he had at Cambridge with Lord Ramsdale. It made me think perhaps I should like to go there. Or perhaps I should go to Oxford—that is where all the Viscounts Wetherell have gone before me. I suppose my father would have wanted me to go there."

"Yes, that's true."

"Well, that would keep me out of trouble, and allow you to move on with your own life. I never before considered what you were giving up to keep looking after me."

Oh, dear. It all made sense to Daphne then. *He thinks that Archer and I might marry if his own situation were not holding me back.* A mixture of love for her stepson and sadness for a future that was not to be swelled Daphne's heart. She could not bear to tell Robbie his mistake now or argue with him over her decision. He would find out soon enough.

"I do not think you should enter university for any reason other than that you wish to do it for yourself," she said carefully, summoning a smile through sheer force of will. "I must say I would be delighted to see you do it, and I know it is what your father wanted."

Clever, subtle Sir Peter. She must remember to thank him. Then she realized with a stab of regret that she was not very likely to see him again. *A note, then.*

"All I have to do is decide which college," Robbie pronounced happily and left her with a lighter step than he had used in days. In his wake Daphne pondered the feasibility of renting a place in the countryside near Oxford, on the river, of course. One could paint anywhere, after all, especially with a well-lit room for a studio. . . .

Archer arrived a short while later, resplendent in crisp, formal white linen and a black evening coat. She had never seen him wear that combination of colors and thought it emphasized his darkly handsome appearance. It also indicated an evening in Town. How could she tell him she had no wish to go out? She definitely *did* want to be with him, for what could be their last time. She had to tell him she would not attend his sister's come-out ball, or any other event from now on.

However, instead of leading her out the front door to his waiting carriage, he led her into the garden behind Grove House.

"Archer, what are we doing?" she asked with a light and slightly unsettled laugh. He always seemed to keep her off-balance.

"You will see," he said mysteriously, leading her down the path to the pier.

In the glow of a lantern, the *Ariadne* nodded gently on the water. Daphne looked down at her pale yellow silk gown. "Surely we are not going sailing? It is nighttime, and our clothes. . . ."

Archer stopped and turned her toward him. Slowly and deliberately, he put his arms around her waist and pulled her against him. "You don't want to go?" he asked teasingly.

"Well, I—"

Unfairly, he didn't allow her to finish her answer. As soon as his lips claimed hers, her resistance melted. His kiss turned into several kisses, and in between he managed to murmur against her cheek, "I hope I am convincing you."

By the time he stopped, Daphne would have gone anywhere he wished. He led her partway down the steps and lifted her into the boat, which was riding high on the full tide.

The night sky was still rimmed with light blue, and the

first stars were just beginning to show. The air was mild and the river at slack water was almost as smooth and still as glass.

"There is little breeze tonight," said Archer, putting up the mainsail. "I hope there is enough." He turned a lazy grin on her. "It was not my intention to merely sit here by the pier, but to cruise the river a little under the stars."

The idea was so lovely, Daphne's eyes pricked with tears. Had he planned this as a farewell cruise? Surely he could look ahead and see the inevitable parting that was coming. *Just enjoy,* said the little voice in her head. *Take each day as it comes.*

The river was very quiet, the only sounds those of the night and the soft ripple of water as the *Ariadne* moved slowly along. Every so often the sail would luff as the breeze left them, but then it would fill out again and the boat would move ahead as if an invisible hand had provided a gentle push.

Daphne tilted her head back and stared up at the sky, watching as more and more stars became visible. Then, beginning with a glow at the skyline, the moon began to rise. "It is so beautiful," she said with a sigh.

"No more beautiful than you," Archer replied.

He had been unusually quiet, sitting at the helm with his hand on the tiller. In the soft moonlight his face looked very serious.

"'I almost lost you yesterday," he said after a brief pause.

"Instead you lost the *Mist.* You had planned her for so long, and had pinned such hopes on her. I am truly sorry."

"Losing her was painful, I admit, but I realized several things during the course of those few hours yesterday. One was that I had pinned my hopes on something that, in the long run, did not matter very much."

"Oh, but—" she started to protest.

He held up his hand to stop her. "No, hear me out. John and I will build another boat, and I will still try to prove my ideas and vindicate Richard Haverthorpe's tragic death. Perhaps I will still win the Duke's Cup, some other year. But it is you on whom I should have pinned my hopes, and pin them now. You are the most extraordinary woman I have ever met—the most beautiful, but also the most resilient, most caring, most proud, most talented. I knew even before yesterday that I loved you. I have loved you almost from the start! But yesterday I knew I could not go on without you. I need you to be in my life, in my arms, every day of every year. I love you. Please, will you marry me?"

Daphne's heart was beating very hard. She closed her eyes against the rush of emotion that threatened to close up her throat. Now was no time not to be able to talk! Choking back the lump, she spoke carefully. "I have tried so hard not to fall in love with you. I am not the wife you need. You are the heir presumptive of the Marquess of Huntington—you need and should have a wife whose reputation is spotless, whose heritage is stellar, whose character is unquestionable. Can you understand that if I love you, I *must* say no?"

She could not stop the tears from spilling over. She did not want to cry in front of him—it only made the whole thing harder.

He let go of the tiller and moved beside her, taking her in his arms. The *Ariadne* drifted, moving more slowly than a pair of swans that passed them in the moonlight.

Kissing her at the end of each sentence, he said, "If you love me, you have no choice but to say yes. You are the wife who will give me children born with courage and character, to raise with love. Your character *is* unquestionable, and when you become the Marquess of Huntington, no one will dare to naysay it. You have never done anything for which you need be ashamed, and you know that in your heart, as do I. If you refuse me, you condemn me to a lifetime of heartache and the loss of a treasure I can never replace. I am offering you my protection and my heart— my very soul. Please do not turn away my gifts."

"I have a gift for you," she answered, pulling away a little, "although it is not yet quite dry. When I give you the painting of Westwater I hope you'll know you have not only my art, but my trust and my heart."

"Can you possibly believe I could accept the painting if you do not come with it? You *must* marry me."

She sighed. "I do love you, more than you can possibly imagine. If you are so certain, then I will agree. In marriage we can give our bodies and link our souls, although those, indeed, belong only to God. I trust you. But I dread to know what your family is going to say."

*   *   *

Winnie's come-out ball was four days later. It was proving to be one of the grandest events of the Season, a rousing finish as Parliament stampeded through its final week of business. With the exception of the most dedicated lawmakers, all the *beau monde* was in attendance, and Fitzwarren Place positively shone.

Lady Ramsdale and the Marquess of Huntington stood at one end of the grand salon, looking on serenely as the dancers went through the figures of the latest country dance. Archer and Daphne were making their way there by a circuitous route around the room, avoiding both dancers and huge urns of flowers as best they could.

"They do not look unhappy," Daphne said tentatively.

"I knew my mother would come around," Archer replied. "She is not a bad sort, really." He had explained Daphne's whole story to his family, even though the facts would never become public knowledge. Galton Meregill had been found dead at the Beaufort Gallery, and Morgan Laybrook's name was in the papers and on every gossip's tongue. Laybrook's hired spy had been allowed to take ship for America and Daphne's footman, Wilson, dismissed.

"It was my great-uncle who surprised me," Archer continued, "when he said he would be ashamed if I let you slip away. He said it is the heart that counts, and he is proud to have yours in our family."

"I think I am going to like your great-uncle very much. You are certain Winnie does not mind having our betrothal announcement made at her ball?"

"She is in alt about it—thrilled down to her toes."

Daphne laughed, and Archer pulled her closer to his side as they continued to walk. "The very first thing that drew me to you was your laughter," he admitted. "I mean to keep you so happy with me, I will hear you laugh every day for the rest of our lives."

Daphne squeezed his elbow, a promise of hugs to come later. "I see Sir Peter dancing with a lively young lady."

"Yes. He had to promise my mother that he would not hide in a corner."

"I should think that would be difficult for one of his size."

Archer chuckled. "I believe Holly has found a new passion besides cards, but the object of his interest does not seem to return his regard. It will be interesting to see how that plays out."

"Speaking of passions, I am going to begin a new painting," Daphne said. "I was thinking perhaps a portrait of the 'yacht' *Ariadne*—would it not surprise people to see a grand painting of such a humble little boat? Or there is a sketch I made of a very handsome man at the helm of the *Mist*—it could be turned into a notable portrait. Whatever I choose, I will make sure passion guides me."

"I can see I have won the prize of a lifetime—an Original as well as a Great Beauty. I hope passion will always rule us. I confess that when I first met you, I thought you would make the perfect mistress. Even better than a boat, would you believe it? But as it happens, I was mistaken. I have learned a great secret since then, one I will pass along to my sons. The most perfect mistress of all should be the greatest love of one's life, the perfect wife."

Author's Note

While I rarely take liberties with history, in the story of
The Rake's Mistake I confess I have taken two small ones—
by setting the story in 1817 (because of another story to
follow), and by making Archer's ship designs a little ahead
of his time.

From 1775 to 1812, small pleasure boats did race on the
Thames, with prizes, pomp, and ceremony. They ranged in
capacity up to seventeen tons, but many were no bigger
than twenty feet long. After 1812, the record stops. I believe the construction of new, more navigable bridges
(Vauxhall, Waterloo, Southwark) complicated sailing on
the Thames during their construction and increased the
river traffic afterward. Significantly, between 1812 and 1815,
forty-two of Britain's most distinguished yachtsmen
founded the Yacht Club (later to become the Royal Yacht
Club). They set a minimum size of ten tons for members'
vessels, and made the racing venue the Solent instead of
the Thames.

As for Archer's "futuristic" design ideas, well, most of
them were known by 1817, in use in America, and under
investigation in Britain. An experimental boat, the *Menai,*
is noted in 1826. However, history has shown repeatedly
that ideas do not catch hold until their time comes. Who
can say why? The character of shipbuilder John Forsyth is
based on two real men, John Fincham of Portsmouth, who
very early tried to break the inherent secrecy among build-
ers by calling for a "scientific examination" of yacht shapes,

and the other, a Scotsman named John Scott Russell, who tried to introduce the sharp-bowed hull model with a cutter he built in the 1840s.

Apparently no one in England saw the new ideas combined in one boat until 1851, when the schooner *America* was shipped across the ocean to compete in what became the first of the America's Cup races. Upon seeing her, the eighty-year-old Marquis of Anglesey, who despite losing a leg at Waterloo had raced yachts since before 1800, commented, "If she's right, we must all be wrong."

The history of yachting could have been quite different if Archer had had his way!

Allison Lane

"A FORMIDABLE TALENT...
MS. LANE NEVER FAILS TO
DELIVER THE GOODS."
—*ROMANTIC TIMES*

THE NOTORIOUS WIDOW
0-451-20166-3
When a scoundrel tries to tarnish a young widow's
reputation, a valiant Earl tries to repair the
damage—and mend her broken heart as well...

BIRDS OF A FEATHER
0-451-19825-5
When a plain, bespectacled young woman keeps
meeting the handsome Lord Wylie, she feels she is not
up to his caliber. A great arbiter of fashion for London
society, Lord Wylie was reputed to be more interseted in
the cut of his clothes than the feelings of others, as the
young woman bore witness to. Degraded by him in
public, she could nevertheless forget his dashing
demeanor. It will take a public scandal, and a private
passion, to bring them together...

To order call: 1-800-788-6262